ALSO AVAILABLE BY BAILEY CATES

THE MAGICAL BAKERY MYSTERIES

Spirits and Sourdough

A Magical Bakery Mystery

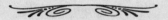

Bailey Cates

BERKLEY PRIME CRIME
New York

BERKLEY PRIME CRIME
Published by Berkley
An imprint of Penguin Random House LLC
penguinrandomhouse.com

Copyright © 2022 by Penguin Random House LLC
Excerpt from *Daisies for Innocence* copyright © 2016 by Bailey Cattrell
Penguin Random House supports copyright. Copyright fuels creativity, encourages
diverse voices, promotes free speech, and creates a vibrant culture. Thank you for buying
an authorized edition of this book and for complying with copyright laws by not
reproducing, scanning, or distributing any part of it in any form without permission.
You are supporting writers and allowing Penguin Random House to continue to
publish books for every reader.

BERKLEY and the BERKLEY & B colophon are registered trademarks and BERKLEY
PRIME CRIME is a trademark of Penguin Random House LLC.

ISBN: 9780593099247

First Edition: January 2022

Printed in the United States of America
1 3 5 7 9 10 8 6 4 2

Chapter 1

Using the tips of my fingers, I gently stripped the tiny, pungent leaves of thyme from their woody stems. The air around me thickened with the scent of herbal goodness. I inhaled deeply with my eyes half closed, and my lips barely moved in a silent invocation to trigger the plant's powers of courage and healing. As a hedgewitch, this kind of green spell was my special talent. As a professional baker, my brand of kitchen magic was a handy addition to my recipes. As part owner of the Honeybee Bakery along with my uncle Ben and aunt Lucy—who was a hedgewitch like me—my gift allowed me to add beneficial dashes of enchantment to the pastries our customers loved so much.

Lucy and I were spending the last hour before the Honeybee closed working on two new recipes. The thyme was for a blood orange thyme cake I'd been fine-tuning for a few days, and Lucy was developing a new treat with Halloween—and the Honeybee Halloween party—right around the corner: gummy worms crawling out of gooey "dirt" brownies made with dark chocolate and a tasty dollop of cherry jam.

Lucy tipped her head and examined her work. "Katie? Come take a look. What do you think?"

Brushing off my hands, I moved to stand beside her. She'd carefully created holes in the brownies, and the worms really did look like they were crawling out.

"Looks yummy but just gross enough that the kids will love them," I said.

"Good." She sounded satisfied. "We'll add them to the mix. So far, we have spiderweb red velvet cookies, homemade marshmallow ghosties, marzipan shortbread jack-o'-lanterns, and nutty popcorn balls."

"We need something with candy corn for the Halloween party. Cupcakes?"

She nodded. "Definitely. We can layer the batter to make the cakes yellow and orange, then frost them with white buttercream and decorate with candy corn. And our usual full-moon sugar cookies will go with the theme. I'll bring my old cast-iron Dutch oven to use as a cauldron. Your uncle has already ordered the dry ice."

At the bakery, we kept things light and fun, but there was another layer to the holiday for the spellbook club—our informal coven of six. Halloween, or All Hallows Eve, was known to us as Samhain (pronounced *sah-win*), one of the four major sabbats. As the witches' New Year, it signified the end of the harvest, gave us the chance to celebrate our departed ancestors, and was the time of year when the veil between this plane and the next was the thinnest—and easiest to breach.

"No one will know the Dutch oven isn't a real cauldron," I said.

"So say you." Lucy's eyes twinkled beneath her loose top bun of graying blond hair.

I grinned. "Touché." Because, of course, she had concocted plenty of enchanted brews in that cast iron, even if they ended up in a mug as a soothing drink or in a bowl as a soup that nourished the soul as well as the body. A kitchen witch's power extends to everything they cook with intention.

The sound of laughter drifted from the bakery's library area. I smoothed the vintage gingham apron I'd chosen for the day and glanced at the clock on the wall. "I'm going to see if the ladies need anything before we start cleaning up."

Lucy murmured absentminded agreement and went back to her brownies.

I walked around the register and past the coffee counter. Uncle Ben looked up, the corners of his brown eyes crinkling in a smile behind frameless glasses. His gaze cut to the women gathered near the floor-to-ceiling bookshelves, and he stroked his beard with his thumb as if speculating about their conversation before going back to cleaning the espresso machine. The next day, it would be ready to create coffee concoctions for our regulars who always showed up first thing in the morning. As I passed, I noted a few more strands of silver glinted from his beard and along his temples. The Honeybee was Ben's second career after he'd retired as Savannah's fire chief. It perfectly suited his outgoing personality and flair for business.

I would be eternally grateful that he and Lucy had convinced me to bring my pastry school training from Akron, Ohio, to Georgia to start up the bakery. Life was certainly different than it had been before I'd relocated almost three years ago. For one thing, I'd learned

3

I was a hereditary hedgewitch like Lucy and that my parents both had magical gifts that they'd hidden from me my entire life. Now I knew who I truly was and why I hadn't fit in for so long. I had heart-filling friendships and five witchy mentors in the spellbook club, a deepening adoration for the richly quirky city of Savannah, and a charmingly updated carriage house in Midtown. Best of all, two months ago I'd married the love of my life, Declan McCarthy.

Life was good. No, make that *great*.

I smiled to myself as I scanned the few customers lingering over steaming cups and empty plates scattered on the blue bistro tables. The late afternoon sun cut through the café curtains that framed the front windows where a local artist had painted a cartoon graveyard scene. The skeleton hand reaching out of the ground toward a headstone marked with RIP U.R. NEX looked more comical than scary, and the floating ghosts reminded me of friendly little Casper.

Fans mounted on the high ceiling lazily stirred the air, and deep amber walls subtly encouraged energy and creativity. The wall behind the register was painted a complementary burnt orange to contrast with the blackboard, where we listed the seasonal menu offerings and daily specials. Fake cobwebs festooned the edges of the sign and dripped from the corner of the glass case full of row upon row of delectable pastries. Silhouettes of mice cut from black felt gamboled along the floor moldings and a few well-placed pipe-cleaner spiders clung to the walls.

At the other end of the bakery, a reading area welcomed anyone who wanted to peruse the eclectic collection of books. Customers were welcome to take any volume they might need or want, or leave behind a title someone else might like. The selection was always full, varied, and interesting. Comfortable chairs in rich jewel-toned brocade invited customers to stay once they'd selected their reading material, arranged along with a poufy sofa around a sturdy coffee table. On one of the bottom shelves, Mungo, my black Cairn terrier and witch's familiar, was curled into a sleepy ball in his sheepskin bed. On the far windowsill, Honeybee, the bakery's feline namesake and Lucy's familiar, sat hunched over her front paws as she watched the goings-on out on Broughton Street. Her orange and white stripes glowed softly in the sun.

It was the perfect place for a book club to meet, and that was exactly what was happening.

Five women gathered around the coffee table, each with a copy of the book they were discussing. Leigh Markes, who had reserved the reading area for their meetings for the last couple of months, closed her copy as I approached. I saw it was a biography of the artist Frida Kahlo. One of Kahlo's self-portraits graced the cover. Since Leigh was the owner of the Markes Gallery and a formidable artist in her own right, I wasn't surprised at her book group's choice.

"Can I get anyone anything?" I asked.

A freckled woman, whose coppery hair was several times brighter than my own short auburn locks, opened her mouth to speak.

Leigh cut her off. "We're good. You close in a few minutes, don't you?"

The redhead frowned. I remembered from their last

meeting that her name was Calista, and I was pretty sure she was Leigh's sister.

I glanced at my watch. "Fifteen. We'll be here for a bit, though, closing up." I did have plans for the evening—spellbook club member Jaida French had invited me and some of our other members to dinner and a ghost tour of Savannah, which she had somehow scored free tickets to. We weren't due at the restaurant for over an hour, though, so there was no rush.

Leigh shook her head. "No. We don't want to inconvenience you. We're finished."

Calista spoke. "But, Leigh, I still want to talk about Kahlo's pantheism and the almost surreal connection to nature her paintings evoke." She looked around at the group. Two of the other ladies nodded. Their dark hair and facial features looked similar enough they had to be related. Given the age difference, I guessed they were mother and daughter. The fifth member of the group, a tanned, athletic-looking blonde, appeared mildly curious.

"That's speculative and irrelevant to this discussion." Leigh stood and adjusted a long silk scarf dyed in blues and greens around her neck. It was obviously expensive and nicely accessorized the elegant seafoam-colored dress that hugged her slender curves. Leigh's hair was solid white and expertly cut to frame her narrow face. With her penetrating eyes and petite nose, she reminded me of Emmylou Harris minus the easygoing manner.

"It's not discussed in the book at all," she said with a note of finality. "And I think we've taken the discussion of her activism and relationship to Diego Rivera as far as we can today."

"But her depiction of animals, her wonderful garden—"

"Not in the book," Leigh repeated in a dismissive tone.

Her sister's cheeks flared bright pink, and her eyes narrowed with obvious anger. "I don't give a . . ." She took a deep breath and glanced around at the other three women. The mother and daughter exchanged nervous glances, seeming equally uncomfortable. The blonde leaned back in her chair and crossed her arms with a bemused expression.

I shuffled back a couple of steps, feeling out of place yet not wanting to call attention to myself. Mungo had quietly left his bed and padded over to stand by my foot. A low whine reached my ears, but the ladies were too caught up in their sudden melodrama to notice.

"Listen, sis," Calista grated, glaring at Leigh. "This is a book *group*, all of us equal, *not* a bunch of toadies like your gallery people you can boss around. You don't have the right to dictate our entire discussion just because you're an artist, or should I say *artiste*, and we're not." She hesitated, glancing at the mother and daughter. "I'm sorry to be so blunt, but someone has to set her straight." Her gaze shunted to the blonde. "But you get what I mean, don't you, Jo?"

Jo responded with a silent but sympathetic smile.

Calista seemed to lose some of her steam. She licked her lips and frowned. "I'm only saying you don't have to be such a bossy moo."

Leigh shrugged. "Usually, the person who chooses the book heads the discussion. At least that's what we've done before." She turned away and picked up the purse strap slung across the back of her chair. As she did so, the end of her scarf flared out, and I clearly saw the intertwined images that made up its blue-and-green pattern.

"You want to do it differently? Fine by me." Leigh turned back and glared at the redhead. "Come up with some new rules, and we can talk about it next time. After all, it's your turn to choose the next book. What will it be?"

Calista looked nonplussed. "Um . . ."

Leigh quirked an eyebrow. "Oh, now. Surely you have something wonderful for us, don't you, little sister? After that scene? Please, tell us all about your fabulous choice for our next meeting."

Her sister's cheeks blazed again, but her chin came up. "I've been looking at a few possibilities but haven't decided yet."

Leigh laughed. "Well, you let us know—"

The older woman with dark hair cut in. "Sorry, all. We have to be going. Let us know your selection for next month when you can, okay, Calista? No hurry." She stood, and her daughter bolted to her feet beside her. "Lovely discussion. See you soon." She waved as they practically ran to the front door.

I couldn't say I blamed them. The air crackled with enmity. I glanced over at Lucy, who had come out to stand by the register. Our eyes met, and I knew she felt it, too. Mungo leaned against my calf, his little body tense and protective.

Calista rose and stiffly packed her book, notebook, and pen into a large quilted tote bag. Without another word or a single look at Leigh or Jo, she turned and stalked out of the Honeybee.

"You should be nicer to Calista." Jo reached down to adjust the strap on one of her sandals. When she stood, I realized how tall she was. Her white cotton shirt was loosely tucked into dark slacks that hugged her sturdy hips. She had the face of a model and the physique of a competitive athlete.

Leigh frowned. "I've tried being nice. Ever since Daddy passed on, no matter what I do, she's against it. I'm sick of it. I'm sick of her."

They began to walk toward the door, and I quickly moved to tidy one of the bookshelves so I wouldn't be caught standing there listening to them.

"Oh, Katie?"

I whirled back to find they'd paused several feet away.

"Thanks for accommodating us this afternoon," Leigh said. "It's lovely in here, and I think I must have eaten my weight in pastries in the last couple of hours. We'd love to meet here again next month."

Relief that she wasn't going to take me to task for eavesdropping whooshed through me, and I started to smile. Then I saw the images on her scarf again.

Dragonflies. *Dozens of dragonflies.*

An oily quiver snaked through my solar plexus.

"Of course," I managed to say. "Just give us a few days' notice so we can put up the RESERVED sign."

"Will do!" She smiled and turned away.

As they continued toward the door, I heard Jo say, "Well, Calista lost a father, too."

They exited the bakery, and I turned toward Lucy. "Did you see?"

Gravely, she nodded. "Your totem. All over her scarf. But dragonflies are everywhere, you know. It could be a coincidence."

"Let's hope so," I said lightly.

Nevertheless, something in me knew better. One of the things I'd learned in my brief journey as a witch was that dragonflies often served as a kind of metaphysical tap on the shoulder. When that happened, it felt different than when the iridescent lovelies simply zinged around my backyard hunting Savannah's ubiquitous mosquitoes.

And it felt different now.

The front door opened, and a muscular man with dark wavy hair and a deliciously strong jaw came in. His ice blue eyes met mine across the room, and I felt my heart give an extra pitty-pat. I wasn't sure how long that sort of reaction was supposed to last, but seeing my new husband still gave me a thrill every time.

Declan wove through the tables, and we met in front of the coffee counter. He wrapped his arms around me, lifting me so I was standing on tiptoe, and then planted a kiss on the side of my mouth.

"Hey, you two. Get a room," Ben growled.

Declan laughed and relaxed his embrace.

Slightly flushed, I protested. "It was just a kiss."

But my uncle was already grinning. Declan McCarthy had been Ben's protégé in the fire department for years before Ben had retired. Now he was a firefighter working out of Five House and would soon begin paramedic training. Declan's father had died when he was young, and Ben and Aunt Lucy had no children. Ben and Declan were very close, and I knew Ben was over the moon that we'd tied the knot. Now one of his favorite people was officially part of our family.

"You ready to go?" Declan asked my uncle.

"Almost," he said. "Just let me put these in the dishwasher." He grabbed a couple of dirty mugs and went into the kitchen.

"You sure you don't want to come on the ghost tour with us?" I asked Declan.

"No way."

"It might be romantic." I drew the last word out, teasing.

"Boring is what it would be," he said. "I grew up here. There's not a haunted house or gruesome ghost story about Savannah I don't already know." His eyes flashed as he looked at me, and he gave me a little squeeze with the arm still draped around my shoulders. "Now, if it were just you and me, and I was giving the tour, well . . . that might be a different story."

"I'd like that." I waggled my eyebrows and slipped out from under his arm. "But not tonight. Jaida already has my ticket, and Lucy's coming, too." Jaida French was my mentor in all things tarot.

"I was surprised by that," Ben said, returning from the kitchen. "But it turns out she's never taken a Savannah ghost tour. Plus: free tickets. Hard to beat that." He came around the counter and said to Declan, "Let's swing by Sandfly BBQ and pick up some ribs and brisket."

"Do *not* get barbeque sauce on the new sofa," I warned. They were taking advantage of Lucy's and my absence to hang out at the carriage house, eat manly food, and watch the Falcons play the Vikings on Monday Night Football.

"I could do with some of their mac and cheese, too. Maybe some fried okra," Declan said, ignoring me. "Where's Mungo?"

Hearing his name, my familiar trotted out from the reading area. He carried something gingerly in his mouth. After dropping it at my feet, he sat back and grinned up at me with unmistakable doggy pride. I bent to pick it up. It appeared to be a bookmark, but not like anything I'd seen before. The metal clip was long and thin, and carved with intricate swirling designs. At the top, the metal expanded into a narrow circle embedded with red jewels. Inside the circle, a tiny sailing ship was etched onto a flat, cream-colored stone.

"Huh," I said, turning it over in my hand. "This looks expensive."

Ben peered over my shoulder. "And old. That's scrimshaw on ivory."

So it wasn't stone. I shuddered as I thought of the poor animal that had sacrificed for this trinket back in the day.

"One of the book club members must have dropped it." I went around the counter and tucked it into the drawer below the register. "I'm sure they'll be back for it."

Lucy came out of the office with Honeybee's designer leather cat tote. Her familiar delicately stepped inside at my aunt's request, and she handed the carrier to Ben. I moved back automatically. I regularly brewed a potion to combat my allergy to cats, a potion powerful enough that Honeybee could hang out at the bakery, but I still couldn't get too close to her.

Declan bent over, picked up Mungo, and tucked him into the crook of his arm. "Come on, big guy. I'll take you home. You can hang out with Honeybee while your, er, owners, are out on the town."

I smiled to myself. Declan still shied away from the term "witch," which was kind of funny given his own complicated connection to the paranormal.

"I'll even give you some brisket for supper," he said.

Yip!

I rolled my eyes. "Not too much. You spoil him more than I do."

Grinning, Declan leaned over and gave me a quick kiss. "I spoil you, too."

"Yeah . . ."

"Don't do anything I wouldn't do," he said over his shoulder as he and Ben left.

"You mean like go on a ghost tour with a bunch of my friends?" I called, but the door had already closed behind them.

Chapter 2

Before we left the bakery, Lucy had changed into funky Thai fisherman pants and a wrap-front blouse. My perfectly coiffed Midwestern mother called her sister *airy-fairy*, usually followed by an eye roll. Lucy did have an aging hippie vibe, but she pulled it off with casual elegance. I'd exchanged my bakery uniform of T-shirt and skort for a pair of white capris and a Breton-striped top. We were the first of our group to arrive at the Cotton Exchange Tavern on River Street. I'd never eaten there, but Jaida, who could be a bit of a food snob, swore they had delicious seafood and the best Reuben sandwich in town.

Passing beneath the green-and-white-striped awning, we entered and paused to let our eyes adjust to the relative darkness. As they did, I took in the rock and brick walls offset with plenty of wood paneling. The air was cool and redolent of garlic and grilling meat, and I suddenly realized I was starving. My aunt and I settled across from each other at a table by a window that overlooked the Savannah River. Soon a waiter had taken our orders for tall glasses of sweet tea and a pile of peel-and-eat shrimp for the table.

Two members of the spellbook club had declined Jaida's invitation to take the ghost tour, so there would only be Lucy, Jaida, Bianca Devereaux and her young daughter, and me. Missing would be Mimsey Carmichael, who had already scheduled a date night with her husband, and Cookie Rios, who had a new baby.

Jaida arrived, striding into the room and spying us immediately. She threaded her way through the tables to join us. She'd changed from her workaday going-to-court attire into denim shorts and a lime green DIRTY DOZEN BRASS BAND T-shirt that popped against her rich brown skin. Her square-framed glasses provided an air of wisdom despite her casual dress.

I rose to give her a hug, inhaling the faint scent of cinnamon that always seemed to accompany her. Since the magical properties of cinnamon were many, including protection, love, and healing, it was a fitting aura to surround one of Savannah's best defense attorneys and a witch who specialized in tarot.

"Whew!" she said, sinking into her seat. "I almost didn't make it. Anubis was very insistent that he wanted to come along."

Anubis was her familiar, a brindle Great Dane as big as a pony. When he got insistent it was no joke.

I raised my eyebrows. "How'd you convince him?"

"Two slices of turkey bacon." She reached for the menu the waiter had left. "And a promise he could watch *The Princess Bride* while I was gone."

I snorted out a laugh. "Yeah. That works on Mungo, too. Except soap operas are his thing."

Lucy, whose feline familiar was far more dignified than either Jaida's canine or mine, rolled her eyes.

Next, Bianca Devereaux and her daughter Colette entered the restaurant. I raised my hand, and they made their way to the table. Colette was nine years old and becoming more like her mother with every passing month. Bianca was the member of the spellbook club who looked the most like an old-school Hollywood-style witch. Even after a long, hot summer, her complexion was so pale it was nearly translucent, and her long dark hair was held off her neck with a silver, sapphire-encrusted hair claw that probably cost more than I made in a month. Her daughter's hair, a shade lighter, was in two braids like a pioneer girl from the past might have worn. They both wore bright cotton sundresses, Bianca's blue and Colette's a light coral.

Bianca had been a single mom ever since her jerk of an ex-husband discovered her burgeoning interest in Wicca and moon magic, and left her *and* his daughter. It turned out Bianca was pretty darn good at magic— and numbers—especially when it came to the stock market. She'd made a small fortune in the years since her ex had skedaddled, and now owned a boutique wine store on Factors Walk called Moon Grapes.

Lucy rose to embrace our friend, who then sat down on my aunt's side of the table with her daughter next to her.

"Hi!" Colette said.

"Hi yourself, pipsqueak," Jaida said with a grin.

Colette wrinkled her nose at her.

"And hello, Puck," I said to the tiny pink snout barely visible at the top of Bianca's Hermès bag.

Colette's eyes grew wide, and she looked apprehensively around the room. "Shhh! It's a secret, and Mom could get in trouble if they find out he's in her purse."

Puck, a smooth white ferret with black markings like a Zorro mask around his eyes, was Bianca's familiar. He'd found her relatively recently, and she hated to be separated from him. Luckily, he was no Anubis, and could fit in her pocket if need be.

Bianca smiled and reached over to fix a strand of her daughter's hair that had escaped its braid. "Don't worry. They know it's a secret."

After a pause, the girl nodded gravely. "Yes, I suppose they do."

The waiter brought our shrimp appetizer and took our orders. When he was gone, I asked Colette, "Are you excited about the ghost tour?"

She grinned and nodded. "Uh-huh. Maybe I'll even get to see one! It's so close to Halloween, the spirits must be out and about more than usual, don't you think?"

The adults exchanged a quick glance, and her mother changed the subject. Colette might be closer to the mark than she realized.

Bringing Colette along was the only reason Bianca had agreed to come at all. Like Declan, our coven mate was a native of Savannah and thought she knew as much as she needed to about the city's haunted history. However, her daughter had lobbied to come, and while Bianca didn't really spoil her, there was no reason to say no. The tour operator had given Jaida the free tickets as a thank-you. I wasn't sure why, so I asked after our supper was delivered to the table.

"How do you know the young woman who'll be giving our tour?"

Jaida swallowed a bite of her fried green tomato BLT and sat back. "Teddy is Gregory's goshdaughter." Gregory was Jaida's partner in love as well as in their small law firm. "Her father's one of his best friends from school. He's not particularly religious, but he and his wife still wanted Gregory to be part of their daughter's life, so: goshdaughter." She licked her lips and took a sip of craft beer. "Teddy's . . . special."

The way she said it made me tip my head to the side. Special? That was like being *interesting*; it could be good or bad. However, Bianca changed the subject, so I let it go.

After a leisurely supper, we strolled along River Street, past the African American Families Monument, and climbed the stairs to Factors Walk. On Bay Street, lots of locals enjoyed the warm air and setting sun, along with the shorts-clad tourists taking advantage of Savannah's ordinance that allowed alcohol to be consumed on the street. As we made our way to the spot where we were to meet Gregory's goshdaughter, we saw a particularly loud cluster of people with the lilt of the upper Midwest in their conversation. A dark green hearse pulled to the curb beside them. I could see the extra seats inside, and the top had been cut off so people could stand and look out at the different haunted sites the tour operator would point out.

Another hearse passed by and then a small, open-sided bus boasting the logo of a haunted pub tour. Savannah offered a variety of ghost tours, along with history tours, architectural tours, cemetery tours, and the ever-present open-bus tours that took visitors all over the city. Unlike many of them, ours was to be a walking version. I hoped the other participants would be less boisterous than the bunch we'd just passed.

"How many other people will be in our group?" I asked Jaida.

She shrugged. "No idea."

Looking over, I considered my friend. Usually vivacious and occasionally acerbic, Jaida was quiet this evening. Her eyes held what I could only interpret as worry.

"Teddy doesn't work for one of the big tour companies," she said. "She has her own operation, which is why she could give me free tickets. I told her it wasn't necessary, but she wanted to do something to pay me back for some minor legal work I did when someone sued her."

"Uh-oh," I said. "I take it things worked out for the best . . . ?"

Jaida sighed. "People will sue about anything anymore. The plaintiff took a ghost tour and became frightened. Very frightened." She glanced at Colette, who was listening avidly. "There was no physical injury and no lasting emotional effects that could be proven, so I managed to get it thrown out."

"Wow!" Colette said. "This is going to be better than I thought!"

"Hmm. I think you'll be fine, pipsqueak, though I understand Teddy's tours can be a little different than the others."

I knew Jaida would never permit Colette to be placed in danger. "You haven't gone on one before?" I asked.

She shook her head. "But after the court case, I suggested Teddy have her clients sign waivers."

I felt a flash of apprehension. "Do you think we'll run into any actual, you know, ghosts?"

Turning her head, Jaida's gaze snagged mine, then flickered down to Colette, who was still watching her. Lucy and Bianca were walking behind us, talking about the book our spellbook club planned to discuss at our next meeting.

"You never can tell, right?" Jaida's tone was light, but her expression wasn't.

That told me she didn't want to frighten Colette. This whole time I'd thought the ghost tours were bunk, but now I wondered. Where there's smoke, there's fire, and all that. Of course, there was no question that souls from the other side of the veil occasionally crossed over to our side. My own nonna had visited me several times when I'd needed her help. Not only that, but a séance had inadvertently revealed the guardian spirit who had attached himself to Declan, allowing him to actually inhabit my husband's physical being on occasion.

Did I mention Declan had his own connection to the paranormal?

I winced inwardly. It seemed like a long time since that had happened. Even though I hadn't liked it at the time, in a way I missed the comforting presence of his guardian. The spirit, a leprechaun named Connell who was somehow caught between the mortal and immortal planes, had sacrificed himself to save me a few months before and was now wandering, lost, someplace in the ether. I'd had contact with him while in a dream state, and Nonna had promised to try to help us find him, but I still hadn't discovered exactly how to get him back. The spellbook club had tried to help at first, but they'd soon run out of ideas, too.

However, I was determined to try to bring Connell back on Samhain, to somehow take advantage of the thin veil between this world and the next during the height of the sabbat, but I still had to figure out a few details. I'd spent many late nights searching and re-searching, looking for solutions, my heart hurting for the man I loved. Not only did Declan feel like a piece of himself was missing, a horrible emptiness I could relate to since I'd lost my own magic for a time, but a man who was a first responder simply couldn't be without his guardian spirit. I tried not to bring it up, but it worried me no end. There had already been a few incidents I felt sure Connell would have steered Declan clear of if he'd been able. So far, my husband had been lucky. I wasn't about to trust to luck forever, though. Not when it came to his safety.

I realized Jaida had been watching me. Smiling weakly, I said, "I guess we'll just have to wait and see what happens tonight."

Bianca came up behind us and pointed at the small group gathered on the corner of Whitaker and Bay. "That's where we're supposed to meet, isn't it?"

Jaida nodded. "And there's Teddy." She lifted her hand in greeting, and a tall young woman responded in kind.

We crossed the street and joined them. There were five others in the group besides us. They introduced themselves.

"I'm Tom," said a short man with a jovial smile, bright blue eyes, and a fringe of dark hair that ran around the back of his otherwise bald head. "And this is my bride, Bridie. Get it?"

I managed not to roll my eyes, but his wife did it for me. "Never mind. Some of his jokes are just for him." The same height as her husband, with a round face and a peaches-and-cream complexion under graying blond hair, she'd no doubt been keeping Tom in line for years. "Though if he doesn't stop with that one, I might have to change my name."

The other couple, Sam and Deanne, were polar opposites to Tom and Bridie. Sam was tall and hovered over his petite wife. Her wide eyes and furtive looks into the shadows made me wonder whether she was a good candidate for this kind of tour.

"We're from Cheyenne, Wyoming!" Sam boomed, and Deanne's chin bobbed in silent agreement. "Don't hold with the idea of ghosts, mind you, but thought we'd see how convincing Teddy here is. Isn't that right?"

The fifth person was the young woman who had waved to Jaida. Our tour guide, who introduced herself to us as Teddy LaRue, was perhaps nineteen or twenty with a mass of dark curly hair, a deep golden complexion, and wide hazel eyes framed by long lashes. She was casually stunning, yet there was a drawn, tense quality in how she held herself. Her eyes roved the shadows like Deanne's did, but she didn't seem nervous.

Rather, she seemed . . . haunted.

Nonetheless, her answer to Sam was easygoing. "Sure enough. But it's not my job to convince you. It's my job to tell you the history and the stories that make Savannah the most haunted city in America."

"Well, I'm a history buff, so I'll enjoy that," Sam responded as he crushed his wife against his hip with a hand as big as a salad plate. "Deanne here has enough truck with the woo-woo stuff for the both of us. Isn't that right, hon?"

Deanne smiled tentatively and nodded again. I began to wonder if she was capable of speech.

"Well, let's get on with the tour, then," Teddy said. An aura of authority had settled over her as she got ready to do her job, masking her tenseness but not eliminating it. "Let me have you sign these waivers, and then we'll start right where we are, with the Moon River Brewing Company. It's not only one of the most haunted places in Savannah, but one of the most haunted places in the entire U.S."

Jaida and Teddy exchanged wry looks as we all read and signed the waivers that released Teddy from liability should any of us be overcome with fright. The out-of-towners didn't comment on that step, not even Sam, and I was glad. Then we moved to stand on the crowded sidewalk in front of the restaurant and bar.

"Built in 1821, this gorgeous building was originally a hotel for the rich and famous. James Audubon liked it so much he lived here for six months. Unfortunately, the hotel closed in 1864, shortly before General Sherman took over the city. It was never a hotel again, but has served other purposes over time, including as a hospital during a series of yellow fever outbreaks in Savannah."

She went on to describe the hauntings on the second floor thought to be the spirits of the hundreds who had died from the horrible disease. Before that, there was the violent and unpunished shooting of a drunken James Stark by Dr. Phillip Minus, which prompted Stark's angry ghost to haunt the main floor, throwing liquor bottles and grabbing patrons. She told us of "Toby," a ghost who showed up in the billiards room so often they'd decided he needed a name. Then there were the upper floors that were under constant renovation, with workers leaving and things going wrong with such regularity that updates were never completed.

"After the tour, I suggest coming back here for a beer, a game of billiards, and to hang out with Toby if you can," she said.

Teddy's tour continued with a stroll through Johnson Square, where she told us why it was the only historical square where you wouldn't find any Spanish moss hanging from the trees. Declan had already told me that one: Nathanael Greene was buried there. He'd hated the heat and hanging moss with such passion that Johnson Square always seemed cool, and the moss didn't dare to grow there. However, I hadn't known the story of little Gracie, a friendly girl who'd lived on the square and greeted all travelers. When she'd died an early death, her spirit had remained and continued to welcome guests.

Teddy smiled down as she related this, as if Gracie were standing right there. I noticed Deanne staring at the same space Teddy seemed to be, wide-eyed, jaw clenched as if she could manifest the little girl's ghost by pure will.

"Come along," our guide said, brushing Deanne's shoulder with her fingertips as she passed by and making her jump. "I have many more stories to tell you."

Chapter 3

We stopped on the sidewalk in front of the Marshall House. Since it was on the same street as the Honeybee, I passed by the upscale Greek Revival hotel often. Declan and I had eaten in the adjoining restaurant a couple of times, and I adored the marble in the front lobby and the cast-iron balconies and veranda outside.

"The Marshall House was originally built by Mary Marshall in 1851, and though subsequent owners changed the name several times, it closed in 1945 and reopened in 1946 as the Marshall Hotel," Teddy said. "It was closed again ten years later, and only in 1999 opened as the luxury hotel you see now, again called the Marshall House. There are many well-documented episodes of haunting in this building."

"Oh!"

The exclamation came from a tall, thin woman walking near the wall. Deanne turned her head to look behind her at the same time the rest of us did. The woman bent to pick her floppy sunhat off the ground where it had apparently fallen. She jammed it back on her head and hurried past us. When we turned back, Teddy was grinning. Then, in a flash, the grin dropped, and she once again focused on our group.

"Well, heck," Tom said. "Turns out this is where me and Bridie are staying!"

Teddy smiled. "Wonderful! Have you had any odd experiences so far?"

"We've only been here one night," Bridie said with a tentative frown. "At the front desk, they told us we might see some strange things, though."

"You just might," Teddy agreed. "Most of these hauntings are attributed to a period of about six months during the Civil War when the building was converted into a hospital for Union soldiers."

Jaida and I exchanged a look.

Another hospital. No wonder it's haunted.

"There have been instances of guests awakening with the feeling of a hand being pressed on their forehead, as if someone were checking their temperature," Teddy said. "And several times the figures of soldiers in Union uniforms have been seen inside."

Sam's lips curved into a wry, unbelieving smile.

Teddy smiled back at him, unfazed. "Then, in the late 1990s when this latest renovation was being made, human remains were found under the floorboards of a downstairs room."

Sam's expression sharpened.

"When they were examined, it turned out they were body parts rather than entire bodies."

Lucy blanched. "Goodness."

"Wow." Colette sounded delighted.

"The downstairs was used as a surgery in the hospital," our guide quickly went on to explain. "The remains that were found were amputated limbs from Union soldiers, you see. In those days, amputations—" She flicked a glance in Colette's general direction. "Well, we don't have to go into detail about that. Anyway, when they cleared out the remains, strange noises—moans, heavy footsteps—began, and the staff would find items and paperwork had been moved around." Her gaze drifted back over Deanne's shoulder, and she appeared to give a little nod. With a tight smile, she said, "But soldiers aren't the only spirits in the Marshall House. There are also children heard playing in the upper hallways, bouncing balls and running up and down."

Bridie gasped. "I heard them in the middle of the night! I wondered why children that age weren't in bed at that hour." She turned and stared at her husband with wide eyes.

He shrugged. "Sorry. Didn't hear a thing. The concierge did mention that guests have been harassed by the ghosts of small children, though."

"Harassed!" Bridie said.

"Oh . . ." Deanne said. Her voice was deeper than I'd expected.

"Nonsense," Sam said in a flat tone. "Just nonsense. Teddy, where would that kind of story come from?"

We all looked at our guide, but she wasn't paying attention to us at all. She stood stock-still, gazing vacantly at a spot on the sidewalk by the corner of the building. Her eyes were round and unblinking, and dark circles had suddenly appeared beneath them. Her skin had taken on a waxy sheen. Then her eyes rolled back, and she swayed. Lucy gasped. I reached out and grabbed her thin wrist, while Jaida put her arm around the young woman's shoulders.

Our touch seemed to steady her. Blinking, her gaze cleared, and she looked around at us. Colette started to move toward her, but Bianca put her hand on her daughter's shoulder.

"Hey, now." Sam's brow furrowed in concern. "You okay?"

Bridie bustled over and looked into Teddy's eyes. "What happened?"

"I'm all right." Teddy's voice quivered, though.

"Now, that might be true, but you just about passed out on us there, right in the middle of the sidewalk. I'm a nurse, hon. Tell me what's going on." The woman's words had taken on a tone of soothing, professional comfort that I'd heard Declan use when he was working.

"I felt a little lightheaded is all," Teddy insisted in a bright voice.

However, I still had my hand on her arm and could feel she was shaking.

She took a deep breath and let it out. Then she looked around at our group again and when she spoke, her words sounded brittle. "I'm so sorry. I do suddenly feel a bit under the weather. I'm afraid I'm going to have to cancel the rest of tonight's tour. Perhaps we could try again tomorrow? In fact, tomorrow I'll contact everyone—you all gave me your cell phone numbers, right?"

At the responding nod, she continued. "I'll get in touch to confirm our rain check tour tomorrow, then. No charge."

Sam stepped forward. "Now, don't you worry about

that. You don't look so good, and besides, we have dinner reservations at the Olde Pink House tomorrow night."

"Oh, I see," Teddy said, her words barely audible. "Yes, of course, you all must have other plans. Give me a moment, and we'll move along. The Olde Pink House is on the tour, and you're going to love those stories."

"I don't think that's a good idea," Jaida said. "You're not well."

"That's right!" Bridie said. "You need to go home and get some rest, young lady." She looked her up and down. "And maybe grab a burger on the way. Have you eaten today?"

Teddy stiffened. "Yes, thank you." She looked down at the ground. "I'll refund your money in full. It should show up on your credit cards in a day or two."

"Then that's that," Sam said. "And don't you worry about a thing, young lady. We sure did enjoy the first part of the tour, isn't that right, Deanne?"

His wife, who had remained silent as she watched the exchange, nodded. Her eyes were narrowed in speculation as she said, "We sure did." She turned her head to look over her shoulder at the wall behind her and then turned back. "Teddy? Did you see something? A spirit of some kind?"

Teddy's face wavered into something resembling a smile. "Well, naturally. I'm good friends with all the spirits on my ghost tour."

Colette nodded emphatically. "I knew it!"

Startled, Bianca looked down at her daughter.

Teddy turned to look at her, too. When their eyes

met, something seemed to pass between them, but I wasn't sure what.

"Now, hon," Bridie said. "Can we call someone for you? We want to make sure you get home all right."

Jaida smiled and stepped forward. "That's so nice. However, we're locals"—her gesture took in Bianca, Lucy, and me as well as herself—"and I happen to be a friend of Teddy's. We can see she gets home all right."

Bridie looked relieved.

"That's fine, then," Tom said. "Bridie, let's go. Maybe we can still salvage some of this evening."

She turned angry eyes on him, and I had a feeling the coming hours might be a little rocky for those two thanks to Tom's callousness.

"Say, why don't you come along with us?" Sam said to the other couple. "I'm sure us out-of-towners can find a little something to entertain us for the next few hours." He winked at Bridie, who blushed. "Let's start inside here, where you folks are staying. We can have a drink and then move on. You can carry your drinks with you on the street here, you know, just like New Orleans." He pronounced it *Noo Or-LEENS*. "We'll make a night of it!"

Tom appeared uncertain but went along with the others as they drifted toward the doors.

Deanne, still quiet, was moving along with her husband and the other couple. However, she was still watching Teddy as she did so.

"Seriously," Jaida said to Teddy as soon as the others were out of hearing range, "are you all right?"

Teddy gave a little nod. "I'm okay. It was just a bit of

a shock when . . ." She trailed off. Her gaze flickered toward me without quite meeting my eyes.

Bianca frowned. "How about we go down to the Honeybee, and you can tell us about it?"

"The Honeybee Bakery?" Teddy asked.

"Sure!" Colette said. "Katie and Lucy own it. They'll open it up just for us. Won't you, Lucy? Please?"

My aunt half smiled at her. "You bet." And then at Teddy. "If you want to?"

The young woman nodded, but I could tell she was still pensive. We started down Broughton Street toward the bakery, Colette marching ahead in the lead while Bianca and Lucy tried to keep up with her. Teddy hung back, though. Jaida and I exchanged a look and slowed our steps as well.

When Colette was out of earshot, Teddy suddenly stopped and turned to me. Quick as a flash, her hand reached out and her fingers curled around my arm.

"Katie."

The intensity of the single word shot ice water through my veins.

Jaida stopped, too, concern radiating from every pore.

"There's a woman. She's dead. She wants you to find out who killed her."

That hung in the air for a few beats until I finally managed to blurt out, "Wh . . . what?"

"She's dead, Katie. *Murdered.*"

I struggled to think through the alarm and curiosity clouding my brain. "When did this murder happen, Teddy?" I asked. After all, we were on a ghost tour.

Could this be part of it? Could her earlier episode be part of the show?

"Tonight."

My mouth dropped open. "*Tonight?*"

"Tonight. And she told me to tell you she wants your help." When she saw my skeptical expression, Teddy said, "Maybe I should put that a different way. She insists on your help. And let me tell you—she's really angry about being dead."

I slowly put my hand over my eyes and murmured, "I don't blame her."

"Hey, you guys!" Colette called from ahead. "Come *on.*"

Chapter 4

Lucy unlocked the door of the Honeybee and disarmed the security system. Jaida shepherded Teddy inside, and the rest of us followed. As she relocked the door behind us, my aunt said she'd start water for tea. I knew she had something soothing in mind for Teddy—probably something with lavender and chamomile.

I hoped she'd bring some for me as well. I'd been expecting an interesting and fun evening with plenty of Savannah history and a sprinkling of ghost lore. I had not been expecting the eerie and ethereal Teddy LaRue, nor her insistence that I was being unceremoniously called to investigate yet another murder.

Maybe this isn't really a call like the others, because after all, the other cases had some kind of link to the paranormal, even old Mrs. Templeton, who was most likely a witch, even though we didn't realize it at the time, and this one . . .

Then I realized two things: I was capable of babbling, even to myself, and being contacted via a medium—or whatever Teddy was—by a very recently created ghost from the other side of the mortal veil did, indeed, count as *paranormal*.

I turned on two lamps in the reading area. They cast a comforting yellow glow along the rows of books and rich fabric of the furniture. Jaida led Teddy to the sofa and sat beside her, while Colette and Bianca squinched into one of the chairs together. I perched on an ottoman, leaving the other chair for Lucy.

"How are you feeling?" Jaida asked.

Teddy took a deep breath and began to rise. "Much better. Please don't make such a fuss. I'm sorry to be such a bother. I can just—"

"Hush," Jaida said as she gently pulled her back to the sofa. "Take it easy for a few minutes. You nearly fainted back there."

Teddy hesitated, then sighed and sank back into the cushions. She was looking at me with a speculative gleam in her eye. She had to be wondering why the ghost thought I could solve its murder.

Lucy bustled up with a tray that held a steaming teapot and mugs for all. "Now, here we go. Chamomile, peppermint, lavender, and just a touch of rosemary. It'll make you good as new. We'll let it steep for a bit first, though."

The young woman offered a small smile. "That's very kind. Really, though, I'm fine now."

"No, you're not," Colette said in a matter-of-fact tone. "You're a mess. Are you sick?"

"Colette!" Bianca admonished in a whisper.

I suppressed a smile.

Teddy did not, however. For the first time, a grin broke out on her face, wide and genuine. "No, Colette. I don't think I'm sick."

"Then what's wrong?" Bianca's daughter leaned forward insistently.

The grin faded. "It's complicated."

"You saw a ghost, didn't you?" Colette asked.

Teddy froze, and the circles under her eyes almost seemed to darken around her hooded gaze. My witchy intuition—or maybe my plain old human empathy— could sense the wave of weariness and sadness coming off Teddy LaRue. There was something else, too.

Loneliness. An intense isolation the likes of which I'd rarely encountered. But I recognized it at once.

Because you used to feel that way, back in the days before you knew who you really were, what your gifts were, or why you never truly belonged anywhere.

Jaida shifted, then seemed to make a decision. "I think you'd better tell the others what you told Katie and me. They'll understand."

"Oh, I don't think so." Teddy made to get up again.

"You did see a ghost!" Colette exclaimed. Her eyes were wide with delight. "It's okay. You can tell us. We're all witches!"

Bianca closed her eyes as if she couldn't believe her offspring's behavior. "Oh, Colette." Her tone was resigned.

I understood her reaction. None of us advertised we were witches. After all, the Honeybee had enough of a reputation since I'd been involved in several local homicide investigations, the first one before we'd even officially opened. Also, we all felt that magic was a private matter. Over time, some people had learned about the spellbook club, but most of them had some connection to magic as well. Bianca's husband's betrayal made her even more secretive than the rest of us.

Bianca wasn't keeping her magic from her daughter, however, and had been actively training her. A flare of envy stabbed through me before I tamped it down. My own parents had kept my magical background from me.

"It's true," I said to Teddy. "And if I'm really being called to . . . help this woman you mentioned, they're going to have to help me."

The other members of the spellbook club exchanged glances at my mention of being called.

At least I think I am.

I needed to know more.

The young woman looked at Jaida, who squeezed her hand. "It's your choice."

Teddy was silent, then took a deep breath, clearly terrified about what she was about to say. "I see dead people."

A thick silence filled the air for a long moment, until Lucy reached over and patted her hand. "No wonder you're such a good ghost tour guide. Do they know you?"

Teddy blinked, obviously not prepared for that reaction. "Um, yes. Most do. I've known some of the ghosts of Savannah my whole life."

"Your whole life?" Bianca leaned forward.

"They're your friends!" Colette pronounced.

Teddy looked rueful. "Well, I wouldn't say that. More like acquaintances. Some are mean or angry, but it's not at me. Some are very sad. And some, like little Gracie, are happy spirits."

"It must be difficult to do the ghost tours," I said.

"It's something I'm really good at," she said. "I mean, the spirits are everywhere. It's not like I can get away from them. They communicate with me sometimes. The ones on my tour often show up because they know I'm there. The people who take my tour have more other-worldly experiences than on any other tour."

I looked at Jaida. "You knew what we were in for. You set us up."

She gave a half smile. "Honestly, the evening didn't go at all how I expected. I did want you all to meet Teddy, though, and I figured if anyone could roll with whatever the evening brought us, it would be my fellow spellbook club members."

"Why didn't you tell us she could see ghosts?" Colette wanted to know.

Jaida tipped her head as she regarded the girl. "That wasn't my story to tell. It's Teddy's, and hers alone."

Colette bit her lip.

"You understand, honey?" Bianca asked.

She looked up at her mother's face, only inches away from her own, and said quietly, "Yes."

"When I was really little," Teddy said to Colette, "I just thought they were other, stranger people. By the time I was your age, I knew other people couldn't see them." She was trying to make Colette feel better for asking so many questions, but that wasn't all. Her voice was husky. What she was saying was intensely important to her.

"Only you could see them," I said. "To other people they weren't real."

Her haunted eyes met mine, and I had to make an effort not to look away.

"So you were all alone with them," I whispered. "All this time? No one else knew?"

She shook her head, her eyes shiny. "Not until Jaida."

My gaze cut to Jaida, but all her attention was on her friend.

"My parents thought it was cute for a while," Teddy said. "Lots of kids go through a stage where they have imaginary friends. Only mine never went away. So they sent me to therapists, and finally to a psychiatrist who prescribed some heavy-duty drugs."

"Oh, no," Lucy breathed, her horror clear.

"It's okay," Teddy said in a tone of forced lightness. "I didn't take them. I mean, I pretended to, and then I said I didn't see anything I wasn't supposed to, and everything was fine again."

I sighed. "Fine for them. Not for you."

She looked at me with intense hazel eyes and gave the slightest shrug. Then one side of her mouth turned up. "You really believe me, don't you?"

"Of course we do." I was firm. "Absolutely."

A deep breath, and then she nodded. "Well, Katie Lightfoot, that's good." She looked at Bianca and Lucy. "Because a new spirit approached me this evening. And by new, I mean brand-new. Like tonight new." She paused and let that sink in for the others.

"You mean . . . someone who had just died?" Lucy asked in a small voice.

Teddy's head inclined in affirmation. She opened her mouth to speak, then glanced at Colette and closed it.

Bianca took the hint. She gave Colette a squeeze and said, "Come on, you. It's a school night and way past your usual bedtime."

"Mommmmm," Colette protested. "I want to hear about the new ghost Teddy saw!"

"I'm sure we can find out the details in the morning." Bianca stood. "We've had enough excitement for this evening. Let's go."

Colette slumped in the chair, glaring up at her mother. Bianca waited as we all looked on. Locked in a battle of wills, her daughter didn't seem to even notice she had an audience. Then Bianca slowly raised one eyebrow and cocked her head to the side.

"Fine!" Colette huffed out and jumped to her feet. "But I think it's rotten that I don't get to hear the rest of the story."

"Noted," Bianca said, her tone mild.

The girl started to march toward the door, then suddenly whirled around and came back to stand in front of Teddy. She threw her arms around the young woman, obviously startling her.

"I'm glad you were our tour guide tonight, even if we didn't get to finish the tour. And I hope your ghosts are nice to you. They ought to be nice to someone who can really see them."

"Um, thanks, Colette. I'm super glad we met," Teddy said.

Colette stepped back. "Sorry we have to go. It's just because I'm a *child*. Maybe you could talk to me more about ghosts another time, though?"

Teddy smiled. "Sure."

Colette sighed. "Okay, Mom. Let's go."

Looking bemused, Bianca shook her head and followed her daughter to the door, but not before shooting me a look of commiseration. She'd no doubt figured out what a brand-new spirit might mean, especially given my propensity for getting dragged into homicide investigations.

"I'll stop by in the morning," she said.

I nodded.

Chapter 5

After they'd left, Lucy topped off our mugs of tea and settled back into her seat. I moved to the chair Bianca and Colette had vacated, and we turned our attention back to Teddy.

"So this new spirit you encountered had just died," I prompted.

"Not just died, Katie. As I started to tell you on the way over here, she was murdered. It had to have been near the Marshall House."

My gentle aunt let out a small sigh. I could sense her automatic compassion for the unknown victim from where I sat.

Jaida's eyes narrowed. "How do you know she was murdered?" She sounded for all the world as if we were in court.

"She told me."

"Oh, dear." Lucy looked over at me, then back at Teddy. "I think you'd better tell us everything."

Teddy frowned. "Well, okay, but it's pretty strange."

"I have no doubt," I muttered.

Jaida's lips twitched. "Go ahead."

"At the Marshall House, I was telling you about the Civil War soldiers who've been tethered to the building for centuries, right?"

We all nodded.

"They're really there, you know. One in particular always comes out when I take a tour there. He has a bit of a sense of humor and likes to play tricks."

"The skinny lady's hat!" Lucy said, remembering the woman who had lost her hat in front of us.

Teddy nodded. "He's never done any harm, and it's good for the tour, so I've never asked him to stop. He'd just flipped her hat to the ground, and his next move was probably going to be to touch someone's cheek or arm—it's a weird feeling for most people."

I shivered. "I bet it is."

"He never got the chance, though. All of a sudden, this spirit comes racing across the porch area, straight for us." She snagged my gaze. "Straight for you, really. But you didn't know she was there, even when she stopped next to you. However, when she saw me looking at her, she realized she could give me a message for you."

"A message," I repeated.

"She wants you to find her killer."

I closed my eyes. "Yes, you mentioned that." I opened them. "Wait. This is someone who knows me? Knew me." I shook my head. "Whatever." My stomach clenched as a parade of women I knew who could be unexpectedly dead flickered across my mental movie screen.

Teddy shrugged. "I don't know. She didn't give a name. They don't exactly *talk*, you see. It's more like a feeling I get from them. A sudden knowledge of whatever they want to communicate comes into my mind. It's wordless. That's how I usually communicate with them, too, with a kind of singular, narrow thought. Though I can just talk to them and that seems to work, too."

All very interesting, but right now I needed to know who was dead. "So how am I supposed to find the killer if I don't even know who they've killed? Can you tell me what she looks like?"

Teddy wrinkled her nose in a kind of apologetic wince. "I know it's a woman. Not young. Not old, but she seems to have very light hair. Angry. Really, really angry. She has a pale aura. Almost white. Maybe that's just her hair, though." Her eyes widened. "Oh! She held something out to me. It was fabric of some kind. It was kind of a pale teal, but swirly." She sighed. "It's hard to explain."

But I was thinking about how blue and green created a kind of teal color, blue and green dragonflies intertwined on a piece of silk fabric. Leigh Markes' beautiful silk scarf, covered with images of my totem.

Svelte, assertive, artistic Leigh Markes with the pure white hair.

"I'm afraid I might I know who it is," I said.

Lucy nodded. Of course. She'd seen the dragonflies on the scarf, too.

Jaida frowned. "Who?"

"A customer at the Honeybee. Leigh Markes. She owns the Markes Gallery."

"She was in the bakery this afternoon with her book club," Lucy all but whispered.

"She has white hair, always reminds me of Emmylou Harris," I said. "Or did, if it was her spirit who approached Teddy." My lips pressed together. "She was wearing a silk scarf covered with dragonflies. Lucy and I both noticed."

The skin around Jaida's eyes tightened. "You don't say." She knew about my totem, too.

Lucy and I nodded.

Teddy was watching us with wide eyes. "A scarf! Yes, that's what she was holding. I . . . I think someone strangled her with it."

I blanched. "Did she tell you that?"

She shook her head. "Not really. But the way she held it . . ." she sighed. "I suppose I sound callous, but most of the souls I see didn't exactly die in their sleep. Many—not all—died tragically. Some violently. That's why they haven't moved on."

We paused to take that in. Then I shook myself. "Hang on. If someone killed Leigh Markes, then there's a body, right? I mean, the police surely must know about it."

Jaida stood. "Of course. I'll call—"

I held up my hand, cutting her off. "I'll call Quinn. If there's been a homicide, he'll know."

Jaida nodded and sat back down. Teddy looked from her to me.

"I've worked with Detective Peter Quinn on some other cases," I explained.

"No wonder the new spirit wanted me to ask you to find who killed her. You've done it before."

I scowled and pulled my cell phone out of my pocket. After selecting Quinn's personal cell number from my contact list, I waited. He didn't answer. Glancing at my watch, I saw it was already after nine thirty. Oops. Over the course of several homicide investigations that I'd been dragged into, I'd become used to being able to call the detective at all hours.

Maybe not the best thing to get used to.

With a grimace, I hung up.

Seconds later, he called me back. "Katie Lightfoot," he drawled when I answered. "Tell me I don't have to leave my rare evening at home because you went and found a dead body."

I couldn't tell if he was being sarcastic or not. Really, it could have gone either way.

"Very funny," I said, hedging my bet. "However . . ." I trailed off, suddenly unsure how to put it.

"However, what?" His tone was flat.

"I was just, you know, wondering . . ."

"Wondering what?" Now an edge of warning had crept into his voice.

"If maybe someone else found a dead body?"

He sighed. Strains of classical music played in the silence that followed, and then I heard a woman ask him if he wanted more wine.

Rare evening at home.

"Quinn, I'm interrupting. I'm so sorry."

Jaida and Lucy exchanged rueful looks.

On the phone, another sigh. "I didn't have to call you back. As a matter of fact, I wish I hadn't. But I did. So what's this about a dead body?"

"Oh, Peter!" his wife said in the background. "Not tonight."

"Never mind," I said in a small voice.

"Tell me."

"It's just that I understand there might have been a

murder somewhere around the Marshall House. A . . . well, a woman."

"And when do you understand this murder occurred?"

"Tonight?" I offered.

"And what, exactly, gave you that understanding?"

"Um." I couldn't tell him about Teddy. He knew I was a witch, but only because he'd seen me do some things that couldn't be explained any other way. He still had a pretty hard time believing in anything related to the paranormal. Expecting him to believe Teddy really could see dead people was a nonstarter. Plus, her ability wasn't mine to reveal.

"A premonition," I said. "You know how I am, with my magical connections and all the woo-woo stuff."

Teddy's eyes widened with a combination of confusion and alarm.

"Oh, for heaven's sake," he said. "Please. A premonition? I have neither the time nor the inclination to have this conversation with you. As the lead homicide detective in the precinct that the Marshall House is in, I'd know if there had been any kind of suspicious death, even on my day off. Which this is. And there weren't any deaths at all, never mind suspicious ones. Good night, Katie." He hung up, but not before I heard him mutter, "Sorry, darlin'" to his wife.

I dropped my cell phone in my lap and rubbed my hands over my face. "Yikes. That wasn't good." When I looked up, the others were staring at me. "There hasn't been any murder reported in this precinct tonight, and now Quinn thinks I'm crazy."

"Well," Jaida said in a matter-of-fact tone. "He already thought you were a little crazy. Nothing to be done about that now. All we can do is wait and see what happens tomorrow."

"Oh, no." Teddy sounded weary. "Isn't there anything we can do tonight? The spirit is still so angry."

"She's here?" I asked, looking around the dark bakery with consternation.

"No, but she's near," Teddy whispered. "I can feel her. And I don't think she's going to leave me alone until you find her killer."

Lucy stood up and put her hand on Teddy's shoulder. "Don't you worry. Katie will find out what happened, and we'll do everything we can to help her."

I opened my mouth to protest but closed it when my aunt shot me a look.

Jaida rose. "But there's really not much we can do tonight. Come on, Teddy. You can come back to our place for the night. Things will look brighter in the morning."

The young woman looked relieved at Jaida's invitation. "I guess you're right. Katie, I'm really sorry to drag you into this whole thing."

"Nonsense," I said. "Leigh Markes dragged me into this."

Or rather, her killer did.

Chapter 6

After retrieving my Volkswagen Beetle from the parking garage, I wended my way through the precise squares of Savannah's historic district and continued down Abercorn Street toward Midtown. As I drove, I mulled over the evening's events. My conversation with Quinn had intensified my misgivings about getting involved in Leigh Markes' death.

Murder, I reminded myself. Even if only a few people knew that so far.

One of whom was her killer.

If Teddy was telling the truth.

I shook my head, remembering the haunted expression on Teddy's face when she spoke of her ability. The shy flutter of her eyelashes when she first admitted to it and the shame that rolled off her as we spoke hurt my heart. Hers was a stunning talent, but I also understood the weight that carried. When I'd been told I was a hereditary witch, I'd resisted for a while but then embraced my gift with everything that I was. It explained why I'd felt alone and out of place for most of my life, why I'd never fit in. Learning about what made me a little different had opened a world of friendship and belonging I'd only dreamed of.

Then when the spellbook club discovered I was also a catalyst, meaning things kind of *happened* more around me than other people, it had explained why since moving to Savannah I'd found myself involved in a ridiculous number of homicide cases for someone not in law enforcement. However, when I'd been told—by a witch hunter and police detective, no less—that I was a *lightwitch*, I'd rebelled. Because he'd told me I was destined to right magical wrongs, I'd felt I didn't have a choice. According to him, I hadn't. Since then, and with the help of my coven mates, I'd come to realize that I could, of course, choose whether or not to answer when I was called.

This situation was one of those. Though I could choose to walk away and a big part of me wanted to, I wouldn't.

Not when Teddy LaRue was Gregory's goshdaughter. Not after seeing the pleading look on her face. Not after the actual murder victim asked for my help.

Okay, demanded. Still.

Suppressing a shudder, I turned my thoughts to how I might go about finding out more about Leigh's life, because by now I'd learned the only way to figure out how someone died was to figure out how they'd lived.

"Mungo, I sure wish you were here right now to bounce things off of," I murmured under my breath. My familiar didn't say much, but he was an invaluable help when I was trying to arrange my thoughts and emotions. Any other night, he'd be strapped into the passenger seat of the Bug, watching me with earnest eyes as I laid it all out for him in my messy, stream-of-consciousness manner. Tonight, he was probably on the sofa in the loft with Declan and Uncle Ben, sleeping off his supper of brisket and ribs.

Ben's pickup was parked at the curb in front of the carriage house when I pulled into the driveway. My husband's even larger truck would be parked inside the new garage, alongside the bench and collection of woodworking tools he'd been adding to once we had the extra room for his burgeoning hobby. It had been his deceased father's hobby, too. Declan had inherited the oldest hand tools from him when only a child, and I was delighted he was learning how to use them.

Though truth be told, I wouldn't have minded him taking up a slightly less dangerous leisure pursuit. Not that woodworking was exactly high risk, but since his guardian spirit had gone missing, I was on high alert for the slightest mishap.

I'd been wrong about Mungo. As soon as I opened the front door, he barreled out of the kitchen and ran to me, toenails skittling as he scrabbled for purchase on the hardwood floorboards.

Yip!

I dropped my tote bag and leaned down as he jumped straight into my arms. Wrapping my arms around him, I nestled my face into the comfort of his fur and squeezed my eyes shut. He instantly fell still, sensing my distress.

I carried him over to the eggplant-colored sofa and sat down. His presence calmed me, as did this space. Dark green bookcases punctuated the gentle sage green walls of the postage stamp–sized living room. Along with the richly hued sofa and matching wingback chairs, Declan's old rocking chair, now painted a dark maroon and festooned with pillows, added to the warm atmosphere of our home. Light wood shutters covered the front windows, and French doors opposite the entrance led out to the backyard, gardens, and gazebo.

"Katie?" Declan called from above. "That you?"

I gave my familiar one last little squeeze, put him on the cushion, and moved out to the middle of the room so I could see up to the loft. "Who else would it be?"

He stood at the top of the stairs. Ben stood next to him.

"How was the game?" I asked.

"Good enough, but we lost," Ben said. "The food and company made up for it."

"And somehow we males managed not to spill barbeque sauce all over the new sofa," Declan said with a smile.

My eyes inexplicably filled with tears.

The two men exchanged looks and quickly came down the stairs.

"Something happened," Declan stated flatly. "On the ghost tour."

I brushed at my eyes and sighed. "A woman was killed."

"What?" Ben took a step toward me. "How?"

I shook my head. "I don't know. Strangled, I think. Detective Quinn said there hasn't been any record of a homicide anywhere near where it happened. He's, uh, not very happy with me right now."

Declan's mouth tightened. "You know what you said makes no sense, right?"

I nodded miserably.

His expression relaxed, and his gaze grew tender. "Okay. Maybe you'd better explain."

"It's weird," I said. "You know. Witchy stuff."

His eyes crinkled at the corners. "I expected nothing less. Ben, you want another beer?"

"Nah. I'm driving." He sat down in one of the chairs opposite the sofa.

"Well, I'm not," Declan said, and went into the kitchen. I heard the sound of the bottle opener. Then he came back with two sweating bottles and handed one to me.

I accepted it gratefully, took a deep breath, and told them what had happened.

After Ben left, Declan and I got ready to go to bed. He'd ended a forty-eight-hour shift at Five House that morning and only had a chance for a brief nap before his evening with Ben and the Falcons. He was practically asleep on his feet. I'd be up by four to go for a run and then get down to the Honeybee to get started on the day's baking, but since I usually only slept a few hours a night, I planned to read for a while.

I came into the bedroom after washing my face and brushing my teeth to find my husband already in bed, covers pulled up to his chin. Mungo lay near his feet, chin resting on his paws, watching for me. Upon seeing me, he immediately huffed out a doggy sigh, closed his eyes, and went to sleep. The dim light from the bedside lamp threw elaborate shadows behind the intricate wrought-iron headboard, a gift from Lucy and Ben, and the waxing gibbous moon hung high in the sky outside the window. A breeze outside brought the scent of night-blooming jasmine into the room, along with the shushing sound of the leaves moving on the magnolia tree at the corner of the house.

Declan pushed himself up on his elbows as I climbed into bed. "Have you decided what to do?" he asked.

I gave a little shrug. "I guess the first thing in finding who killed Leigh Markes is making sure Leigh is actually dead. It would be a heck of a thing to run into her on the street after all this."

"But you don't think that's going to happen, do you?"

"Nope. I believe Teddy LaRue, and I saw those dragonflies on Leigh's scarf."

"So then what?"

"Call in the spellbook club," I said. "Six heads are better than one, after all. Besides, the way Savannah works, at least one of them is bound to know something about Leigh Markes or her family or her gallery. At least I hope so because I sure don't."

"Once you have a thread, though, you can start pulling it and see where it leads," he said.

I grinned. "That's how it seems to have worked before, eh?"

"Pretty much." He reached over and stroked his finger down my arm. "Are you sure about this one? It seems a little . . . spooky, I guess. Someone who talks to dead people and all."

I gave him a look. "Seriously? Worse than a voodoo curse? Worse than someone trying to unleash an evil spirit from the other side to give them unlimited power? Worse than . . ." I trailed off.

"Worse than a séance that brought my not-quite-dead leprechaun guardian spirit out of the woodwork?" Declan asked with a gentle smile. "I guess not."

I was silent for several seconds.

"Katie?"

Might as well bring it up.

"You know how I said I wanted to help the murder victim, and that I wanted to help Teddy LaRue, too?" I'd pretty much told Declan and Ben everything I'd been thinking as I drove home from the Honeybee in order to justify getting involved in another murder case.

But not quite everything.

"Yeah . . . ?"

"Something else occurred to me. On the one hand, I'm not proud of it, because it feels selfish and maybe even wrong to ask someone to do. On the other hand, it might be just what we're looking for, you know?"

Declan's eyes sparked. "You think Teddy could be the tether we're looking for?"

Though I didn't know exactly how to get Connell back, one thing I had discovered was that the process would require a *tether*—someone who could straddle the veil between this world and the next, someone with access to both planes at the same time. From what she'd said, it seemed to me that Teddy LaRue had that access most if not all of the time.

"Would she do it?" Declan asked.

I lifted one shoulder and let it drop. "No idea. It can't hurt to ask, though." Which was true, but there was something about the young woman that made me hesitate to approach her with what could be a trying, even potentially dangerous proposition. I sensed that she had a deep core of strength, but there was also a delicacy, a fragility. A smile lit up Declan's face then, and I pushed away my uncertainty. Getting Connell back was really important.

"Well, then! Things are looking up." He reached for me, still grinning.

"I thought you were exhausted after your shift," I teased.

"Why don't you just turn out the light and see?" he asked.

I turned off the light.

The next morning Declan was still fast asleep by the time I left for the Honeybee. I propped a little love note alongside a lime poppyseed muffin, loaded the French press coffeemaker with freshly ground dark roast, and filled the electric kettle. Outside, Mungo trundled across the dark yard and jumped into the Bug as soon as I opened the driver's side door. He settled into the back seat next to my ginormous tote bag and promptly took his first nap of the day as I drove to work.

The edge of the eastern sky was lightening toward dawn, and the streets were still mostly empty. After parking, I hauled my tote bag, now mostly full of Mungo, onto my shoulder and made my way to the bakery. All the while, my senses were pinging around me, alert to danger in the dark. Usually, it was so automatic I didn't notice myself doing it. *Most women would re-*

late, I thought. I also knew I drew on my witchy intuition to augment my vigilance. However, this morning the feeling of danger was palpable. A woman had been murdered last night, just down the street. At least I thought she had.

Not to mention that for all I knew, otherworldly spirits surrounded me on my journey from the car to the front door.

Maybe even inside.

That was a disconcerting thought.

After locking the door behind me, I revved up the ovens to crackling hot for the sourdough loaves that had risen overnight. Then I started in on the buttermilk batter base for the different muffins our breakfast crowd went for first thing—lime poppyseed, banana pecan, blueberry maple, and brown butter oatmeal with a brown sugar crust. After the first batches were in the oven, I mixed up dough for the cathead biscuits we served our specialty breakfast sandwiches on. The Lucy was piled with sausage, swiss cheese, spinach, and egg, the Iris was a delectable combination of tasso ham and homemade pimiento cheese, and the Ben was bacon, lettuce, and tomato, slathered with avocado and topped with a fried egg. The Katie was our vegetarian version, with soft brie cheese, sauteed mushrooms, and fig jam.

My phone buzzed in my pocket. It was a text from Quinn.

Call me ASAP.

I called him and he answered immediately. "Katie, you will be pleased to know a dead body was discovered this morning near the Marshall House."

"*Pleased?* Are you kidding me?"

He sighed. "Sorry. Bad choice of language. But I want to know about this, er, premonition you had last night."

"Um."

"Katie, I'm looking at a murdered woman as we speak. Stop 'umming' and tell me why you called me last night."

"I just had a feeling?"

Another sigh.

I barreled on. "And since you're, you know, a homicide detective, and you've always been so nice to me, I thought I'd check in with you about my, um . . . feeling." He hadn't always been so nice to me, of course, and indeed had tried to pin a murder on Uncle Ben before we'd even managed to open the Honeybee, but now wasn't a good time to bring that up. "How did she die?" I asked.

"*She* was strangled," Quinn said. "How did you know—"

"The dragonfly scarf," I said without thinking. "Dang it."

"Katie! How did you know the victim was strangled with a scarf? And yes, those do look like dragonflies!" Apparently, he was looking at the murder weapon as he spoke to me.

"I told you," I said. "A premonition. Can you tell me the victim's identity? Was she found inside the Marshall House?"

He swore. Quinn seemed to swear a lot when he talked with me. Then a few seconds of silence passed before he said, "I guess it can't hurt to tell you. After all, the time of death was determined to be at least a couple of hours after you called me last night, so I'll have to take your word as a"—he took a deep breath—"a *witch*, that you experienced some kind of clairvoyant . . . something. The victim is named Leigh Markes, and she was found strangled inside her car in the parking garage behind the Marshall House."

My vision seemed to contract, and I felt lightheaded. Leigh Markes was dead. It had all been theoretical until Quinn said it out loud, but now it was all too real. She had been murdered, strangled with the lovely silk scarf she'd been wearing when last I saw her, and now any slight doubt I might have harbored that her spirit had been in contact with Teddy was gone.

Quinn broke the spell. "What else can you tell me?"

"Nothing," I answered honestly. "I've told you all I know."

He harrumphed. "More like I told you all I know."

Then I realized just what he *had* told me. "Are you sure she was killed after I called you?" I asked.

"Our people know how to do their jobs."

"Of course." My voice sounded faraway to my own ears. Distracted. Could Leigh's spirit have contacted Teddy before Leigh died? It didn't seem possible.

I heard the key turning in the lock of the door that led to the alley. "I have to go, Quinn. Talk to you later, okay?"

"Are you sure you can't tell me anything useful to the investigation, Katie?"

"Sorry. If I come across anything, I'll let you know."

"Well, don't go looking, all right?"

I made a noncommittal noise.

"Katie!"

"Gotta go. Bye." This time I was the one who hung up first.

Chapter 7

Turning, I found my aunt and uncle shrugging off their jackets. Honeybee sat in her carrier on the floor at Lucy's feet.

"Who were you talking to?" Ben asked.

"Detective Quinn," I answered.

They both paused and gave me questioning looks.

I nodded. "Quinn just confirmed it. Leigh Markes was found dead in her car, strangled with her own scarf."

My aunt closed her eyes, and Ben wrapped his arm around her shoulders.

"He says they determined the time of death to be a couple of hours after I called him last night."

Lucy's eyes opened. "That doesn't make any sense."

"I know." I looked at my watch. It was just coming up seven o'clock. "I'll start calling the spellbook club in an hour or so."

"I'll do it." Lucy picked up Honeybee and carried her to the reading area, where she exited her carrier and leaped to the windowsill to watch the activity starting up on Broughton Street. "I've already spoken with Mimsey."

If we'd been a formal coven, Mimsey Carmichael would have been our high priestess. As it was, she was our de facto leader due to her considerable experience in the Craft, her gentle wisdom, and the simple fact that we all loved her to pieces.

Before she came back to the kitchen, my aunt hung the RESERVED sign by the reading area, ensuring a modicum of privacy when the other witches arrived.

Our part-time employee, Iris Grant, showed up as Lucy was rolling out the pale, sugary dough for moon and stars cookies. Nineteen and studying at the Savannah College of Art and Design, she had come to work at the bakery after I met her while investigating a murder on a movie set in the historic district. She had brown eyes, multiple piercings, an elaborate fairy tattoo on her upper arm, a talent for both baking and magic that was perfect for our work at the Honeybee, and a sweet disposition. Since just the day before, she'd dyed her ever-changing hair, currently cut in a short bob, bright orange around her face and black with orange streaks in the back.

"Nice," Lucy said with an approving nod at her hair.

"Very Halloween-y," I said with a grin.

"Samhain," Iris corrected me, her face serious. "I've been paying attention."

"Are things going okay, sweetie?" Lucy's eyes traveled over our employee's young face. Sure enough, once I looked past the brightly colored hair, Iris's eyes appeared red-rimmed and swollen.

Iris began to nod, but suddenly tears welled up.

"Oh, honey." Lucy hurried over and gave her a big hug. Iris let out a little sob as the tears spilled over.

"That's it. Tell us what's wrong," my aunt demanded.

But Iris pulled away, vehemently shaking her head. "No. I can't. I'll just lose it, and I have work to do. I'm not going to think about it for a while. Oh, that jerk!" The tears threatened again, but she quickly wiped them away and strode back to the office. I heard her greet Mungo in a shaky voice, then blow her nose. When she returned, she calmly asked me what I'd like her to do.

After a moment's hesitation, I suggested she could start making pastry for pumpkin hand pies. As she gathered ingredients, Lucy gave me a look. I nodded and went over to the counter, where a pan of cookies were cooling. One of Iris' recipes, they were on the menu as that day's special and were studded with delicate petals of roses, lavender, and violets—all triggered with a spell to activate their ability to promote love and comfort heartbreak. From our brief exchange, my guess was that Iris was having trouble with her recent boyfriend. I didn't know how bad it was, but the cookies might help. I picked one up and took it over to her.

"Care to try the daily special?" I asked.

She took with it with a grateful moue. "Thanks," she whispered. "Maybe this will do the trick."

Things were settling down as they generally did midmorning. I was restocking the pastry case, and Lucy was patrolling the tables for crumbs and spills before the lunch wave hit. Ben was on the phone with the farm that supplied our eggs, and Iris was shifting fragrant molasses cookies from a baking sheet to a rack to cool.

When the door opened, I looked up and felt a smile bloom on my face. "Mrs. Standish! How are you today?"

"Oh, I'm fine, fine, fine. Why, what have you heard?" She waggled her painted eyebrows and they disappeared into the zebra-print turban snugged on her head. A few iron gray curls escaped artfully around the edge. The loose belt on her orange caftan matched the turban, giving her a safari-meets-jack-o'-lantern vibe. Her dark orange lipstick matched the caftan.

Edna Standish had been one of our very first customers and was now one of our most loyal. Her enthusiastic love of the Honeybee pastries had spread to her wide-reaching social network and had been influential to the bakery's quick success in the community. Almost every day she stopped by with her companion, Skipper Dean. They had met shortly after Lucy and I had boosted the possibility of love for a very lonely widow Standish with a special vanilla-laced treat. Today, however, she was alone.

"I've only heard good things about you, dear." I laughed. "Where's Dean?"

"The Skipper is at a meeting of the Savannah Arts Association. I was supposed to go, but those things can be so terribly boring, you know. They're discussing something about graffiti along the riverfront and whether it's vandalism or art."

Ben had finished with his telephone conversation and came to stand beside me. "Edna, how long have you been involved with SAA?"

"Oh, heavens." She waved a manicured hand that glittered with rings. "Years and years. My husband, bless his departed soul, was a great patron of the arts. He just loved helping up-and-coming talent, you know. Quite the expert. I'm afraid I don't really know much about art, though."

"But you know what you like?" Ben's eyes flashed humor as he smiled.

She laughed. "Indeed. I've continued my involvement with the organization as a tribute to Harry. Skipper Dean, on the other hand, has a particular interest in something called 'outsider art.' To me, it looks like something a kindergartener came up with, but what do I know?"

"Are you familiar with the Markes Gallery?" Ben's demeanor was so deliberately casual I thought she'd peg to it, but she didn't seem to.

"Well, I know Leigh Markes from other organizations I'm involved with—she's always been a contributor to my animal welfare fundraisers. And of course, I've been in her gallery. Bought a lovely painting for the guesthouse from her." Now she squinted at him. "Why do you ask, Ben?"

I started to break in with a rundown of the freshest additions to the pastry case, but Ben answered easily, "Her book club met here, and we chatted a bit."

Mrs. Standish continued to regard him for a long moment, then turned that razor-sharp attention to me. I smiled and kept my mouth shut. She had an instinct for gossip that was almost otherworldly.

Lucy bustled by with the cloth she'd been using to wipe down the tables. No doubt she'd heard every word. "Edna! How lovely to see you. It's a warm one out there, isn't it? Perhaps you'd like a glass of sweet tea? Today's is mint. It goes especially well with the double chocolate chip cookies."

Mrs. Standish's face lit up. "Oh, yes. Please. And I'll take a half dozen of those decadent cookies. They're the ones with the weensy little marshmallows in them? Excellent. The Skipper loves those. And I'll take a small loaf of sourdough today. It will be a nice accompaniment to our rack of lamb luncheon. Now, don't look so surprised, Katie. We generally eat a very light supper."

I hadn't realized my expression had been so transparent. Embarrassed, I set to putting her order into a bakery bag decorated with our logo of a certain orange cat.

Mimsey Carmichael came in the door as Mrs. Standish was leaving. Old friends, they greeted each other and took the time to exchange pleasantries. The door closed behind Mrs. Standish, and Mimsey made her way to the counter where we stood, her stride and posture full of purpose.

"Where is everyone?"

"You're the first to arrive," Lucy said. "Shall I bring you a cup of tea?"

Mimsey gave a ladylike snort. "Heavens, no. But I'll take a double espresso and a sage scone, if you're offering."

Laughing, Ben hurried to make her caffeine supplement, and Lucy put a scone on a plate for our friend.

Shorter even than my aunt, who was several inches shorter than my five feet eight, Mimsey referred to herself as comfortably padded. A witch who specialized in color and flower magic, she owned a florist shop a few blocks away from the Honeybee called Vase Value. The oldest of our group, she'd officially become an octogenarian since I'd met her two and half years before, but looked at least ten, if not fifteen, years younger than that. Though I'd once wondered if she employed a glamour to augment her looks, I'd come to realize they were simply a result of how she cheerfully and enthusiastically embraced every single day. She tended to dress in magically strategic colors, and today she wore a tunic swirled with yellow and orange over white slacks. An orange bow perched on the side of her white pageboy as if by . . . magic.

Probably a hidden hair clip, though.

The color combo made me think of a piece of Halloween candy corn, but I knew the yellow was for focus and creativity—both good for solving problems—and the orange for success and justice. The white would be for clarity.

I'd learned a lot from Mimsey. And we were going to need all the help we could get if we were really going to find out who had killed Leigh Markes.

Armed with her scone and napkin, she wove her way through the tables toward the reading area, calling over her shoulder, "I brought a couple books for your library. I'll just find a place for them and wait for the others in here."

Jaida and Bianca came in together as Ben took Mimsey her espresso. They made their selections—a chocolate croissant for Bianca and a pumpkin spice muffin for Jaida—and joined Mimsey. By the time Lucy and I left Ben and Iris in charge of customers and went into the reading area, Bianca had her laptop open on the coffee table. It turned out Cookie Rios, the youngest member of the spellbook club, was able to attend our impromptu meeting virtually—along with her new baby, Isabella. Lucy and I sat down and added our cooing and exclamations over the beautiful little girl. Amid the hubbub over her sweet little self, Isabella's eyes drifted closed, and she slept.

"Whew," Cookie said, her voice hushed as she centered the camera on her own face. "It's amazing how she just up and checks out with no warning. Of course, pretty much everything she does is amazing." She grinned, and the mothers around the table grinned back in understanding camaraderie.

"Even the middle-of-the-night feedings?" Bianca asked.

"Even those," Cookie said. "Though having my mother around has helped so much. And Oscar does his part." She looked down at the baby in her arms. "He loves his little girl, oh, yes, he does." Her words held the slight lilt of her early childhood in Haiti.

I smiled. Cookie had changed a great deal since we'd met. In the beginning she had been known to go through boyfriends every three months or so, as well as jobs, skittering from man to man and everything from being a waitress to managing a shoe store. She'd even worked at the Honeybee for a little while. Then she'd come back from a trip to Europe with a husband and settled into a career in real estate as if she'd been born to it.

She had moved to the US with her mother and brother when she was nine, after her father, a voodoo priest in Port-au-Prince, had been killed. A witch who had always been more comfortable than the rest of us dabbling in what I thought of as "gray" magic, she'd recently reconnected with her voodoo past and was deepening her connection to those roots.

Right now, though, she was all about little Isabella. She looked happy but tired, with no makeup on her light brown skin, dark circles around her eyes, and her dark tresses clamped back in a messy ponytail.

"Let me just take care of something, and we'll get started," Mimsey said.

She rose and went to where a thick, braided tieback held a floor-to-ceiling curtain against the wall. She unhooked it and drew the curtain across on the rod Ben had installed above, essentially closing off the reading area from the rest of the bakery. Then she murmured under her breath and made a few hand gestures. Bianca rose and moved to stand beside her, repeating the gestures with her.

When they sat back down, I asked, "Privacy spell?"

Mimsey nodded. "Silencing spell. People will be able to hear voices, but not what we're saying."

Just when I think I've learned so much, I realize I have so much more to learn.

Tamping down the resentment that rose whenever I thought about how my parents hadn't told me about my magical gifts—in an attempt to protect me, but still—I made a note to ask the others about that spell later.

"So everyone is up to speed on what happened last night?" I asked.

Everyone nodded, even Cookie. The spellbook club had a very efficient internal grapevine.

"Okay. What do we know about Leigh Markes?" I didn't have any kind of a plan and hoped someone would know something that we could grab on to, a thread to pull and see what unraveled, as Declan had said.

Bianca looked around at the others. "Well, I was acquainted with Leigh from her gallery."

That didn't surprise me. Bianca, though nouveau riche, had made her way into Savannah's old-school society scene as well as the arts community.

She continued. "But I hadn't seen her for a while. She hadn't been running things there for over a year. She returned a few weeks ago. While she was gone, her assistant had full control of the place."

"Leigh was taking time off?" I asked.

Bianca nodded. "Her father was ill. She moved him into her house and took care of him." She made a sympathetic noise. "He recently passed away."

"I knew James Markes," Mimsey said. "Leigh, too, in passing. But James was my generation, part of my crowd growing up. We even dated for a bit in our early twenties."

"My condolences, dear," Lucy said.

Mimsey waved a hand. "Death is but a journey to the next plane. James was a card, though. Funny as all getout. Loved a practical joke, teased his poor wife to distraction. They were very much in love. Over fifty years they were married. She passed six or seven years ago."

"Leigh has a sister," I said.

"Oh, yes. Calista. Bit of a flibbertigibbet. Leigh was the artist, but she was also a hard-core businesswoman. Calista missed out on both talents. I heard there were issues between her and James in his later years."

I made a mental note. Calista and Leigh hadn't exactly parted on friendly terms, and that had been only hours before Leigh had been killed.

"Um?" A voice from the corner near where the curtain had been drawn made me jump. We all turned to find Iris standing just inside the curtain, looking pained. "I'm sorry. I know this is an important meeting and private and all, but Ben told me Ms. Markes died suddenly. I just wanted to say . . ." She trailed off.

"Say what?" Jaida's tone was kind.

"I knew Ms. Markes. Well, sort of. I'm friends with her daughter, Zoe Stokes. We were in the same year of high school. She's away at college now. She's cool. Her mom was cool, too." She looked down at the floor, and my heart went out to her. Then she looked back up and squared her shoulders. "Her dad isn't so great, though. Kind of a"—she searched for a word—"jerk." I had a feeling that wasn't the first word that came to her mind. "He and Ms. Markes divorced about four years ago. I guess it was messy. He was pretty mean when they split up."

The spellbook club members exchanged glances.

"Yes," Mimsey said. "I'm afraid Iris is right about Walker Stokes. James did not approve of his marriage to Leigh, not at all. I don't know details other than Walker's reputation as a ladies' man—and a cad."

Chapter 8

I suppressed a smile at the term *cad* and leaned forward. "What does he do for a living?"

Mimsey looked surprised. "You know, I'm not really sure."

"He manages things," Iris said.

"What kind of things?" Jaida asked.

Iris shrugged. "I don't know. It's just something Zoe said once. Her mom was involved in all sorts of stuff, but her dad just seemed to be, you know, around." She sighed. "I guess she'll be coming back from college for a while. I'm going to text her. I'd like to see her, tell her I'm sorry about her mom."

Suddenly I realized the connection: Iris had lost her mother when she was quite young. She lived with her stepmom, whom she adored, in the small basement apartment of her stepmom's house.

Lucy nodded. "I think it would be nice for you to connect with her."

Iris reached for the curtain, then paused. "Katie?

Ben said Zoe's mom didn't die accidentally. That she was killed. Are you going to find out who did it?"

I met her eyes. She'd worked for us long enough that she knew I sometimes got involved with police cases.

"If I can help, I'll do what I can," I said.

"We all will," Jaida said.

A smile fluttered at the corners of Iris' lips. Her voice was strong. "Good." She turned and slipped back out.

"Oh, poor Zoe," Cookie said. "Do you think she might accept an amulet of comfort? I could make it and give it to Iris to give to her."

"That would be a kindness," Bianca said. "But do you have time?"

"Don't worry. I'll make time," Cookie said, gazing down at the tiny person resting in her arms.

Mimsey shook her head ruefully. "Death is so hard on the young ones." When she looked around at all of us, her eyes were bright with determination. "Now, what's the plan?"

I took a deep breath, thinking. "We need more information. I could ask Steve Dawes if he knows anything about Leigh, the gallery, any possible enemies. He's reporting on crime now, but he had the downtown arts and business beat for a long time."

Silence fell over the group. Steve and I had almost been a thing, about the same time Declan and I were becoming a thing, and there had been a history of bad blood between them even before I'd stepped into the picture. Plus, Steve was a member of the local druid clan, who were not exactly rivals of the spellbook club, but not exactly friends, either.

"Do you have a better suggestion?" I asked.

"No, it's a good idea," Lucy said in a brisk tone.

"Okay," I said. "I'd like to talk with Leigh's ex-husband. Detective Quinn has likely already spoken with him, since in murder cases it makes sense to look at the spouse, or in this case, ex-spouse, first. Maybe I could ask Quinn—" I stopped myself and shook my head. "No, he won't tell me anything without good reason. And to him, there isn't a good reason."

"Yet." Mimsey quirked an eyebrow.

I looked at Bianca. "Do you think Leigh's assistant would be at the gallery? Or do you think it's closed?"

She gave a kind of facial shrug. "Easy enough to call and find out."

"Right. If it's open, you and I can stop by and chat with her. Wait—her?"

"Yes, her. Paisley Long," Bianca said.

"I can do a little digging through public records on Walker Stokes," Jaida offered. "Gregory offered to take over whatever I might need him to at our practice so I can help out his goshdaughter." She made a face. "I know this is about Leigh, but it's about Teddy, too."

We all murmured agreement.

"Katie, what about Leigh's friends?" Lucy asked. "The others in their book club?"

"There was Leigh's sister, Calista." I thought back. "But I don't know the names of the others. I think two of them were mother and daughter. Oh, wait. I heard them call the tall one Jo. No idea about last name, though."

"Could the bookmark Mungo found belong to Calista?" my aunt asked.

I felt my lips twitch. "Indeed, it could. Maybe I'll track down her number and give her a call."

"Would her last name be Markes?" Cookie asked from the computer screen.

I looked over and saw Isabella now slumbering in a bassinet while Cookie typed furiously.

"Yes, it's Markes." She answered her own question. "I'm sending you her address." She made a noise of speculation. "Nice digs. In the Victorian district."

Mimsey said, "That's the home that's been in the family for generations. She must be living there."

"I wonder if Leigh was as well," I said.

Cookie typed some more. "No, she has a house in Midtown."

We heard a flurry of voices out in the Honeybee proper. Apparently, the spell Mimsey and Bianca had placed on the barrier worked both ways, because we couldn't make out a single word being said. Lucy jumped up and looked around the edge of the curtain.

"Tour group," she exclaimed, and that was all it took.

The curtain slid back and was pinned to the wall, and Lucy and I hurried out to help Ben and Iris with the rush. The other members of the spellbook club said goodbye to Cookie and Isabella, brought our dishes back to the kitchen, and removed the RESERVED sign. Soon customers drifted in to peruse books and lounge on the comfy furniture.

The members of the spellbook club left, beginning with Mimsey. Jaida was next, and I waved to her as I saw her moving toward the door. She started to wave goodbye but then realized I wanted to talk to her. I held up two fingers, and she gave a nod and gestured toward the street. I also nodded, and two minutes later had left my coworkers to deal with the last of the customers while I slipped out to the sidewalk.

Jaida was next door, looking at the offerings in the window of the Fox and Hound Bookshop. When she saw me, she sauntered back, and we met halfway.

"I was just going to get back to the office to do an online check on Walker Stokes," she said.

"Thanks for doing that. I didn't like the way Iris described him."

"I didn't either, but that doesn't make him a murderer."

"True." I fell quiet.

"Katie?" She waited.

I took a deep breath and plunged in. "So, you know about how Connell is, well, missing."

"Yeah."

"And we all talked about how Nonna told me we needed help to get him back, right? But then there was the wedding, and Declan's sister was a suspect in killing her ex, and finding Connell kind of fell by the wayside."

Her gaze softened. "It did. I'm sorry. We didn't forget. We just don't know what to do next."

"Oh, I know. It's not anyone's fault." I licked my lips. "Jaida, Declan needs Connell. *I* need him to have Connell. He serves as Declan's intuition, the red flag when there's danger. After my dear husband is finished with his paramedic training, can you imagine the situations he's going to find himself in?"

Slowly, she nodded. I could tell she was thinking. I barreled on.

"The help we need is a *tether*. It has to be someone who can straddle both sides of the veil, who has access to both worlds."

I watched the realization dawn on her face.

"Do you think Teddy could serve as that tether?" I asked. "I mean, she's kind of the perfect person to do it. She regularly sees spirits on the other side, and if we perform the ritual at midnight on Halloween, it should be extra easy for her to help us find Connell and bring him . . ." My growing hope died as I saw the look on Jaida's face.

"I don't know, Katie. Teddy's special, as you well know. But she's fragile. Skittish. I don't know all the details, but I don't think it's been easy growing up with her ability, and I don't think it's easy to walk around with it day in and day out, either."

I bit my lip. "She does make a living from it, though."

Jaida didn't say anything.

"Do I have your permission to ask her?"

My friend stepped in and wrapped me in a hug. "You don't need my permission. She's a grown woman and so are you. I'd be glad if she can help bring Connell back to Declan. I just don't want you to count on it."

I gave her a squeeze and stepped back. "Right. I won't put all my eggs in that basket. But Connell wouldn't be gone if he hadn't stepped in to save my magic for me. I'm going to try anything I can to fix this for Declan—and Connell. He can't be happy stuck in whatever between-world he's in."

"I'm behind you all the way, honey." She smiled. "Let me know what Teddy says."

Her words were encouraging, but as she turned to

leave, I saw the worry pinching the skin around her eyes. I tried to remain hopeful as I went back inside the Honeybee.

Half an hour later, the traffic had dwindled to normal. Bianca had stuck around, helping out as she could. Lucy was in the kitchen, and Ben moved among the tables, tidying and pushing in the chairs. I had begun to restock the pastry case in preparation for the lunch crowd starting to trickle in when I heard Bianca on the phone.

"Hello, Paisley? Bianca Devereaux here." I noticed her Southern accent was strong. Paisley was in for the gentlest hard sell around. "I was wondering what time the gallery will open today. I have a friend in town who might be interested in that Hanta sculpture. It's such a lovely piece, and I was telling her all about it. The lines! Tell me you still have it." There was a pause as she listened. "Oh, dear. That's terrible. Just awful. This morning, you say? No, I haven't seen the paper yet. Yes, I understand, of course . . . Oh? . . . Well, that's very kind of you . . . Two o'clock should be fine." She looked over at me, and I nodded. "I'm so sorry to hear about Leigh. A tragedy indeed."

She ended the call and came over to where I stood waiting behind fresh rows of assorted muffins. "It was in the *Savannah Morning News*."

Juggling two plates and a half-empty mug of coffee, Ben walked by. "I looked. Nothing in there about a murder."

"It wouldn't have made the presses for the print paper," I said over my shoulder as I returned the tray to the kitchen. "It must be online."

Bianca was already tapping on her phone. By the time I returned she was scanning the screen. "Not much info here. They found her body in her car in the parking garage behind the Marshall House. Nothing about how she died, only that it's being investigated as a homicide. Reference to her family roots here in Savannah and the gallery, but not much else." She looked up. "Pretty spare reporting, really. For Steve Dawes."

I sighed. "Quinn must have put a damper on the story. Usually, Steve is quite thorough."

"Maybe they just don't know much yet."

"At least not that they're telling anyone at this point."

"I'll be back to pick you up at one forty-five. I can drive us to the gallery." She grinned.

I grinned back. I'd never refused a ride in Bianca's car yet. "See you then."

Chapter 9

I leaned back against the leather upholstery and sighed. Sitting in Bianca's cherry red convertible Jaguar was first class in every way—lush and plush, wood trimmed, the soft purr of the engine as it idled at the light.

Then the light turned green, and I was gripping the edge of my seat, adrenaline surging, breathless and trying not to smile stupidly. The Jag had been one of her first big purchases after she'd found her calling in the stock market. She kept it in perfect condition and drove it as if we were at Le Mans, even though we were just tooling down Bull Street.

The Markes Gallery was on a side street off Whitaker. The exterior eschewed the antebellum architecture of the historic district, instead embracing a modern look with clean lines, an asymmetrical roofline, and double metal doors at the entrance. We'd left early in case parking was hard to find but lucked out with a spot right in front of the gallery. Bianca pulled into it, and we got out and paused on the sidewalk in front.

"What am I supposed to be looking at again?" I asked.

"It's a sculpture of spirit or love or transcendence. Something like that. I don't really remember. All her work is conceptually representational. The artist is named Hanta, just one name. Actually, I think you'll like it."

"Well, I should have brought my checkbook, then."

Bianca side-eyed me. "Funny."

"Too spendy for the likes of me, eh?" I grinned.

She shook her head. "No one uses checks anymore, silly."

The door handles were massive isosceles triangles painted lime green. A CLOSED sign hung in the tall, narrow window above the right one. I stopped in front of it and looked at my watch. Bianca rolled her eyes at my Luddite tendencies and pulled out her phone to check the time.

"We're early," I said.

"Well, I have to pick up Colette, and I'll be cutting it close. Let's knock."

Instead, I reached out and pulled on the door. It opened, smooth and silent, and the cool interior beckoned.

"Or we could just go right in." I gestured for her to precede me.

We entered a room with displays of postcards, books, jewelry, posters, and artistic knickknacks along with a few Savannah-centric souvenirs. It looked more like a museum gift shop than a gallery entrance. A small reception desk sat on the far side of the room next to a large archway that led into the gallery proper. I could see bright, framed prints hanging on butter-colored walls. The overhead lights hadn't been turned on, but enough natural light spilled in from the other room that we could make our way between the tables and cases.

I opened my mouth to call out, when a woman in the gallery said, "Oh, Aldo. It's not right."

My mouth closed as I looked over at Bianca. She froze in her tracks, and her eyes moved to meet mine. It was a woman's voice, clear and high, accompanied by the sound of approaching footsteps.

The footsteps stopped. "Why not?" a man answered in a deep baritone.

I raised one eyebrow at Bianca. Were we interrupting a tryst?

"Now there's no reason to cancel my show," he said. "And you promised."

"I just don't feel good about it, that's all," the woman answered.

"We had an agreement! At least until she messed things up." I could hear the pout in his voice.

"But she's dead," she said.

"Exactly!"

"Aldo—"

"That means she never had a chance to cancel the publicity. The ads are going to run. The public will expect my art to be on display when they visit the gallery. As they should. She *never* should have refused to show my work."

"Oh, wow. That is cold." She sighed. "Really cold. And for all I know, the gallery won't open for a while. If ever."

"Listen, hon." Wheedling. "Simply go ahead and have

the show. There's no one to stop you. You've been running this whole place for a year. You've shown a profit. You're getting a reputation in the arts community. No one will question you, Paisley."

"Her ex-husband is coming here tomorrow. He wants to take over the gallery himself. Says he still has a legal stake in it, but I'm not sure."

He cut her off. "Let him. Just tell him Leigh wanted my show, and you're honoring her memory."

"When it's exactly the opposite?"

"Who cares? She's dead. She'll never know. And no one else needs to, either. You were already going to defy her when she was distracted by her dad."

"Well . . ."

"So stick with the plan, hon. Because this could really make it for both of us."

She snorted. "I think outsider art is important, and I wanted to bring it into the gallery, but if you think having a single show will guarantee success, you have another think coming, mister."

"I promise it will be a success. The show will sell out. And that's after I jack up some of the prices, too."

"Oh, please. You can't possibly promise something like that."

"But I can. And I do."

"Well, I don't see how. Listen, you need to go. I have a client coming in for a private look-see at a piece."

The footsteps started up again, coming toward us.

Bianca sucked her breath in. Quickly, I pulled her toward the front door, then turned back with my hand on it.

"Hello?" I called. "Is anyone here?"

A woman came around the corner and flipped a switch on the wall. Light flooded the walls, illuminating the gallery wares with a gentle yellow glow.

"Ms. Devereaux!" she exclaimed, her eyes darting to me and back to my friend again. "Did you just get here?"

Bianca nodded. "I hope you don't mind that we let ourselves in."

"Not at all!"

"This is my friend, Katie Lightfoot. Katie, this is Paisley Long. She runs the gallery and agreed to show us that sculpture I was telling you about."

"No problem," Paisley said brightly. "It's nice to meet you, Ms. Lightfoot. Please follow me, and I'll show you the Hanta piece Ms. Devereaux wanted you to see." She turned so quickly that her ponytail flared out before settling between her shoulder blades once again.

Paisley was a tall, slender African American woman clad in blue jeans, a light blue T-shirt, and boots. I hadn't seen a flicker of suspicion when Bianca told her we'd just arrived, and she strode to the back of the gallery with purpose, looking back at us a couple of times as if to hurry us along. The impression was that she was very busy, but I had to wonder if she didn't want us to see the man she'd been talking with.

The main gallery had twelve-foot-high ceilings and stretched back at least a hundred feet. It was wide enough to accommodate a series of eight-foot walls at staggered intervals that provided more display space and broke up the space into cozy nooks. The whole room was the same light yellow, except the back wall, which was made up of lovely mottled red bricks. I looked up as we walked and noticed small security cameras mounted in each corner of the room.

As we approached the rear of the building, I heard a noise and looked left to see a man removing a painting from the wall and setting it on the floor next to several framed pieces leaning haphazardly against the bricks.

Paisley saw him, too, because she paused and cleared her throat.

"Let's wait on that, shall we?" she said to him. He frowned but walked back to a small room that looked like an office with the door ajar.

She smiled and didn't explain, simply gesturing to a small metal statue on a pillar stand. "*Compassion.*"

I moved closer and bent to squint at the piece as if I knew anything about what I was looking at. The material looked like steel or maybe pewter. The solid, flat base was roughly a foot in diameter and appeared stained and worn. Tendrils of metal reached up from it in all directions, some of them wide, some narrow, some only beginning to sprout from the base. Their surfaces ranged from smooth and shiny to hash marked and grayed. The longer I examined it, the more I felt the calming effect of the swooping lines, while the disparate surface textures conveyed the transition of fresh newness into wisdom and persistence.

I stood and looked at Bianca. "Wow."

She nodded. "I thought you'd like it."

So it hadn't just been a ruse to get us into the Markes Gallery. Well, it had been, but the bonus was experiencing a truly moving piece of art.

That would look fantastic in our living room.

I began mentally placing it around the room. Perhaps in the center of the built-in shelving? On the end table by the new sofa?

Then I saw the price tag. Any vague notion I'd had of actually purchasing the piece flew out the proverbial window. With a jolt, I pulled my attention back to Paisley Long and our real purpose for being in the gallery.

"This is truly lovely. Do you have any other Hanta pieces?"

Paisley shook her head. "I'm afraid this is the only one left. There were originally three."

I nodded sagely and tried to look as if I knew what I was talking about. "I see. I'm not surprised Leigh homed in on this artist. She had such impeccable taste and a genius for scouting out talent."

A soft snort sounded from the direction of the office.

"You knew Leigh?" Paisley asked, her eyes wide.

"We were acquaintances. She frequented my bakery, the Honeybee. Her book club met there . . . recently."

Paisley looked confused, and I recalled Bianca had said she had a friend in town who wanted to see the Hanta sculpture. That did sound like someone visiting from out of town, but it could also mean someone already in town, so I let it go.

"I'm so very sorry for your loss," I said, and wondered if some of the sudden compassion I felt for this young woman who was obviously in distress might be augmented by the sculpture of that name. "You see, I saw the story in the online edition of the *News* this morning."

The gallery assistant nodded, her ponytail swinging gently over her shoulder. "Thank you."

Bianca reached out and touched her arm.

Paisley smiled up at her with a wavery gaze, then seemed to pull herself together and glanced from Bianca to me. "Ahem. Yes. It's a terrible loss—for the gallery, for her family, and for the whole community."

"I do hope the gallery will be able to continue as part of Leigh's legacy," Bianca said.

The assistant smiled a bright but brittle smile. "Yes, I hope it works out that way, too. I'm hoping to stay on. It's too early for such discussions, though. I'm still trying to decide whether to open the gallery or not. I need to talk with Leigh's ex-husband." She looked troubled at the thought.

"Oh, is he a patron of the arts as well?" I asked.

"Not . . . exactly," she said.

The phone rang in the office, and a male voice answered, "Markes Gallery."

The skin tightened across Paisley's face. "Are you interested in the sculpture, Ms. Lightfoot?"

"I am, but I'd like my husband to see it. Do you mind if I take a photo?"

"Not at all," she said. "You go ahead, and I'll be right back." She smiled again, then hurried into the office and closed the door behind her. We heard her arguing with a man, but this time we couldn't make out the words.

I took out my smartphone and took a couple of pictures of *Compassion*. Then I quickly strode over to the items on the floor next to the bricks where the man I assumed was "Aldo" had been taking down the painting. I took several pictures and tucked my phone back into my pocket before bending down for a closer look.

Each was a white canvas board that I recognized as the kind you could buy ready-made in craft stores. Objects had been glued onto them in a seemingly haphazard way. One was food wrappers—candy bars, gum, power bars, the bright stripes of a Life Savers roll with some of the candy inside. They were all dirty, as if rescued from a street corner garbage can. Another was just . . . stuff. A cotton ball, a broken piece of plastic, part of a Coke can, some shiny cellophane, interspersed with a few pennies and what looked like dryer lint.

I was about to look at the third one when the office door opened, and Paisley and the man came out. Startled, I looked up but didn't move. I tried a smile instead. Bianca joined me as they approached.

The man seemed pleased that I was looking at the collages. "Like them?" he asked.

"Indeed," I said. "Outsider art is so interesting." Never mind that I'd never even heard of outsider art before Mrs. Standish had mentioned it to me that morning, or that I wouldn't know this junk-laden stuff qualified as such if Bianca and I hadn't eavesdropped on their earlier conversation.

"I'm glad you think so." He strode over and stuck out his hand.

This close, I could see the frayed edge of his shirt-sleeve, the worn shoes, his need for a shave. However, when I shook his hand, it was soft and uncalloused, his nails were clean and tidy, he smelled of Old Spice, and I caught the edge of what looked like an expensive watch.

Something is off about this guy. It's like he's dressed up as a bum for Halloween.

"Aldo Bracket," he said, "outsider artist. I do hope you'll come to my show here next week."

Paisley looked agitated but didn't say anything.

"Next week?" I asked. "I'll certainly try to make it. There are more pieces like this?" I gestured vaguely toward the candy wrappers.

"Oh, sure," he said. "Lots!"

Paisley stepped forward. "I'm so glad you came by, Ms. Devereaux, Ms. Lightfoot. However, I'm afraid I have some calls to make."

"Of course," Bianca said smoothly. "We appreciate that you let us in when the gallery is closed. And I'm so sorry about Leigh. I know she's been instrumental to your career as well as a great friend. I'm sure you'll miss her."

A flicker of discomfort flashed across the assistant's face before her usual smile returned. "Thank you. And, Ms. Lightfoot, please feel free to call if your husband wants to see the Hanta. Pictures don't do it justice."

I nodded. "I'll do that."

She led us to the door, and I heard the lock turn behind us as we left.

"Who the heck is Aldo Bracket?" I asked Bianca as she pulled away from the curb.

"Never heard of him."

"Do you know anything about outsider art?"

She shook her head and pressed on the accelerator. "Not really."

"Well, apparently Skipper Dean does. I'll ask him."

"Did you really, um, like that stuff?" she asked tentatively.

"Are you kidding? Total junk. But Mr. Bracket seemed

pretty full of himself, and he also seemed determined to have a show in Leigh's gallery whether Leigh wanted him to or not."

Bianca slowed for a traffic light and glanced over at me. "Motive for murder?"

"You never know." I sighed. "People have some awfully strange reasons for doing awful things."

Chapter 10

Bianca dropped me off in front of the Honeybee, and I hurried inside. Sure enough, the place was hopping. A line had formed at the register, and Iris was taking orders while Lucy filled pastry bags and Ben filled drink requests. The murmur of conversation rose and fell, punctuated by the squeal of hot steam foaming milk for lattes and cappuccinos.

One of those cappuccinos was already sitting on a bistro table in the far corner. Steve Dawes lifted it to his lips and took a sip, observing the room over the rim of the mug. His eyes caught mine and lit up as he lowered his drink. He gestured me over. I shook my head, pointing at the register and mouthing, *After this rush*. He nodded and pulled out his cell phone.

I assessed what needed to be stocked in the pastry case and ducked into the kitchen. Lucy and I swerved to miss each other, a dance that was automatic after working together for so long. A fresh batch of molasses cookies was cooling on a rack. I scooped several of the still-warm goodies onto a tray, along with muffins and our standard cheddar sage scones that seemed to sell out every day. As I stocked the display case, I watched Steve.

He was reading something on his smartphone, scrolling with one thumb, brown eyes flicking over the screen. His honey-colored hair had grown long enough to pull back and fasten with a leather cord. He wore a weathered blue T-shirt, cargo shorts, and sandals, looking for all the world as if he belonged on a beach or a mountain trail, but I was used to how he dressed when he was working.

And today he was definitely working. I could tell by the set of his shoulders and the way his jaw worked. He was a crime reporter, a crime had been committed, and I was already involved. He often turned up at the nexus of those circumstances, and I was glad enough to see him because I'd already planned to call him and pump him for information about Detective Quinn's murder investigation. I simply hadn't had the chance yet. So how had Steve known to come see me? I mean, he was a member of the oldest druid clan in Savannah and a powerful sorcerer in his own right, but I didn't see how that came into play. Maybe there was something else going on? Or . . .

Quinn. He would have been up in Detective Quinn's grill as soon as he learned they'd found Leigh's body. And Quinn had foisted him off on me.

It just fit.

Smiling at a customer and turning back to help Lucy fill an order, I spied a familiar face on the other side of the bakery, way over in the reading area.

Teddy.

She sat with her hands folded on her lap, still as a cat, radiating anxiety, her eyes glued to me. I glanced at Steve, saw he wasn't looking, and smiled at her. I indicated the line, and she nodded her understanding. She'd wait.

Great. I needed to keep Steve away from her. She didn't need him to find out she was in contact with Leigh's ghost. He'd feel compelled to interrogate her, which wouldn't even help him in the end. It wasn't as if he could put in the paper that the murder victim had contacted a medium of sorts when she'd been killed.

Then a horrible thought occurred to me. What if he did report such a thing? It was salacious and might gain readers, however cruel it might be. Steve and I had been good friends—more than that for a short while when I'd first moved to Savannah—and over the years I'd learned more and more about him. He could be kind and helpful and sweet. He was a good journalist, even though his very wealthy father wanted him to ditch the newspaper business altogether and come back to work at Dawes Corporation.

But.

Steve was also a member of that druid clan, and they were not always nice people. Not at all. He'd done a few things to me personally, too. Things that had betrayed my trust in him. It had been in the name of love, supposedly, but still. It was a stretch, but I could see him exploiting Teddy for a good story.

The need to keep them apart hummed under my skin as the crowd quieted and customers drifted out of the bakery laden with treats and caffeine. When Lucy reached for a towel and tray to bus tables, I held out my hands to take them.

"I'll do it," I said.

"Oh, hon. I've got it!" Her bright smile faded when I shook my head.

"Teddy's over there." I gestured with my chin. "And Steve's over there. I need to check in with her without him knowing."

My aunt looked momentarily puzzled, but then understanding dawned. "Right. You want me to go talk to her?"

"Oh, that would be even better. See if she can stick around for a while. I want to find out what Steve wants, but I need to talk to her, too."

"On it," Lucy said with a decisive nod.

I moved around the counter, still wiping my hands on a dishtowel, and went out to where Steve was waiting. I slid into the seat across from him and tipped my head to the side.

"Nice to see you," I said.

That was true. We hadn't seen much of each other since Declan and I had gotten married. Steve had come to the wedding after one last-ditch effort to get me to marry him instead. Our few encounters since then had been slightly strained.

"Nice to see you, too, Katie-girl."

I frowned.

"Sorry. I forgot you don't want me to call you that."

I stopped frowning but didn't smile. Instead, I leaned against the back of the chair and regarded him silently.

"So," he began. Then he shrugged and gave a little laugh. "You probably know why I'm here."

"Hm. Maybe."

"There was a murder last night. Not far from here."

"Not far indeed. I saw your story in the *News*. I suppose there will be a follow-up in tomorrow's paper?"

"I hope so," he said. "If you can help me out."

"And why do you think I can help you out?"

"Oh, come on, Katie . . ."

I lifted my eyebrows.

"You know, and I know, that you get involved in certain kinds of . . . crimes . . ." He trailed off with a chagrined look on his face.

"If you're referencing how I've contributed to police investigations of homicides with a paranormal element, well, you're right." I leaned forward, wide-eyed. "Are you saying there was something magical related to Leigh Markes' death?"

He looked uncomfortable. "Well, no. Not that they could tell right away, I mean. It's just that—"

"Just that what?" I asked, unable to keep a twinkle out of my eye.

"Quinn said you called him."

"Did he also tell you I had a premonition?"

"He did."

I held my hands up, palms to the ceiling. "Well, there you go!"

His eyes narrowed in suspicion. "As I recall, you aren't given to premonitions."

I smiled apologetically and shrugged. Of course, he was right. I'd never had a premonition in my life, but I couldn't tell him the truth.

"Where were you, exactly, when you received this premonition?" he asked.

"Um, here." I knew I sounded lame.

"At the Honeybee?"

I nodded.

"At one in the morning?"

"Nooo. It was earlier than that."

"Well, that was the time of death." He sat back and considered me. "I guess you could be telling me the truth. Quinn did say you'd called him last evening, not this morning." He gave a little half frown as he worked it out. "So you called him before Leigh was actually dead." He leaned over the table so fast I jumped. "How did this premonition come to you?"

"I'm sorry, Steve. I can't tell you any more about that. I'm asking you to trust me." My voice was quiet. "You called the victim by her first name. Did you know her?"

He held my gaze for a long time before his shoulders slumped. "I did, in passing. She gave Brandon a showing before he went international." Brandon was a member of his druid clan and a very successful artist. Also, one of Cookie's many old boyfriends. "And you know I used to cover the downtown arts and business scene."

"Do you know Leigh's family?" I asked.

"Again, in passing. Her father and my father knew each other. James Markes recently passed away, though. He was very ill." He took a sip of his cappuccino, then asked, "Do you know how she died?"

"Well, Quinn called me this morning. You know, to let me know I'd been right last night. He told me she was strangled. With a scarf, I think?"

"A scarf," he confirmed. "I saw it."

I tried to look curious but then realized that might

seem callous—was, in fact, callous given that a woman we both knew was dead. "That's awful."

"It wasn't pleasant, that's for sure. Especially given that they were moving the body from her car to the medical examiner's van at the time."

I shuddered.

"It had an interesting pattern on it," he said.

I felt the confused look on my face. "The body?"

"No, the *scarf*."

I sighed. He knew about my dragonfly totem. "I have to get back to work, Steve. I've told you what I know." And I had. Sort of. And he wasn't exactly proving to be a font of information.

He drained the dregs of his cappuccino. "If you say so." However, I knew he wouldn't let it go for long.

I started to rise, then sat back down. "Do you know anything about outsider art?"

He tucked his phone back into his shorts pocket. "A little. Why?"

Should I come clean about where I'd been that morning? It would invite a whole bunch of questions I didn't want to answer.

So I fudged. "I recently heard of an artist who creates outsider art. His name is Aldo Bracket. Do you know him from when you worked that beat?"

He shook his head, then stopped mid-shake. "Hang on. Aldo Bracket? I know an Alessandro Bracket from back in high school. Aldo is sometimes short for Alessandro. Is he about my age?"

"Yeah, mid-thirties sounds about right." I went on to describe the man I'd met that morning in the Markes Gallery.

He laughed. "That's him. What a dufus. I haven't seen him in forever. I heard he moved out of town. He didn't get along with his father." He shrugged. "Of course, his father is a lot like mine."

"Difficult," I said.

"Mm."

"And wealthy."

"Quite. Not Dawes wealthy, but very well off." He wasn't bragging, just stating a fact.

I thought of the man I'd met that morning and how the combination of old clothes and nice watch and soft hands had seemed off.

Steve said, "I'll ask Father if he knows anything about Alessandro being back in town and suddenly taking up art." He rolled his eyes. "Are you thinking of buying one of his pieces?"

"God, no. They're terrible."

"Then why . . . ?"

"I'd never heard of outsider art. I was just curious."

"Outsider art is typically created by someone without formal training and no real association with the mainstream art world. It's unconventional, but some of it is quite evocative and interesting. What does Aldo's art look like?"

"Like someone threw up a bunch of garbage and framed it. Here. See for yourself." I reached into my apron pocket and took out my phone. In seconds I had the pictures I'd taken of Aldo's collages on the screen.

Steve flipped through the photos, then went back and did it again. "Yikes. I'd say that's an unfortunately accurate description." He handed the phone back to me.

"Maybe you can buy one for your father to put on his

office wall." Steve's father was more the type to have an original Constable behind his desk.

He laughed and rose to his feet.

"I'll see you soon, Katie-girl."

I frowned.

Hc laughed again. "Oops. Sorry."

Chapter 11

I watched through the window as Steve crossed the street before I made my way over to where Teddy waited. She still looked pensive but seemed less jittery. Steam fragrant with the herbs from the Honeybee relaxing green tea blend—peppermint, chamomile, holy basil, and fennel—wafted up from the mug she held in front of her hands. Lucy at work again. The half-eaten profiterole filled with lemon balm and ginger custard was another nice touch: tasty calories tinged with calming magic.

I sat down next to the young woman on the sofa and looked into her eyes. The circles around them were so dark I wondered if she'd slept at all the night before.

"How are you holding up?"

"Okay." Her voice sounded reedy. Then she shook her head. "No. That's not true." She looked away as she set down her mug, paused, then met my gaze again. This time I saw a new determination. "Katie, I've dealt with spirits my whole life, sometimes less and certainly more since I started my ghost tour business. But none of them have hounded me like the woman who was killed last night."

"Hounded you? What do you mean?"

She took a deep breath, looking thoughtful. "Spirits usually stick to a locale, you know. The place where they died, or at least a place that has meaning for them."

I nodded. "That makes sense." It was also what I'd heard before.

"I've heard of spirits that are attached to people, though."

A gasp escaped from my lips before I could stop it. She looked at me curiously.

"What?"

Shaking my head, I said, "Nothing. At least nothing to do with what happened to Leigh Markes." At least I didn't think so. "Are you telling me she has attached to you?"

Teddy closed her eyes and gave a little nod. When she opened them, she was looking over my shoulder toward a bookshelf.

Slowly, I turned my head to look. Mungo was standing there, next to his bed. But he was looking up as if someone was standing next to him.

My lips parted as a shiver ran down my spine.

"She's here?" I whispered.

"She's here." Teddy reached for her mug without looking away from the shelf and took a couple of big gulps from it. "And she's still pretty mad." She tore her gaze away from whatever she was looking at and directed it at me. "Have you found anything out? Anything at all?"

I settled back onto the cushion, feeling odd about

facing away from the dead woman's ghost. "I went to her gallery this morning and met her assistant. She seemed very upset about Leigh." I glanced behind me. "Is she reacting to anything I'm saying?"

Teddy gave a quick shake of her head. "No. I don't know if she even understands. She's simply here—or wherever I am—and she's angry, and she wants revenge. You're lucky she didn't attach to you instead since you're the one she thinks can find her killer."

"Well, I'm not sensitive in the same way you are," I said. "She must know that somehow. If she attached to me, I might never even know. Right?"

Teddy sighed, which I took to be agreement.

But how had Leigh known to have Teddy ask for my help in finding her killer? Was there something I already knew but didn't realize? Or had someone on the other side told her I investigated homicides? Who? Nonna? Connell?

That gave me pause. "Teddy, do you think Leigh might be in contact with other spirits on her side of the veil?"

She blinked, giving it some thought. "I honestly don't know. I don't see spirits talking to each other, really. They seem very . . . alone."

"Lonely?"

Her lips pressed together, and her eyes grew sad. "A lot of times. Not always. Remember me talking about Little Gracie last night? In Johnson Square?"

I nodded.

"She's not lonely. She greets everyone, still cheerful, oblivious to the fact that they're unaware of her. Most of them, at least. I've run across quite a few sensitives on my tours."

"But not like you are."

"No. Not like I am."

I let the thoughts ping-pong around my brain for a few moments. "You're sure that if Leigh Markes' killer is brought to justice, then she'll leave you alone?"

"I am. I can't tell you why I know that, but I do. Experience, maybe. Her entire connection to this plane is due to her desire to have exactly that: justice. She'll fully move on to the next plane once she has it."

"Okay, then. I'm working on it, along with the other members of the spellbook club, and we're going to do the best we can." I looked over my shoulder again. "I hope she understands that. We're going to do the best we can," I repeated a little louder.

Ben looked over at me from behind the coffee counter, and I felt my cheeks redden.

Teddy looked relieved. "Thanks. She seems to understand—a little, at least. She's not so angry."

"But she's sticking with you, regardless."

The young woman looked unhappy. "Please hurry," she whispered.

As if a ghost couldn't hear her.

As if I knew anything about ghosts.

Teddy reached for her boho bag, ready to leave.

"Um," I said.

She paused.

"So you know how you said you'd heard about spirits attaching themselves to people? Even before this"—I gestured vaguely behind me—"happened to you?"

Suddenly wary, she nodded.

"Have you ever heard of a guardian spirit attaching itself to someone? A good one, you know? That chooses its, er, host?" It was as good a word as any to describe Declan. "One that actually chooses him at birth, maybe does so in each generation. Sticks to one family?"

She sat back, at ease. In her element. "Is this someone you know?"

I debated for a nanosecond how much to tell her, but the truth was I was desperate and needed all the help I could get to bring Connell back for Declan. And I needed it soon. Samhain was in only a few days.

So I told her the story, as succinctly as I could.

"At a séance a few years ago, the medium inadvertently contacted a spirit named Connell, who, it turned out, had been attached to my husband—this was before we were married—ever since he'd been born. He'd been a kind of guardian angel, warning him away from danger, pushing him toward opportunity, keeping him safe. This séance brought Connell out of the woodwork, so to speak."

"How?" Teddy interrupted.

"He, er, takes over Declan's physical body."

She stared at me. "Seriously?"

"Seriously. It didn't happen often, but it was clear when Connell was front and center. See, he has a distinct Irish brogue, and a certain way of . . ." I trailed off. Oh, well, in for a penny, in for a pound. "We're pretty sure he's a leprechaun, actually. He was attached to the McCarthy family— there are some very old photographs that show him, and I've, well, I actually met him in the Otherworld—shamanic journey, long story—and it's the same guy."

Teddy was frowning, but her voice was amused. "And I thought I had a weird life."

"Yeah. Well. Anyway. Connell saved Declan's life more than once, as well as mine. And a few months ago, he . . ." I rubbed my hands over my face. "Oh, goddess. How do I put this so I don't sound too nuts?"

For the first time, I heard her laugh. It was full and throaty and genuine, bringing a smile to my own face. "I think you're way too far past nuts to worry about it," she said.

I grinned. "You might be right." I paused. "So you know I'm a witch."

She nodded, looking curious.

"And that means, well, *magic*."

Another nod, a little slower.

"Now, everyone has access to magic. Not everyone does access it, and some people do it automatically without realizing it."

Now she was studying me with interest.

"It's all about intention, about focusing that intention in order to manifest an outcome. Rituals and spells and the like help do that."

"So anyone can be a witch?"

My turn to nod. "I believe so. See, the Craft is about a certain way of harnessing the magic that's in the world, a certain way of directing intention, with rules. When you're working with others, like, say, a coven, then the sum is greater than the parts. And while everyone can access magic, there are some people who have a particular affinity for it. A gift. A talent."

"Like a musician."

I pointed at her. "Exactly! Anyone can learn an instrument and play tunes, but some people are gifted at it."

"And I'm guessing you're gifted at magic," she said.

"I am," I admitted. "So are the others in the spell-book club."

"What does this have to do with your husband's leprechaun guardian?"

"Right. Well, a few months back, my gift for magic was taken away. It would be like a musician not being able to play anymore, going suddenly tone deaf."

"That sounds awful."

"You have no idea." I shuddered, remembering, then brought myself back to the point. "Connell was able to retrieve my gift and give it back to me. Thank goddess. But in the process, he was flung into the ether."

She looked skeptical. "Wasn't he already in the ether?"

"I guess. Yeah. But wherever he is now, he doesn't have access to Declan. He's too far away. I don't know where that is, but it's not too far to get him back from. See, I've been in contact with him, in a way. He's not hurt. He's just lost. And unhappy. And he's not here to help Declan, who, by the way, is a firefighter. He's had Connell guiding him for his whole life, and now he's gone. Connell acted as his intuition, helped his instincts, steered him away from danger."

Teddy was frowning. "That doesn't sound good at all."

"It isn't."

She leaned back against the arm of the sofa. "Why are you telling me all this?"

I leaned forward. "Because I want to try to bring Connell back, and I want to do it this Samhain."

She looked confused.

"Halloween. At midnight if possible. And I need your help."

"My help?" she yelped. Heads in the main seating area turned toward us.

"I'm putting together a spell to reach to the other side. But in order to not lose myself while I'm searching for Connell to bring him back, I need someone to ground me here, someone who can straddle the two planes. A tether. Someone like you."

Teddy suddenly stood. "Oh, no. I'm sorry, but I can't help you." She grabbed her bag and was backing away.

I rose, too. "I really think you can, hon. If only—"

She turned and hurried to the door, bursting through it to the street outside. I started to follow, but stopped. I'd only frighten her more if I ran after her.

Our resident author, who always worked with his earbuds in, turned his head from the still-closing door and looked at me with raised eyebrows. The other two customers had stopped their conversation and were staring across the room.

"Good lord, Katie! What did you say to that poor girl?" Lucy asked as she bustled over.

My voice was low. "I asked if she'd help us get Connell back on Samhain. It didn't go over well." I was surprised to hear tears in my voice. I hadn't realized how much I'd been counting on Teddy's help ever since the idea had occurred to me.

"Oh, Katie." My aunt gave me a big hug, then held

me at arm's length. "You told her all about what happened?"

"I did."

"It probably sounded a little, you know"—she smiled—"crazy?"

"I don't think that was it. I mean, the woman sees dead people, for heaven's sake. Has her whole life."

Lucy led me back to the kitchen. "True. Something about the idea frightened her badly, though. It was all over her face."

I frowned. On the one hand, I felt terrible for Teddy, the lonely outsider with a gift that was also part curse.

On the other hand, that gift/curse was the one thing I wanted—no, *needed*—to help retrieve the guardian spirit of the man I loved.

"That was Teddy LaRue," Iris said as soon as we entered the kitchen.

Surprised, I asked, "You know her?"

Iris half shrugged. "Sort of. She was a year ahead of me in high school." She squinted at me. "How do you know her?"

"She's Gregory's goshdaughter." Seeing her confusion, I added, "You know, Jaida's Gregory?"

Her face cleared. "Right. I hadn't heard the term *goshdaughter*, but I like it. So, um . . . do you know Teddy very well?" She asked the question with such careful casualness, I paused in getting out the ingredients for a batch of cookies and turned to her.

"We just met the other night. She guides ghost tours."

"Oh." She made a little face. "Yeah, that makes sense."

I leaned toward her. "Why is that?"

Instead of answering my question, Iris parried with another. "Is she involved in Zoe's mom's death?"

Behind her, I saw Lucy whirl in alarm.

"She hasn't done anything wrong," I said easily. "Now, why on earth would you ask such a thing?"

Iris looked away. When she looked back, she shrugged again. "I don't know. I mean, I know you're looking into what happened, along with the other spellbook club members. So I figure there's something witchy involved. Because that's what you do, right? And Teddy is . . ." She trailed off.

"Teddy is . . ." I prompted as Lucy came to stand beside me.

"She's weird," Iris said. "Everyone knows she's strange. I mean, I know we're supposed to accept everyone for who they are and how they act, but there's something's off about that girl. Always has been." She took a deep breath. "Sorry."

Lucy and I exchanged a glance, and then Lucy said, "I daresay you're right. There is something different about Teddy. Just as there's something different about Katie and me and you."

Iris' eyes widened. "Ohmagosh. She's a witch?"

"No, that's not what I mean."

I tensed, hoping she wasn't about to tell Iris about Teddy's unique talent. I needn't have worried about my kind and tactful aunt spilling any beans, though.

"All I mean is that everyone has their own gifts, their own burdens, and their own stories. You don't know Teddy very well, at least from what you said. It might be best not to judge. People aren't always who you think they are."

Iris blinked, and suddenly her eyes filled with tears. "They sure aren't!" She angrily wiped at her eyes with the back of her hand.

Bewildered, Lucy and I went to where she stood on the other side of the counter.

"Something's been going on the last couple of days," I said. "Spill."

She sniffled, then whirled and ran into the office.

Chapter 12

"Do we follow?" I asked Lucy.

She looked out at the bakery, which was half full of seated customers, all involved in their own conversations or what was on their laptop screens. Ben was at the register, and she raised her eyebrows after catching his eye. He gave a little shake of his head, indicating he didn't need our help right then.

"No," she said, moving to the counter that ran along the back wall behind one of the industrial ovens. "She'll be back."

Sure enough, Iris returned. Her eyes were a little red, but the sniffles were gone. She still looked mad, though. She came over and crossed her arms over her chest. "Sorry."

"It's okay," I said with a mild smile.

"It's Taylor," she said. "He's being a jerk."

"Yes, you did use that word a few times yesterday," Lucy said.

"I did?" She seemed surprised.

"Under your breath, mostly, but yes."

"Oh. Well, he is."

"And what flavor of jerk is he being?" I asked. After all, there were several. I'd once had a jerk practically leave me at the altar, and I was pretty sure this wasn't that bad.

"So, he's studying sound design, right? At SCAD."

We nodded. Savannah College of Art and Design was also where Iris had decided to focus on studying graphic design.

"Well, he's working on a movie project, and there's this girl who's also working on it, and I happen to know she really, really likes him." She took a deep breath. "And they're in Atlanta." She paused.

"Atlanta," Lucy said.

"The film's being edited there. It's not a SCAD project. They're both interning for an editing company. It's some kind of nature documentary."

"Okay," I said.

Iris looked between us. "Don't you *see*?"

"There's a girl there with your boyfriend, and she's got some kind of crush on him," I said.

"Yes!"

Lucy frowned. "Does he like her?"

Iris blew out a breath between pursed lips. "He says he doesn't. But he's still there with her." She hesitated, then said in a small voice, "And she's cute. Really cute. Long blond hair and blue eyes and perfect skin and super skinny. I know she's going to make a play for him. I just know it." She grimaced. "If she hasn't already."

"Oh, dear," Lucy said.

"I know, right?" Iris exclaimed.

But I knew where Lucy was going and was already shaking my head. "Iris, since he's a sound engineer who, from what you've told us, wants to work on films for a living, isn't Taylor going to be in a lot of situations where he's out of town and around women?"

She looked down at the floor. "Well, yeah. But this is different."

"How?"

"She's . . . she's . . . he's . . ." She trailed off.

"Don't you trust Taylor?" Lucy asked in a gentle voice.

"Yes!" She frowned. "Well, mostly. But Shawna's so pretty and—"

"Iris, there are lots of pretty women out there. And another standing right in front of me," Lucy said, pointing at her. "I don't know Taylor very well, but if he's a player, then you are better off without him. And if he's not, and he is trustworthy, then you don't need to make yourself miserable with all this jealousy."

"But how can I *tell?*" Her voice was full of anguish. "How do I know whether to trust him or not?"

Lucy put her hand on the young woman's arm. "You trust yourself first. Your gut. And then you make a decision. If you decide not to trust him in the end, then that's a very shaky foundation to try and build a relationship on. And if you do trust him—"

"And I'm wrong?"

My aunt sighed. "Then you're wrong. Seriously, Iris. You have very powerful intuition. It's a gift of yours, which we recognized as soon as we met you. So did the other spellbook club members, as a matter of fact."

"Really?" Iris asked in a small voice.

"Yes! Really! And you know it, deep down. You just don't trust it yet. Once you do, you'll know what to do about Taylor."

"But—"

"No buts," Lucy said firmly, ending the conversation. "Now, we've got baking to do. Iris, you start in on the sourdough levain for tomorrow's loaves, and Katie and I will make the candy corn cupcakes for the Halloween party. We'll freeze them unfrosted. Katie? How do you want to flavor the cupcakes?"

"I think a simple vanilla batter will do. What's better than yummy cupcakes that encourage luck and love?"

"Indeed." My aunt grinned and gave a brisk nod. She went into the pantry to retrieve the ingredients, and I reached for the yellow and orange food coloring.

I was tired when I pulled into the driveway that evening. It had been a twelve-hour day at the bakery, which wasn't all that unusual since I generally went in early to get things started in the kitchen and often stayed until we closed. However, today I felt the extra weight of Leigh Markes' murder, her ghost demanding that I find her killer, the look in Teddy's eyes as she asked me to hurry, and the urgent hum of needing to bring Connell back for Declan.

Suppressing a sigh, I turned off the engine and leaned over to give Mungo a kiss on top of his head and scratch behind his ears. He responded by wiggling closer and leaning his forehead against my shoulder. We sat that way for a few calm moments before getting out of the car.

As I was hauling my tote bag out of the back seat, I heard the sound of children's voices from next door. I straightened and closed the door, turning toward them. Margie Coopersmith waved at me from her porch, and I saw her towheaded twins, Julia and Jonathan—known collectively as the JJs—playing a beanbag toss game on the far side of their front yard. Their little brother, Bart, helped by running back and forth to retrieve the beanbags for his siblings. Mungo nudged my leg and looked up at me. I nodded, and he took off to join the fun with a loud *yip!*

Margie came down the steps and hurried across the lawn to where I stood. "Got time for a quick glass of wine?" she asked by way of greeting. "I hardly ever see you these days." She blew a stray strand of her white-blond hair off her forehead, looking hopeful.

"Oh, I wish." I glanced over my shoulder at the carriage house.

"I take it Declan is on days off and waiting eagerly for his bride to come home." It could have sounded sarcastic, but I knew it wasn't. Margie was all about family.

"Something like that," I said. "Mostly I'm just tired. If I drink a glass of your pink wine, I might not make it through supper."

She squinted and looked me up and down. "You're working too hard."

I waved my hand. "Nah. Just one of those days." I

gestured over her shoulder to the kids playing. "Are you guys still coming to the Halloween party?"

"Of course! Redding will be out of town, surprise, surprise, but Evelyn will help me wrangle the kids." Redding was Margie's husband and a long-haul truck driver. He was often gone for days at a time, though he checked in via computer every evening and read to his children before bed. Evelyn was Margie's mother-in-law, and they got along famously.

"Oh, Evelyn made Julia the cutest skeleton costume! Painted a black leotard with glow-in-the-dark paint. She's so talented. Researched how the bones should look and it's cute and creepy at the same time. Julia wanted to wear it to school this morning." The JJs were six.

"Sounds adorable. Do they let them wear their costumes to school on Halloween?"

"Of course! Though I don't think Jonathan will manage to wear his all day. He insisted he wanted to be a school bus."

"A school bus," I repeated.

"Uh-huh. It's . . . cumbersome. Took me a while, but I figured out how to make it light enough that he could wear it with straps over his shoulders."

"You made it?"

"Oh, sure. I can't cook a lick, darlin', as we both know, but I can make a Halloween costume with the best of them. Hot glue gun at the ready." She pantomimed drawing a gun from her hip.

"What's Bart going as?"

"A bumblebee."

"Again?"

"Yep. We were going through the trunk looking for

ideas, and he saw his wings from last year and wanted to wear it again. Lucky break for me."

Some moms might have been disappointed at their child wearing the same costume two years in a row, but Margie just wanted her boy to be happy. I loved that about her.

"Well, I'd better go inside and see what my husband has been up to all day," I said.

"He worked in the garage most of the afternoon, I can tell you that. And I don't know what that man is cooking up for you, but I can smell it from here. I'll think of you as we eat our mac and cheese and hotdogs for supper." She rolled her eyes. "Kid food."

Now that she mentioned it, there was a savory fragrance riding the evening air, and it did seem to be coming from our place.

I said goodbye, called for Mungo, and headed inside.

The full effect of Declan's culinary efforts hit me like a cartoon anvil when we stepped inside. Even Mungo made a little noise in the back of his throat.

Mmmm. Onion, something smoky—sausage? Something else . . . aha! Filé powder!

Made from the crushed leaves of the sassafras tree, filé powder had a distinctive scent. Declan had made us one of his delectable firehouse recipes—gumbo.

I stashed my tote in the corner as my husband came out from the short hallway that led to the bedroom and bathroom. He was wrapping a thick piece of gauze around his hand.

Rushing to him, I demanded, "What happened?"

"Knife slipped in the kitchen. No big deal." He kissed me.

"Since when does no big deal require enough gauze to wrap a mummy?"

He raised an eyebrow. "Will you relax? The cut is in an awkward place, that's all. And yes, I would have done the exact same stupid thing with Connell around. It's not like I was in a plastic bubble my whole life."

I bit my lip, chagrined that he had read my mind so well. "Sorry."

"No worries," he said, trying to keep it light. But I could hear the irritation under the words. "Now come on. I've set the table, and the rice should be ready now."

I let it drop and followed him into the kitchen. The table was set for two, and he'd added a vase of the rambling Cherokee roses that grew beside the house. I didn't know how long this romance stuff was expected to last in a marriage, but I sure liked it.

Lifting the lid of the pot, I inhaled the fragrant steam. "What a treat!" Chicken, sausage, shrimp, crab, and okra swam in a combination of beef and chicken broth flavored with spices and aromatics and thickened with the classic filé powder.

I fished out a chunk of chicken from the gumbo, added a few pieces of okra—which my familiar loved—and placed the bowl on Mungo's placemat on the floor. He started in on it at once.

"Rude," I noted, but he ignored me.

Declan and I dished up and dug in.

After dinner, we both washed up, and I asked Declan if he would mind giving some of our leftovers to Margie. I knew she'd welcome the respite from kid food. He readily agreed and took the dish over himself. By the time he got back, I was already in my pjs and had a movie queued up in the loft. Two hours and a light comedy later, Declan was snoring in bed beside me while I perused the pile of spellbooks I'd gathered.

I was tired, but there was work to do.

Chapter 13

For months, I'd been kicking around some ideas for how to create the best spell to get Connell back. The spellbook club had agreed with the ones I'd run by them. Now I needed some particulars.

Particulars that didn't rely on Teddy acting as a tether.

I refused to wait to find someone else who could exist on both planes at once. Who knew how long that would take? I'd thought about trying to find a medium who could do the job, but there were two problems with that. First off, how would I know if they were legit? The medium who had inadvertently brought Connell to the fore was out of the country again, working on a movie set, and since that had been an accident, I didn't think she'd be able to help us anyway. Which brought up the second objection, which was that mediums invited spirits to visit them of their own free will. Connell didn't need an invitation. He was happy to come back. No, he needed to be neatly caught in the net of a spell and brought back.

So. How to combine a spell for finding lost objects with one designed to pierce the veil? Would it be a spell within a cast circle, or something different?

A cast circle, I thought. That was what I knew so well, and what felt most natural. Spells and rituals were about intention in the end, intention augmented by harnessing the power of the elements and of nature. Best to focus on that. Besides, that was how the spellbook club was used to working, too, and I was going to need their help.

After a bit, I came across a list of herbs that helped reach the other side. I opened my grimoire, my personal book of spells that I'd added to ever since learning I was a witch. I thought of it as my recipe book, complete with notes, comments, and possible additions to the rituals I performed or wanted to try. I was keeping all my research on the spell I was developing there. I made a note to add cinnamon, allspice, frankincense, and myrrh into the mix.

Nothing else caught my attention. I closed the book and gently tapped the end of the pen against my teeth. Mungo grunted and rolled over, looking at me upside down from the end of the bed. Then he righted himself and trundled up to snuggle in next to my hip.

Mimsey had suggested using graveyard dirt in the spell, which made sense. It might seem gory, but she'd explained that it was traditionally used in any kind of spell involving transition. Not only that, but it was used in all sorts of Samhain spells as a matter of course, to connect with departed ancestors and friends.

I made another note.

Need to ask Jaida to bring the right tarot card . . .

Another note.

Lucy and I needed to bring our hedgewitchery into play, too. I grabbed another spellbook and found what I was looking for—Samhain ritual cakes made with pumpkin, ginger, and cinnamon.

What else? Maybe I could find a suggestion online. I slipped out of bed, lifted Mungo to the floor, and padded out of the bedroom to trade out the spellbooks for my laptop. Rather than risk disturbing Declan, I settled on the sofa, tucking my legs beneath me. Mungo jumped up to join me, for all the world looking as if he were checking out the websites I brought up.

After ten minutes, I'd found nothing of interest and closed the laptop. I opened my grimoire to my notes on Connell. Next to those, the page was blank. Soon I found myself doodling names.

Leigh Markes. Aldo Bracket. Walker Stokes. Zoe Stokes. Paisley Long. Calista Markes. Jo . . . something.

All suspects. Perhaps. Not Zoe. No, I was pretty sure Zoe Stokes hadn't snuck home from college to kill her mother, though it wasn't impossible. But what possible motive could she have?

I couldn't even guess.

Aldo Bracket, though. Could he have killed Leigh because she didn't want to give him a show in her gallery? Really? He'd been promised the show, had apparently talked Leigh's assistant into it once, and was trying again now that Leigh was dead. How important was that show to him? He didn't seem, well, *artistic*. From what Steve had told me, he was a spoiled rich kid, possibly with a chip on his shoulder, and stranger still, he hadn't even seemed to connect with his art.

I wonder if I could act like I was interested in purchasing a piece and get him to talk to me more about it. Maybe he'd let something slip . . .

And then there was Paisley herself. She'd been running Leigh's gallery for a long time while Leigh took care of her father. Then, boom! Suddenly Leigh was back in charge, and one of the first things she did was reverse a decision Paisley had made about Aldo's show. Who knew what other decisions she'd questioned, what she might have said to Paisley. I hadn't known Leigh well, but she was no-nonsense and blunt. That wouldn't go over well with everyone.

I wondered if it had contributed to her divorce. But her ex must have understood from the beginning that he was marrying an assertive woman. She didn't exactly hide who she was. And from what Iris had said, Walker Stokes was hardly blameless. I hoped Jaida would find something in the public records or through her lawyerly channels that would help to unmuddy the picture I had of him.

Calista Markes and her sister hadn't been on the best of terms, but I had no way to know if that was their normal relationship. I was an only child, but I knew sisters often squabbled without meaning much by it. But as they'd left the Honeybee, Leigh had said something to her friend Jo about how difficult Calista had become since their father had died. Perhaps the rift between them had ended in violence.

For all I knew, Jo had been the last person to see Leigh that evening. I didn't know her last name, but she'd looked vaguely familiar. Without much hope, I opened my laptop again and considered. Leigh and Jo had seemed comfortable with each other. Jo knew Calista, too, and had easily commented on their father's death.

So probably a family friend. At least a good friend.

I input Leigh's name and simply "Jo," then clicked on Images. Sure enough, a picture of Leigh and Jo taken at a fundraiser came up. The caption said her last name was Sterling.

When I searched for Jo Sterling, I found a treasure trove of information.

I'd thought she looked like a professional athlete, and it turned out I was right. Or at least she had been. Jo Sterling was thirty-seven and had been prominent on the women's golf tour until a few years ago. Then a television viewer had emailed the golf powers that be, sure she'd seen a rule infraction during a tournament Jo was playing in. It had resulted in a multiple-stroke penalty the next day and had cost Jo the win. Two weeks later, she'd torn her rotator cuff and shortly after that announced her retirement.

Now she and her husband owned a fitness center on the north side of town.

I closed the laptop, placed it on the coffee table, and picked up Mungo. I needed more information about Walker Stokes, Calista Markes, and Aldo Bracket, as well as Jo Sterling. But more than anything, I needed to get some sleep. Tomorrow was going to be a busy day.

The next morning, Iris and Lucy both came in early, and we got the regular baking done in short order. Then we started preparing what we could for the Halloween party. The candy corn cupcakes were already baked, wrapped, and frozen. I loved that when frozen cake thawed, it was not only easier to frost or ice, but even moister than it would have been without freezing. It was the same for Lucy's "dirt" brownies. Now we made up sugar cookie dough for extra moon and star cookies, cut out the shapes, and froze those so we could bake them the morning of Halloween. By the time the mid-morning rush hit the bakery, things were well in hand.

Lucy had brought her Dutch oven, an impressive black cast-iron beast that looked great perched on the coffee counter surrounded by garlands of autumn leaves and a few hairy spiders.

"Hey, Ben," I said to my uncle as I arranged the last spider. He was lounging behind the counter with that morning's paper. "Anything in there about Leigh's murder?"

He made a wry face. "Plenty about her and her family, old-school, upstanding members of Savannah society that they were, but not much about the murder investigation. It's officially 'ongoing.'"

"Hm. I guess that doesn't mean much. Detective Quinn isn't going to give Steve any information that might endanger official inquiries." He wouldn't give me any, either, at least not intentionally. But it wasn't time to give him a call yet. I still had more to find out on my own.

I tucked a spider leg behind a maple leaf and called it good. "You know the blonde who was here the other day with Leigh?"

Ben looked interested.

"I was poking around online last night and discovered she used to be a professional golfer." Ben was a regular Sunday golfer and, to Lucy's chagrin, often watched golf on television.

He snapped his fingers. "I thought I recognized her, but I didn't know from where. What's her name?"

"Jo Sterling."

"Of course! Crazy what happened to her."

"I saw the thing about a television viewer costing her a big win. That seemed pretty strange. How can that be legal? I mean, in the rules of golf or whatever."

He shook his head. "Weird, huh. I think she tried to fight it, but it's allowed. She retired soon after that. I wonder if that tournament is why."

"She tore her rotator cuff," I said.

He shrugged. "Either way, she's out of the game now."

My phone buzzed in my apron pocket. When I saw it was Jaida, I ducked into the kitchen to answer it.

"Hey."

"Hey yourself," she said. "I've been going through public records. I started with Leigh's ex, since the police always look at the spouse or ex-spouse first."

"Right. I've been wondering about him ever since Iris mentioned him." I moved back to the office and closed the door. "Find anything?"

"A couple of things. First off, their divorce was final about two years ago. Two months later, he married again."

I let out a low whistle. "That was fast."

Mungo sat up on his club chair and cocked his head at me.

"Wasn't it? Then again, we don't know if Walker and Leigh had been separated for a while before the divorce—there were no separation papers filed, mind you, but that doesn't mean they didn't try a trial separation."

"You're right. Best not to jump to conclusions."

"When they divorced, their daughter was eighteen and off to college, so there were no custody issues. However, nothing was mentioned about who was supposed to pay for her college. It wouldn't be Walker, though, because he declared bankruptcy right after the divorce."

"Ouch." I sat down in the office chair. "Do you think Leigh took him for a lot of money?"

And would that be a motive for murder?

"It doesn't look that way. On the other hand, he didn't get much money from her, either, though he still retains part-ownership of the gallery. Hers was old family money, and her father made darn sure it was protected when she married Walker."

"So he lost the benefit of that money when they split. Who filed for the divorce?" I asked.

"Leigh did," Jaida said. "So that's what I have so far. I checked to see if her father's will has been probated yet, but it hasn't. He only passed away last month, and it takes a while. He did, however, quit-claim the family home to Leigh's sister, Calista Markes. It looks like he did that when he moved in with Leigh, presumably so she could care for him. Her address was on the papers he filed."

"Katie!" Lucy opened the door. "You need to come out here. Cookie brought the baby by!"

"Oh, Jaida, I have to go. Cookie's here with Isabella. Thank you so much for digging this info up. I know it's taking time away from your work."

"No problem. Like I said, Gregory's covering for me. Let me know if you think of anything else I can do to help. And give that baby a kiss for me."

"Will do!" I hung up and hurried out.

Cookie was standing by the coffee counter with Isabella in a baby sling wrapped around her chest, and Lucy was already cooing over the three-week-old bundle of joy. Isabella gurgled and smiled at my aunt, and a brilliant smile erupted on Lucy's face. She and Ben had married relatively late in life and hadn't had any children. Lucy was one of the most nurturing women I knew, gentle and thoughtful of others almost to a fault, but when I'd asked her if she missed having children, she'd been philosophical about it, telling me that it had been a choice she and Ben had made.

Nevertheless, I knew Cookie now had yet another built-in babysitter anytime she wanted one.

As I approached them, also melting a little at Isabella's bright dark eyes and button nose, the thought of having my own child with Declan flashed across my mind. But that was for later. We'd already decided to wait at least a year or two after marrying.

"Oh, Katie. Look at this little one," Lucy breathed.

I smiled at Cookie, who looked down at her daughter with a mellow expression of pure love. "She's adorable."

"Yes," she said. "Yes, she is."

Then she looked up. "We haven't been out much, but I thought this would be a good time to start. My man-man will be leaving soon, and Oscar and I will be on our own." Another doting glance down at Isabella, whose eyes were starting to blink sleepily. "Anyway, I brought this for Iris' friend Zoe." She reached into her pocket and held out her hand. A beaded leather necklace dangled from her fingers. "The comfort amulet I mentioned yesterday."

Lucy's eyes quickly raked the customers in the bakery and said, "Come into the office. You can tell us all about it. Iris!"

Our friend followed us back to the office, but there was no way all four of us could fit in the small space. Instead, we gathered just outside, hidden from view and being overheard by a bank of cabinets.

"Yes, Lucy?" Iris came around the corner. "Oh, look at her!" she exclaimed as soon as she saw the baby. "Ooh." She bent and gently stroked Isabella's perfect, plump cheek with the back of her finger. "Hi, baby."

Cookie smiled indulgently as Iris straightened, then held out the necklace to her. "Hi, honey. Listen, I wanted to drop this by for your friend Zoe. It's a comfort amulet. Not in the traditional form, but perhaps something she might wear. I'll leave it up to you whether to tell her the significance of the crystals and that it's been magicked."

"Magicked," Iris repeated, her eyes wide. "And the crystals?"

Cookie had strung several different kinds on the leather cord, and now she listed them off. "There's Apache tear to help with grief, rose quartz for calm and to feel the love of the universe, smoky quartz for sadness, clear quartz for clarity, onyx and carnelian to help ground her, moonstone for strength, and several amethysts mixed in. Amethyst is a soul stone, to help with balance, peace, sadness, and so many other things."

"Wow." Iris looked thoughtful. "I don't know how

open Zoe would be to the idea of a necklace with a spell on it, though. It can't do any harm, can it?"

We all shook our heads.

"This is entirely white magic," Cookie said with a smile.

Iris nodded. "I think I'll just tell her I got it for her birthday, which was last month, and this is the first chance I've had to give it to her."

"That's fine," Lucy said. "She doesn't have to know what it is in order for it to help her."

Iris' eyes suddenly filled with tears. "Thanks, Cookie. I really appreciate you going to all this trouble for someone you don't even know."

Our friend waved her hand. "No worries." An expression of sorrow came into her eyes. "I know what it's like to lose someone." She looked around at us. "We all do."

Nods from each of us.

The rising sounds of voices out front alerted us to new customers. As we went back out to help Ben, Iris tucked the necklace Cookie had given her into her pocket. "Say, can I ask you a question?"

I looked back and saw Iris drawing Cookie aside. "Listen, I know you, um, dated quite a bit before you got married. How did you know Oscar was the one?"

Cookie grinned and said something. I didn't know what it was, but I saw the look in her eye and suspected it was something along the lines of what she'd told me when I'd asked her the same question before marrying Declan.

When you knew, you knew.

Chapter 14

After the lunch crowd had thinned out, I was in the reading area tidying books. Iris came in, tucking her cell phone into the pocket of her shorts.

"Katie?"

"Hmm?"

"I was wondering if I could borrow your car."

I stopped what I was doing and turned to give her my full attention.

"See, Patsy's using mine because hers is in the shop, and she's helping to cater a cocktail party over in Pooler this evening." Patsy was Iris' stepmother and managed the Welsh Wabbit Cheese Shop where I'd originally met Iris. "And Zoe Stokes called me and wondered if I'd mind picking her up at the airport. Her plane just got in, but she has to pick up her luggage, so if I leave now . . ."

"Sure," I said. "Is she doing okay? I'm a little surprised her dad isn't picking her up."

Iris made a face. "He was supposed to, but for some reason he texted her that he couldn't make it."

I wondered if Leigh's ex might be busy making the arrangements for a memorial or the like.

Iris added, "She's staying at his house, though. So it's okay?"

"Of course. I'll get my keys."

A smile bloomed on her face. "Thanks. I didn't want her to have to take a cab. But maybe I could bring Zoe here before taking her home. For a cup of tea or something?" She raised her eyebrows.

Something with a little touch of beneficial magic.

"I think that's a very good idea," I said. "In fact, I just harvested some betony from my garden. It's in the mint family and will help with how unsettled and sad she must feel. I'll brew some for her. Does she like sweet tea?"

"I'm pretty sure she does. Oh, thank you!" Iris came over and gave me a big hug. "I knew you'd be able to help."

While Iris went to get Zoe, I considered the goodies on offer for the day. We regularly rotated the selection in response to the seasons, what local foods were available, and customer demand. Recently, Iris had been experimenting with flowers in our baked goods. She'd developed a rose-petal-and-violet-studded shortbread that people raved over, and it was what I'd offered her when she'd been so upset about Taylor. Both flowers could promote love and comfort heartbreak, and that was what Iris had triggered as she baked the selection in the pastry case. However, violet could also be used for peace and healing—it was also called heartsease—and rose had qualities of well-being and protection.

I removed a half dozen of the cookies and took them back to the kitchen. Arranging them on a plate, I murmured under my breath:

Petals purple and pink
Blooms of beauty, link
To peace and ease
And appease
Loss and distress.
So mote it be.

I put the plate aside and returned to tidying the reading area. I'd just finished the self-help section when Steve Dawes came in. He spied me right away and beelined over.

"Hey," he said.

"Hey," I responded. "What's up?"

"I came to ask you that. Any news from Quinn? On the Markes case?"

My head tipped to the side. "Why would Quinn update me about anything? He thinks I'm crazy for having a premonition, and he doesn't want me to investigate."

"But you are, aren't you?"

I gave an infinitesimal shrug.

"It wasn't a premonition, was it?"

"Steve." I was unable to keep the frustration out of my voice. "I can't tell you anything for your story. I'm sorry."

He considered me for a long moment. "Well, maybe I can tell you something, then."

I folded my arms and waited.

"I have a friend in the crime tech lab."

Of course you do.

"And she says they declared the murder victim's car as the primary crime scene. So they hauled it in and went through it with a fine-tooth comb."

I tried to keep my expression neutral, though I was raging with curiosity. "As they should. And, uh"—I examined my fingernails—"did they find anything interesting?"

He smiled. "The usual stuff—hair, fingerprints, fibers. They're checking out where any of that might lead. There was one other thing, though."

I uncrossed my arms. "What?"

"The heater was on."

I blinked.

"The heater wasn't just on, it was on high. And the battery was completely run down."

"In October? But why . . ." Turning away, I walked over to the window. Honeybee cracked a green eye at me as I thought. Then I had it.

I came back. "Time of death. The heater kept the body temperature higher for a longer period of time."

He pointed at me. "Bingo."

"And that means she was killed earlier than they thought."

"You've got it. Which means"—his eyes narrowed—"you didn't have a premonition at all. She was dead when you called Quinn, wasn't she?"

"It doesn't matter whether my, um, clairvoyant experience was before or after her death, does it?"

He shook his head. "I still don't think that's what happened."

"Well, I can't do anything about what you think, Steve."

He took a deep breath and held my eye for several seconds. "Promise me you're not in danger."

"I promise." At least I was pretty sure I wasn't. Unless Leigh's ghost got really cranky. Even then, I wasn't sure what she could do.

Still, the idea gave me pause.

The door opened, and Declan walked in. Steve saw me looking over his shoulder and turned.

"Ah. I'll be going now. But, Katie-girl?"

My lips pressed together, but he didn't notice.

"I'm still around, you know. If you run into trouble."

I nodded.

He turned to go, then turned back and flashed a white-toothed smile. "Oh, and if you find out anything fit for print, you have my number."

"Noted," I said wryly. Couldn't blame the guy for doing his job, though.

Steve and Declan took a step away from each other as they passed, as if by animal instinct. I suppressed a sigh as the door closed behind Steve, and Declan joined me by the bookshelves.

"What did he want?" Declan asked, looking after his former rival.

"To tell me police forensics found Leigh's car heater was on for a while after she died. She really was dead when her spirit approached Teddy outside the Marshall House."

"Hmph. Does that change anything?"

"Maybe. At least Quinn will be looking for alibis for the right time."

"Whose alibis?" Declan asked.

"Well, I have my list, and I bet the same people are on his." I led him away from the reading area and changed the subject. "The Halloween party starts at seven tomorrow night. There will be a costume parade for the little ones earlier, and then the downtown businesses are having trick-or-treat for a while after that. We'll be open late, until nine, but then—"

"I'm working Halloween. Sorry. Didn't meant to cut you off, but that's what I came by to tell you."

I stared at him. "You can't work on Halloween."

"You know how crazy it gets out there. We have three times as many calls that night. It's almost as bad as the Fourth of July, only with fewer fires and a different kind of stupid."

"No, you *can't* work on Halloween, Declan!"

He frowned, and I suddenly became aware that my voice had risen.

Closing my eyes, I said, "Sorry," in a lower tone. "Have you known this for a while?"

"I just volunteered. Katie, what's wrong? I've worked other Halloween nights and you didn't worry."

"That's not it." I rubbed my palm over my face. "I should have told you earlier, but I wanted it to be kind of a surprise, and I wanted to make sure I could pull it off. But I have a plan, and the spellbook club is going to help."

He looked confused. Then his face cleared. "Does this have something to do with Connell?"

I gave a little nod and looked around. No one within earshot would know we were talking about retrieving the spirit of a sort-of-immortal leprechaun. "Yes. Connell. That's the best time to . . . do the thing."

He grinned. "So your new friend Teddy said she'd help?"

"Um . . . no."

His face fell.

"But we can still do it." Another glance to make sure no one was paying attention. "*I'll* serve as the tether if I have to." The desperate thought had occurred to me in passing a couple of times, but I'd never said it out loud until right then.

"You can't—"

"I've been both places," I said. "Here and there, at the same time." Well, sort of. I'd had a guide—my father—during a shamanic journey. I knew that if I were the first choice to be the tether between the veil between this world and the next in this endeavor, my grandmother's spirit would have told me so when we discussed it during a lucid dream. But she hadn't; she'd said we needed to *find* a tether.

Maybe she just didn't want me to risk it. However, looking into the ice-blue eyes of my husband, I knew I'd risk anything for him. And I felt confident I could pull it off.

Somehow.

Pretty confident, at least.

Declan took a deep breath. "I don't like it."

I bit my lip before I said something I shouldn't. "Nothing terrible will happen. I promise. The worst that can happen is that we end up right where we are now."

He looked down at his hands. "I could lose you, too."

He looked up. "Katie, I couldn't bear that. I'd rather go the rest of my life without Connell than risk that."

I made a face. "Honey, it's totally different. Connell is already in the ether. I'm right here, with a corporeal body and everything." I smiled, hoping desperately that I was right. "Can you get the night off?"

He sighed. "When do you want to try this stunt?"

I let the stunt comment go. "Midnight."

"Okay. I'll talk to my lieutenant. They will probably only need me during the hours before midnight. It's not like Halloween falls on a weekend this year, so most of the really dumb things people do will be before that. Does that work?"

I nodded, immensely relieved. "Yes. Thank you." I leaned forward and took his hand. "Just a couple more days, love. And then, hello, Connell!"

Chapter 15

It wasn't long before Iris came in, followed by another young woman. Her petite nose, wide mouth, and slim build were like her mother's, but her hair was light brown with lots of highlights. I was happy to see Zoe already wore the spelled necklace Cookie had made. I called out a greeting and went back to ringing up two loaves of sourdough bread for one of our regular customers.

I'd told Lucy they would be stopping by on their way to Zoe's dad's house. As soon as she saw the young women, she hurried over and led them to the sofa, which she'd had the foresight to place the RESERVED sign by. Soon they were drinking the special herbal sweet tea I'd brewed and nibbling on rose-and-violet shortbread cookies.

The herbal goodness appeared to work its magic—literally—on both Iris and Zoe, as they visibly relaxed and even laughed a few times. After about ten minutes, I went over and introduced myself.

"Hi, Katie," Zoe responded. "It's nice to meet you. Thanks for letting Iris borrow your car."

"No problem. I'm sorry about your mom."

She gave a sad smile. "Thanks. I'm still taking it in."

"Oh, hon. I can only imagine." I picked up her empty glass. "Can I get you more tea?"

"No, thanks. I think we need to get going. As it is, Iris is going to miss her class this afternoon. If I'd realized—"

"Don't worry about it," Iris said. "Please."

I frowned. "Your class isn't until three thirty, is it?"

"Yeah," Iris answered. "But I'd have to take the bus after I drop your car back here, and it would be half over by then. It's no biggie."

I thought for a moment. "Ben and Lucy can handle things here until closing. Would I be imposing if I came along? We can drop Zoe at her dad's, and then I'll drop you right at school, Iris. You'll have lots of time that way."

They looked at each other.

"I totally get it if you guys want more one-on-one time, though," I said. "It was just a thought." Also, it would be a good way for me to meet Leigh's ex.

Zoe smiled. "I'm happy for the ride, and I don't want Iris to miss class. Thank you so much."

I looked at Iris, and she nodded enthusiastically. "That would be great, Katie. If you don't mind."

"Not at all." I reached back to untie my apron strings. "I'll just get my bag and we can go. Iris, did you park in the garage?"

"Found a spot right across the street." She stood and gathered their dishes. "We'll meet you out there."

"Perfect," I said, and hurried back to tell Lucy—and Mungo—I'd be gone for a while.

I followed Zoe's directions to a newly built neighborhood on the edge of Midtown. After a couple of wrong turns, we stopped in front of a beige-gray two-story with a two-car garage and a flowering plum in the middle of the neatly trimmed front lawn.

"Sorry I had you turn a street too soon," she said as she exited the passenger seat. "It was Juliette's house, and I was already in college when they got married. I've only been here a couple of times."

"No worries," I said cheerfully. I was sure I couldn't have found it again without feeding the address into GPS. All the houses looked the same, from the cookie-cutter architecture to the single tree planted in the front yard to the font of the house number spray-painted on the curb next to the driveways. Every garage door had the same window configuration, and every entry door had three poured-concrete steps leading to it. This neighborhood's HOA had to be downright militant.

Iris unfolded herself from the back seat of the Bug and joined us on the sidewalk. I retrieved Zoe's bag from the trunk, and we walked up the steps. Zoe seemed suddenly nervous, and she stopped without reaching for the doorbell.

"Your dad's expecting you, isn't he?" Iris asked, apparently picking up on the same thing I was.

Zoe nodded and opened her mouth to speak when the door flew open. Startled, she stood slack-jawed for a few moments before snapping her lips back together and narrowing her eyes.

"Juliette," she said by way of greeting. Her tone wasn't exactly friendly.

Neither was the response. "Saw you out here on my doorbell camera. Took you long enough to get here. Was your plane late or something?"

The speaker was a woman in her mid-forties who was about my height. She wore a sundress with a floral paisley pattern, and her wedge sandals boasted rhinestones while showing off bright pink toenails. The white-blond hair that fell to her shoulders looked dry and overprocessed, with flyaway strands that surrounded her head like a nimbus in the backlit doorway. Her skin had the tint of a not-great spray tan. But it was her eyelashes that made it hard not to stare—they were thick, a third of an inch long, and jet black. Combined with her blond hair, they made her look just a wee bit like a Muppet.

Unkind, but true. Plus, I didn't like how she talked to Leigh's daughter.

"No," Zoe said. "My plane was on time. This is right about when I said I'd arrive." She leaned to the side, trying to see around Juliette. "Dad texted and said he couldn't come get me. Is he here?"

Juliette half smiled. "Nope."

Zoe looked puzzled. "But he knew—"

"He's over at Finkel, Bumgartner, and Tott."

The skin tightened across Zoe's face, and the color drained from her cheeks.

"What's wrong?" I rested my fingertips lightly on her arm.

"Who're you?" Juliette demanded, as if she suddenly realized Zoe hadn't arrived alone.

"We're friends of Zoe's," I said shortly and turned my attention back to the young woman beside me.

Zoe turned and looked at me full-on. "FBT is the law firm that handles my trust."

I must have looked confused.

"My grandfather left money to me in the form of a trust that was administered by my mother until I'm twenty-one. I suppose my father will take over now."

"Darn tootin' he will," Juliette said.

I felt my dislike of her blooming with every word that came out of her mouth.

Zoe looked at her with alarm, then her eyes hardened in suspicion.

Juliette smiled.

"He had to go today?" Zoe asked. "Instead of meeting me at the airport?"

"No time like the present and all that," Juliette said with a wave of her hand. "You coming in or not? Walker made me make up the guest bedroom."

I stared, stunned by this woman who had apparently taken the place of Leigh in Zoe's father's heart.

Unbelievable.

"Not." Zoe said the word with quiet emphasis and turned back toward the Bug.

She marched down the steps, dragging her roller bag behind her. After one glance back at the startled woman in the doorway, Iris and I quickly followed. Without a word, I opened the trunk and tossed the bag back in, and by the time I got to the driver's side, the other two were already pulling on their seat belts.

"Hey!" Juliette called. "You can't do that! Your dad's gonna be pretty mad."

Zoe ignored her. I glanced over as we pulled away and saw her eyes were filled with tears and her jaw was clamped so tight the muscles stood out in her neck.

"You can come to my house," Iris said. "I have an apartment, sort of, in my stepmother's basement. It's not very big, but you can stay as long as you want."

"Zoe," I said, before she could take Iris up on her offer, "you have an aunt in town, don't you? Your mother's sister?"

She swallowed and managed to unclench her jaw enough to say, "Yes. Aunt Calista lives in Grandpa's old house."

"Would you like me to take you there?"

A few seconds passed, and then she nodded. "I think so. I don't know if she'll want me, either, but I guess I can try."

Her words broke my heart, and I sent out a prayer to the universe that Aunt Calista would welcome this grieving young woman with open arms.

"Thanks for offering, Iris. I might have to take you up on it. But if Calista will let me stay with her for a few days, she's got tons of room. Besides, she's family, and I feel like, well, you know . . ." She trailed off.

"Of course." Iris reached forward from the back seat and put her hand on Zoe's shoulder. "Why don't you call her?"

Zoe blinked, then said, "Duh. My brain isn't working very well."

"Go easy on yourself," I said.

She made the call, which was picked up immediately.

When Zoe explained the situation and asked her aunt if she could stay with her, we could all hear the enthusiastic response on the other end.

I guess I don't have to use the excuse of returning the scrimshaw bookmark to talk to Calista after all. I'll have to remember to ask her if it's hers.

However, I'd hoped to meet Leigh's ex on this venture, and now I had no idea how to manage that.

Zoe was smiling when she hung up. "She's kind of kooky, but I love her."

"She's got to be better than Juliette," Iris muttered from behind us.

I shot her a look in the rearview mirror.

However, Zoe tipped her head to the side and looked thoughtful. "I don't know Juliette very well, but I don't think she likes the idea of sharing Dad with me. Honestly, I was pretty upset when they married so quickly after Mom and Dad got the divorce, didn't want to go to the wedding or have anything to do with them. But I did go, and she seemed nice enough, and Dad seemed happy. I had to admit he wasn't happy with Mom." She fell quiet for a few seconds and then said, "He complained a lot about how she kept total control of her family's money. I guess that's not a problem anymore." She sighed. "At least until I turn twenty-one in another year and a half."

Iris and I exchanged a glance in the rearview mirror.

"What does your dad do for a living?" I asked.

"He manages things."

That was what Iris had said. "What kinds of things?" I asked.

"He used to manage a bookstore, but was let go.

145

Then he managed an appliance store until the owners decided to close it, and for a little while a restaurant, but then that went under. He's looking for another position." She sighed. "Or he might decide he just wants to manage my trust. It's pretty big."

The thought made my stomach turn. It didn't sound like Walker Stokes was very good at managing things.

I changed the subject. "Did your mom have a boyfriend? Or whatever you'd call it. Was she seeing anyone?"

Zoe gave the tiniest of shrugs. "She didn't say anything, but that was like her, even with me. I don't think she'd talk about anyone she was involved with unless it got pretty serious. Mom was a very private person."

I nodded and drove in silence for another block.

Suddenly Zoe said, "You know, I think there might have been someone."

"Something she said?" Iris asked from the back seat.

"No . . ." her friend said, staring out the windshield as if looking at a memory. "It's just that when I came home the Friday before Labor Day, she told me to come by the gallery when I got into town. I'd driven down from Atlanta with friends instead of flying like today," Zoe explained. "Anyway, I went there, but no one answered. I don't have a key to the gallery, so I went around to the back entrance. No answer there, either, so I went on to the house. She came home a little later— said she'd just missed me. But when I went around to the back of the gallery, I heard voices inside. A man's and a woman's. I didn't hear much of what they were saying, but it sounded . . . intimate." She swallowed.

"That's when I left. The last thing I wanted was to interrupt something like that."

"Ugh," Iris said.

Zoe made a face. "She had a right to see anyone she wanted, I guess. I hinted around the next day, but she never admitted to anything. I let it drop."

A boyfriend would be on Quinn's suspect list—if he knew about him. It didn't seem like it would be that hard to find out who he was. Maybe it was about time I checked in with the detective.

We had to park a few doors down from the large house in the Victorian district where Zoe's aunt lived. It was a beautiful structure with a huge bay window half hidden by overgrown lilacs, painted a creamy light yellow with decorative gingerbread trim in two shades of green, orange, and blue. A round turret rose from the second story on the right, and to the left, the deep porch, supported by wide columns, had been recently painted traditional haint blue. Comfortable outdoor furniture sprawled across the porch, and the far end was completely shadowed by a huge, twisting wisteria. The gardens near the house were messes of bright overgrown blooms and tangles of weeds, all thriving together in chaotic neglect. Clumps of weeds, mostly yellow nutsedge and purple blooming mallow, studded the small lawn, which was in desperate need of a mower. The place had an air of neglect, but with the tidy, inviting porch and sparkling birdbath, I could see it was a kind of curated neglect.

Some things were important to the inhabitant, but a lot of things simply weren't.

As we approached, the front door flew open, and Calista Markes ran down the steps.

"Zoe! Honey!" She wrapped the young woman in a bear hug. I could feel the genuine love she felt for the girl, and some of my worry abated.

Zoe dropped her bag and returned the embrace, burying her face into her aunt's shoulder and murmuring, "Hi, Calista," in a muffled voice.

Suddenly, Calista pushed away and held her niece at arm's length. "How are you holding up, honey?"

"I'm okay." She sounded a little tentative, but I thought she really would be okay with time—and the help of her aunt.

Anger flared at her father, but I tried to tamp it down. I didn't know the whole situation, and I wasn't in a position to judge.

Honestly, I judged anyway.

So did Calista, apparently, because she said. "What the heck is the matter with your dad?"

Zoe opened her mouth to speak, but her aunt barreled on.

"And why did he have to pick now to be so hardhearted? Though for all I know, he never stopped, you know? Oh, honey, I'm so sorry. He's such a narcissist. I mean, your mama was, too, pretty self-involved, but at least she wasn't cruel. But don't you worry—" Her gaze fell on Iris and me standing there, and she stopped herself, realizing she had an audience. Her expression sharpened as she tried to place me.

I stepped forward and held out my hand. "Katie Lightfoot. I work at the Honeybee Bakery. And this is

Iris Grant. She's an old friend of Zoe's and picked her up from the airport. She works at the bakery, too."

Recognition flooded Calista's face, and she stepped right past my outstretched hand to give me a big hug, and then did the same to a surprised Iris.

"Thank you so much, girls, for taking care of little Zoe here!"

Behind her, Zoe rolled her eyes.

"I guess you were friends of Leigh's, too?" The last words came out as a question. She was wondering why I was there.

"We were acquainted with Leigh," I clarified. "I came along to give Zoe a ride."

Zoe's hand rose, and she fingered the crystal beads on her new necklace. She seemed calm in spite of everything, and I silently thanked Cookie for her foresight in making the comfort amulet.

"I'll call Dad later," she said. "Calista, can we go inside? I'm melting out here."

"Of course, honey. Let's all go in. I have some fresh lemonade."

Iris started to protest, but I spoke before she could. "We have a few minutes before we need to get you to class, don't we?"

She followed my lead. "A few."

"Okay, then. Come on inside," Calista said.

The inside of Calista's house had the same flavor as the outside—expensive antiques, worn carpet, a fine layer of dust on various knickknacks and picture frames, ornate woodwork carved more than a century before—all suffering from a kind of benign neglect. Beneath the scent of recently made toast, the air smelled like an old lady's closet, a mix of mothballs and cedar and age.

We went through the living room to the dining room. The table was piled high with bolts of vinyl in bright patterns—zebra and leopard print, brilliant florals, paisleys, and various leaf prints. Among them were several completed head coverings, ranging from cutesy bow-laden versions to a design I could imagine Nefertiti wearing.

"What's all this, Calista?" Zoe asked.

Her aunt stopped in the doorway of the kitchen and turned. "Oh, that's my new business! Designer shower caps! They're awesome."

I walked over and picked up a finished cap. "This is beautiful." Rather than the ruffle-edged type I'd seen before, this cap looked more like a turban, classy and fashionable. Mrs. Standish came to mind. "Seriously, I know people who would wear this as a hat."

"Oh, thank you! I want them to be different, you know? To stand out, but still be practical." She wrinkled her nose. "Of course, Leigh thought I was crazy, refused to invest in my business, or in me, but I'll get the money anyway." She made a wide gesture. "This old house is worth something, after all."

"You *sold* Grandpa's house?" Zoe asked, obviously aghast at the idea.

"It's not his house now." Calista sounded bitter. "I'm going to mortgage it. Leigh had some notion of trying to stop me, some legal maneuver, but I'm going ahead. Carpe diem, right? Oh, don't look like that, hon! I'll be able to pay off the family digs in no time, once my shower caps hit the market."

Zoe looked sick, and I figured her confidence regarding her aunt's business acumen matched her mother's. Calista didn't seem to notice. She blithely continued into the kitchen and started pulling glasses from the cupboard.

Soon we were all sitting around the enormous butcher block kitchen table, sipping lemonade and learning about the shower cap business. Calista assured us there was a market, and a very upscale one at that.

"Leigh just never believed in me," she said with a sigh.

I wondered if Zoe was getting tired of her aunt complaining about her sister, so I bluntly changed the subject to the one we'd been talking about in the car.

"Was Leigh seeing anyone?" I asked.

Calista blinked, then looked at her niece. "I'd heard a rumor that she was seeing someone. Maybe someone she shouldn't have been, as a matter of fact."

Zoe lifted an eyebrow. "Are you saying my mother was involved with a married man?"

Her aunt shrugged. "Where there's smoke there's fire, you know."

"That doesn't exactly sound like her," Zoe said, fingering her necklace. I was glad to see she didn't appear upset.

Iris did, though. I could sense her discomfort as she rose. "I'm sorry. I need to be getting to class now."

I stood up as well. "Right. Calista, it was nice chatting with you. Best of luck with your shower caps. Zoe, you give us a shout if you need anything, all right?"

Calista waved that away. "Don't worry. Daddy's old car is in the garage. She can drive that to her heart's content."

Zoe smiled at me, aware that I hadn't just been talking about transportation. "Thanks. I will."

As we showed ourselves out, I heard Calista say, "I have an Etsy shop for now, but I'm working on getting a manufacturing contract, and they'll be everywhere! I call them Shower Chapeaus. They have PEVA linings, which is way better for the environment."

At the door, I turned and went back to the kitchen. "Calista?"

They looked up from the table.

"We found a pretty fancy bookmark at the Honeybee after your meeting there. It's scrimshaw on ivory, surrounded by red stone—ruby or garnet. Is it yours?"

She shook her head. "Oh, no. That's Jo's. It's a family heirloom."

"I'll get it back to her. What's the best way to get a hold of her?"

Calista considered. "Most of the time, she's at the gym she runs with her husband. Sterling Fitness. I think I have her number here somewhere, though." She started to get up.

"No worries," I said. "I'll drop the bookmark by the gym. Thanks."

Iris was waiting outside. "Are you sure it's okay to leave Zoe here?"

I sighed. "For now. She knows she can call. I don't think Calista means any harm. She's just oblivious that her comments about Leigh might make Zoe uncomfortable."

"Seems to run in that family," Iris muttered.

Though I agreed, I kept silent. I also kept silent about the possible new murder motive we'd uncovered. Leigh had been going to throw a monkey wrench into Calista's big Shower Chapeaus business plans.

Now she wouldn't be a problem.

Chapter 16

I dropped Iris at SCAD and got back to the bakery in time to help with prep for the next day. Ben had already left, and Lucy and I were getting things ready to close down when Mrs. Standish and Skipper Dean came in.

"Yoo-hoo! Lucille!" Mrs. Standish called as if my aunt were down the block and not just in the kitchen. "We're having a fundraiser for the animal shelter next month, and I'm hoping you can provide some yummy treats. Do you have a moment to chat?"

Lucy came out, wiping her hands on a towel. "Sure. Let's go in here."

They went into the reading area, and Skipper Dean sauntered over to where I was emptying the tip jar by the register. He was a wiry man, thin and muscular, with thick gray hair and impeccable taste in clothes.

"Are you in the market for a yummy treat yourself?" I asked with a smile.

He returned the smile. "Always. I believe Edna wanted some of your cheddar sage scones to go with our vichyssoise this evening. And I wouldn't mind a bit of cake for dessert. What do you have?"

I popped into the kitchen to wash my hands, then came back to load the scones into a Honeybee bag. "We don't have much cake left this late in the day, but I've been experimenting with a blood orange and thyme cake, and I think I've got it about right."

His eyes brightened. "That sounds delightful."

"It's on the house as long as you give me your honest opinion about it."

He gave a single, firm nod. "Deal."

I went back into the kitchen and loaded the cake into a box for him to take. Back at the register, I rang up the scones, and he paid.

"Say, Dean," I said, "I understand from Mrs. Standish that you're interested in something called outsider art."

"Indeed I am."

"What can you tell me about it?" I asked.

After telling me more or less the same thing Steve had regarding how the form was defined, he went on to tell me why he was so interested in it. "It's unconventional, but a lot of art could be called that. Outsiders, however, bring to their pieces an honesty, a rawness that transcends tradition and expectation. Sometimes it's very odd, sometimes whimsical, sometimes folksy. It apparently started among asylum inmates in the early twentieth century, and today outsider art often comes from those who suffer from mental illness. Their art provides a kind of window into their souls, a new twist on creativity."

I blinked. "Wow. When you put it that way, it really is interesting. The stuff I saw the other day didn't seem all that creative, though."

"Oh? Where was this?"

"At the Markes Gallery."

"Ah. Yes. Poor Leigh." He paused thoughtfully. "I don't believe she was much of a fan of outsider art, though. She was quite traditional in that way and believed all artists should have extensive and proper training."

"I'm not sure she wanted this artist to have a show in her gallery. Have you heard of Aldo Bracket?"

Skipper Dean made a very rude noise in the back of his throat. "I have."

I waited.

"Aldo Bracket is an ignorant troglodyte."

"Oh?"

"He does not create art. He does not *create* anything. He buys things, including favor."

I leaned forward, remembering how Aldo had guaranteed Paisley his work would sell out if she gave him a show. "Favor, you say. Do you think he'd buy his own work—through someone else, of course? To gain something, a reputation in the art community, maybe?"

Dean made the noise again. "I wouldn't put it past him. Not that selling his work would gain him anything in the true art community. Especially not that garbage he claims is outsider art. After all, outsider art isn't about commerce at all, not at its heart. However, his father might take him more seriously. His father is all about money."

I pushed away from the counter. "If he sold out a show at a reputable place like the Markes Gallery, his dad might respect him more?"

He shrugged. "I'm only speculating." Puzzlement creased his brow. "I don't see any way that Leigh would give him a show in her gallery, though."

Her assistant, Paisley, on the other hand . . .

"Skipper!" Mrs. Standish waved him over to where she and Lucy had stopped by the door. "Are we supplied for the evening?"

"Indeed we are." He bestowed an indulgent smile on her, then turned to me before going. "Thank you for the cake, Katie, and for the discussion. Let me know if you have any other questions about outsider art."

I agreed that he'd be the first one I'd call.

Before I started the Bug, I texted Declan.

Will be a little late. Going to drop by Sterling Fitness to return an item Jo Sterling left at the bakery.

He replied immediately.

Okay. Grilling salmon tonight. Grab some wine if you get a chance. Love you.

I replied with a heart emoji, then turned the key in the engine.

Sterling Fitness was on the north side of Savannah and overlooked the river and the Talmadge Memorial Bridge. I parked at the back of the lot and rolled all the windows down for Mungo.

"I won't be long."

He stood on his hind legs and looked at the door of the gym, then back at me.

"Believe me, you don't want to go in there. You don't even like to go for a run with me. This is a perfect opportunity for you to take a nap."

Yip!

He sat back down in the passenger seat. I grabbed my tote and headed inside.

The place was beautiful. The entire back wall, which faced the river, was floor-to-ceiling windows. Treadmills, spinning bikes, and the like were arranged to take advantage of the view. The walls and ceiling were painted bright white, and the floor was a rich hardwood. Shelving units against the walls held neat rolls of towels, subtle sconce lighting was tucked into the columns that marched down the center of the space, and weightlifting equipment stood in a long, tidy row. Off to the right, doorways punctuated the wall at regular intervals. The nearest one was closed and had a sign that read PILATES, and I assumed the rest led to activity-specific studios. To the left was a long counter with stools—a juice and oxygen bar to serve the clientele. And everywhere, ferns of all kinds hung from the ceiling and spilled from wall planters, creating a verdant oasis for luxury workouts.

The gym was about a third full, and every single person was trim and thin, lithe, and dressed to the nines in designer athletic clothes. Near the front door, a glassed-off area offered items for sale. I went in and saw where some of the clothing on the well-dressed gymgoers came from. I checked a couple of price tags and nearly gasped out loud before backing out.

I turned to scan the room for Jo but didn't see her. A man stood behind the juice bar counter, watching me.

When I caught his eye, he smiled a brilliant, white-toothed smile that belonged on a magazine cover. As I approached him, I saw all of him belonged on a magazine cover. The man was gorgeous, with sandy hair, hazel eyes that crinkled just enough at the corners to make them spark when he smiled, and even features that were both masculine and boyish. He wore a light blue polo shirt and chino shorts.

"Well, hello there," he said in a rich baritone. Three words, and I could already tell he was flirting. "Haven't seen you in here before." He cocked his head to the side. "Are you interested in joining?"

"Actually, I was hoping—"

The door opened and three women came in and rushed over to the juice bar.

"Oh, Rhett, there you are. You naughty boy. You weren't here yesterday when we came for spin class." The speaker was a very well maintained middle-aged woman with perfectly coiffed hair and an impressive amount of eye makeup for a gym workout. Her friends were carbon copies. All of them ignored me completely, focusing their considerable attention on . . . *Rhett*.

Slowly, I backed away and looked around again. This time I spied Jo. She had exited the Pilates room and stood leaning against the wall next to the door, arms crossed over her chest. Her straight blonde hair fell over her face as she watched the shenanigans at the juice bar. I walked over and joined her against the wall.

"Quite the show, isn't it?" she asked, with a glance my way. She wore dark slacks and a white button-down shirt much like what she'd had on during the book club meeting. Maybe it was a kind of uniform to her.

"They seem to really like the guy," I agreed. "Rhett, is it?"

"Mm. My mother-in-law had a real thing for *Gone with the Wind*."

I turned to look at her full-on. "That's your husband?"

"Mm. Not that you can tell."

I squinted. "Well, he is wearing a wedding ring."

She snorted. "Yeah, that holds them off." Then she sighed. "It's harmless, though. And he does bring in the paying customers. Lots of them."

"How much does it cost to join?" I asked.

She told me.

Despite being prepared for a big number, my jaw slackened in surprise.

Jo laughed. "What the market will bear, right? You're from the bakery, aren't you?"

Still stunned, my head bobbed in affirmation. Then I mentally gave myself a shake. "Yes. Katie Lightfoot from the Honeybee, where you had your book club meeting. That's why I'm here."

Surprise widened her eyes. "You want us to sell your pastries here? Because that's a terrible idea. I mean, they're absolutely delicious, but no one would buy them." She gestured with her chin. "I'm pretty sure those women only eat avocados and almonds."

I smiled. "No, that's not why I dropped by." Fishing in my tote bag, I said, "You left this at the bakery. Calista Markes told me that it's yours." I handed her the bookmark.

Relief flooded her face. "Oh! Yes, that was my mother's. I had no idea where I'd left it, though now that I think about it, of course I must have dropped it at the book club meeting." She took a deep breath. "It's been a hard couple of days. If you've seen Calista, you've heard about Leigh."

"I have. I'm sorry for your loss."

"Thanks." She looked into the distance for a few seconds. "I might be one of the only people who will miss her."

"Really?"

She blinked and came out of her reverie. "Never mind. Come back to the office."

Puzzled, I followed her to the far door along the right wall. Inside, a large desk took up most of the room. She sat behind it, opened a drawer, and took out a checkbook.

Ha! And Bianca thinks no one writes checks anymore. Wait . . .

"What are you doing?" I asked.

She looked up at me from under her brows. "Giving you a reward. For returning the bookmark. It's quite valuable."

"Oh, for Pete's sake. You don't have to do that."

"But—"

"No. Seriously. I don't want anything for returning something you lost."

"Are you sure?"

"Absolutely."

"Well, okay." She stood and held out her hand. "Thanks."

I shook it. "No problem."

As she came back out from behind the desk, I said, "Can I ask you a question?"

She quirked an eyebrow. "You can try."

"You said you were the only one who would miss Leigh. It just struck me as, well, as sad mostly. What about her daughter?"

She crossed her arms over her chest and considered me. "Do you know Zoe?"

"We've met." Earlier that same day, but still. "She's friends with one of the Honeybee employees, Iris Grant."

Her arms dropped. Even with all my witchy intuition, I found her very difficult to read.

"You're right. Zoe will miss her mother. They were pretty close, I guess. But Zoe's part of . . . that family. And that family is all about how things look. Zoe is sturdy. She'll be okay."

"And Calista?" I was fishing. From the way she'd talked earlier, I didn't think Leigh's sister seemed all that broken up over her death.

Jo made a face. "Nah. Leigh was a thorn in her side her whole life. I mean, she didn't want her dead or anything. Don't get me wrong. She won't have to compete anymore, though. See, Leigh tended to rub people the wrong way. She was blunt, she could be rude, and she could be bossy."

"You were her friend," I said.

Tears suddenly filled her eyes, and she swallowed. "We met in high school. We had our differences, for sure, but we'd known each other for such a long time it didn't matter anymore."

"I'm sorry," I said.

She nodded, swiped the back of her hand across her eyes, and opened the door.

"Calista said her sister was seeing someone. Do you know who it was?" I asked.

Jo turned in the doorway. "She told you that?"

"Uh-huh."

"Did she know who?"

"No." I didn't elaborate.

"Well, she's right. Leigh was seeing someone."

"He'll miss her, then, won't he?"

"He might. He just might." She started to walk away but stopped and looked back at me over her shoulder. "I'm not so sure about his wife, though." She began walking again. "Whoever she was."

Chapter 17

On the way home, I headed back downtown to Bianca's wine shop on Factors Walk for a nice bottle of wine to go with Declan's supper. We had fallen into a routine, with him taking over supper duties three nights a week when he was off shift, and I loved it. Partly because I worked in a kitchen all day, but also because my husband was a fantastic cook.

Bianca, who concentrated on finding amazing wines and running the business side of things, had already left. Her knowledgeable clerk suggested a pinot noir since the salmon would be grilled. I also grabbed a bottle of rosé to share with Margie when we finally got the chance.

On impulse, I turned toward Whitaker Street on my way home. There was plenty of parking by the Markes Gallery so late in the day. I'd been hoping to ask Paisley if the gallery would be opening soon and perhaps ply her with a few casual questions about Leigh's ex-husband. The door was locked, but there was a sign on the door: UNDER NEW MANAGEMENT.

And below that the information that the gallery would be open to the public again as of tomorrow.

New management. Ugh.

I was more curious than ever to meet Walker Stokes.

As I pulled away from the curb, another car going in the opposite direction slowed to a crawl. I turned my head to look at the driver, and there was Detective Peter Quinn peering into my eyes.

He didn't look happy.

Declan had glazed the salmon with hoisin and soy sauce and grilled it on our little hibachi on the back patio. Sitting at the small table outside, we ate it with fragrant jasmine rice cooked with lime, a marinated tomato and cucumber salad, and the pinot noir I'd picked up at Moon Grapes. Mungo had already finished his own unseasoned salmon and rice and was making his rounds in the backyard, sniffing here and there to see if there were any updates.

"The way Jo talked about Leigh made me sad. I didn't know her well, but the way her friend—her best friend, mind you—made her sound, Leigh must have been quite unhappy."

He put his fork down and took a sip of wine. "She was a very successful woman."

"There are a lot of ways to define success."

"True. She did take off work to care for her father, though."

"There's that," I said. "Mimsey said James Markes didn't approve of her marriage to Walker Stokes. I wish I could have met him when we took Zoe to his house."

"You don't know where he works?"

"He doesn't, according to Zoe. He's taking over managing the trust her grandfather left her, it sounds like, and Bianca and I heard Leigh's assistant say Walker wanted to reopen the Markes Gallery. I went by this evening and saw it's 'under new management,' which I assume means his management."

"Can he do that?"

"Jaida said he had a financial interest in the business. Now, maybe he's the full owner."

"Hmm. Leigh is killed and suddenly her husband owns her successful art gallery and has access to his daughter's money. A lot of money, I imagine."

"It's a motive, for sure," I agreed. "Say, what time do you have to go to work tomorrow?"

"Not until three."

"Do you want to take a look at a sculpture?"

His eyebrows lifted. "I don't know. Do I?"

"Yep, I think you do. If I can swing it. When Bianca and I went to the gallery to check out Leigh's assistant, the idea was that Bianca wanted me to see a sculpture. Turns out it's kind of amazing."

He tipped his head to the side. "And you want to buy it?"

"Nah. It's way too expensive. I took pictures, but the assistant, Paisley Long, said my husband should see it in person. And the gallery is reopening tomorrow."

It took him a minute, but he put it together. "And you think Walker Stokes might be at the gallery."

I nodded. "It's worth a shot."

"Okay. Set it up, and I'll be there."

*　　*　　*

That night I tried to contact Nonna. When I'd done it before, it had been through a lucid dream. However, try as I might, I couldn't drift off enough to dream. Instead, I spent the night in a fitful, half-awake state that provided little rest. I gave up at four a.m.

It was officially Halloween. Tonight, we'd finally try to get Connell back.

No. Tonight we *would* get Connell back.

Normally I would have gone for a run to energize myself after a poor night's sleep. Instead, I quickly showered and dressed, then silently went up the stairs to the loft and turned on a lamp. I opened the cupboard where Declan kept some of the sentimental items from his past. Reaching past the baseball trophies and ticket stubs, I grasped the thick photo album full of old family photos his mother had given him. Opening it, I found what I was looking for. After several seconds of hesitation, I slipped the photo out of the corners that held it in place. Turning on the printer, I scanned the picture and printed it out on photo paper. I tucked the copy in the front of the album, closed it, and returned it to the shelf. Rummaging through the desk, I found an empty envelope and put the original photo inside, then headed back downstairs.

After a few sips of coffee, I slid open the door to the patio and slipped out with a bag of supplies. Mungo followed, and I closed the door behind us. The sun was still below the horizon, and there was a crisp bite to the air. It carried the scent of the Cherokee roses, even this late in the year, along with mint, sage, and lavender from the herb garden.

Soon after I'd purchased the carriage house, Declan had helped me to carve out flowing garden beds along the edges of the yard. There was one for vegetables, another with herbs, and one exclusively devoted to magical plants and gardening spells. A small rowan grew in the middle of that one, along with the witch hazel from which I'd made my wand. Of course, all the herbs were magical, too. I'd tucked flowers in all the gardens, chosen so there would be something blooming all year. As I went out to the small stream that ran diagonally across the very back corner of the lot—natural running water was invaluable to the spell work of a hedgewitch—I noticed the fuzzy blooms of blue mistflower mixed in with purple false foxglove and white boneset.

A flicker drew my attention, and I turned to see Mungo lying in the lush grass, chin down and staring at a very unseasonal firefly glowing right in front of his nose. Shaking my head and smiling, I filled a large plastic jug with water from the stream and twisted the cap on. Fireflies seemed to be attracted to Mungo the same way dragonflies were to me, and I was always amazed when they appeared out of nowhere when he was around, even in the dead of winter. During the early summer there were so many in the yard and surrounding trees that Declan joked we could read by their light.

In the middle of the yard stood a cedar gazebo, and nearby was the firepit. I checked the wood supply and found Declan had filled the rack after our last fire. I retrieved the rough straw broom, or *besom* in witch talk, from the gazebo and carefully swept the three-foot-wide circle of rocks around the pit, clearing it of dried leaves and debris while chanting a cleansing spell.

Usually, I did solo spell work inside the gazebo, but there would be too many of us, and I wanted to be able to move around. We'd cast the salt circle around the outside of the rock ring, with a small fire burning in the center. To the neighbors it would look like an autumn backyard gathering, albeit rather late at night. I could only hope Margie and the kids would be fast asleep by then.

I put the jug of water on the small table in the center of the gazebo, along with a canister of salt, four white candles, and four black candles in holders. Satisfied with the preparations for tonight's spell so far, I sat on the top step of the gazebo and scratched Mungo's ears while considering what else we'd need. I stood, and he gamboled after me, his firefly forgotten, as I went back inside. Sipping coffee, I composed a quick email to the others in the spellbook club to confirm what they'd be bringing that evening and when we'd meet.

Minutes later, my familiar and I were buzzing toward the Savannah River in the Bug. There was one more thing I wanted to do before going to work.

On Bay Street, I parked and reached for Mungo's leash. He graciously allowed me to put it on him, then scrambled over to the driver's seat and jumped to the ground when I got out. I locked the car, and we headed toward Rousakis Plaza.

The sun wouldn't even start to rise for more than an hour, so we navigated by streetlights until we got to River Street. We saw few others out that early—a couple of runners, a slow-moving police car half a block away, drivers on their way to early work shifts, and another dog walker. Reflected light from the imposing Westin Hotel and Golf Resort on the other side of the river painted the water with multicolored streaks that reached nearly to where Mungo and I stood on the shore. Without the smells of restaurant food and car exhaust tainting the air, the slight smell of sulfur from the river reached my nose. The sound of a boat horn drifted toward where we stood.

Shaking myself out of my reverie, we continued to Rousakis Plaza and Echo Square. Mungo padded beside me as I walked to the center of the red and black bricks laid out in a circle in the center of the square and paused.

Echo Square was a favorite destination of tourists because it possessed a unique quality. It functioned as an echo chamber. If you spoke while standing inside it, people outside the square couldn't hear you, but your own voice reverberated in your own ears. It was in all the guidebooks and a favorite feature of many tours. However, I had stumbled upon another feature of Echo Square quite by accident.

The spirit of my deceased grandmother had once answered me as I spoke out loud, trying to parse my thoughts on another paranormal murder case in which I'd been involved.

Now, as I stood there with Mungo, I figured it couldn't hurt to try. I was anxious about the spell I was going to attempt that night. I was basing it on advice she'd given me the last time we'd been in contact, and I had questions.

"Nonna?" I whispered. Then I repeated it louder, even though my voice sounded to me as if I were shouting. "Nonna? Are you there?"

After my question echoed back to me, all I heard was the sound of a light breeze and Mungo panting beside me.

For the most part, Nonna had only been in contact when I was in danger or desperate. I definitely felt desperate, but not in danger.

At least not really. Not yet.

"Nonna, I'm going to do what you told me. I'm going to go after Connell tonight, when the veil is thin. I haven't found a tether, though. Well, I did, sort of, but she won't help. Can't help, I guess. So I'm going to do it myself. Act as the tether, I mean. Will that work?"

Truck tires clattered over a grate in the road several hundred feet away.

"Nonna, *please* talk to me." Despair leaked into every word.

Mungo whined low in his throat, and it reverberated back to us, loud and unhappy.

I took a deep breath. "Well, I guess it's okay, then. Maybe you'll be around tonight. I hope you will be. I'd love to hear from you."

And I need all the help I can get.

Sighing, I reached down and ruffled the fur on Mungo's head. Then we started back to the car.

After the sourdough loaves were in the oven, I started in on the Samhain cakes for that evening's ritual. As I gathered ingredients, I decided to make them more like scones than regular cakes. Rubbing the butter into the flour and brown sugar, I thought about the spices to use. Cinnamon was useful in love spells, but I wanted to trigger its protective qualities. Ginger was also protective, and helpful in augmenting any magic. The spellbook club often drank ginger tea before casting.

Nutmeg was often used in travel spells, which would be perfect in a ritual to help a lost spirit travel back home. It was also a spice that could be used to promote justice. Getting Connell back could be considered a kind of justice, as I felt it was absolutely the right thing to do. He'd saved my magic and deserved my gratitude and help. I also made a note to myself that perhaps nutmeg would be helpful in a spell to bring justice to Leigh Markes. I felt like I'd gotten almost nowhere trying to find her killer. Casting a spell to try to break that logjam couldn't hurt.

Tomorrow. Tonight I had to concentrate on Connell.

I brought my attention back to the task at hand, grating fresh nutmeg into pumpkin puree. I reached for the powdered ginger, then stopped. Barmbrack was a traditional Irish Halloween treat, a kind of fruitcake made with dried fruit. Crystalized ginger would have more of that vibe, and besides, it was delicious. I grabbed a jar and chopped the pieces finely before adding them, along with some candied orange peel, to the pumpkin. As I stirred, I whispered under my breath, invoking the ability of pumpkin to protect from evil spirits—a handy thing, it seemed, if someone was planning to visit the next plane.

Not someone. Me. I'm going to be the tether.

And I had no idea how to do it.

I pushed the thought out of my mind. Right now, I needed to concentrate on my intentions for this recipe.

The first batch of customers had come and gone, and I was loading still-warm loaves of sourdough into the pastry case. The door opened, and I looked up in anticipation, as we had come to know most of our early-morning regulars. It turned out to be someone I knew, all right.

"Hello, Detective Quinn," I said.

"Why, hello, Katie Lightfoot." The words sounded so friendly, except he wasn't smiling.

Peter Quinn was fit, boasted a shock of thick gray hair and piercing eyes, and had rather expensive taste in clothing.

"What can I get you, Detective?" I asked.

In the kitchen behind me, Lucy snorted quietly. Despite her respect for law enforcement, after the situation with Ben, she had mixed feelings about Quinn. Luckily, I was pretty sure he hadn't heard her.

"Some information might be nice."

I smiled. "Perhaps with a side of sweet tea and a muffin?"

His lips twitched. "Perhaps with a side of espresso."

"Nothing sweet?"

"Not today."

Well, that told me what kind of mood he was in. I asked Ben for an espresso, and he started brewing it with a smile. Unlike Lucy and me, Ben acted as if Quinn had never accused him of murder.

I led Quinn to a table in the corner and sat down. He slid into the seat across from me.

"How's Mrs. Quinn?" I asked.

He blinked. "She's fine."

"I'm so sorry I interrupted your date night with my premonition."

"Hmm. Not exactly a premonition, it turns out. The time of death was earlier than the medical examiner initially thought."

"I know." It came out a bit smug.

He looked surprised. "Oh?"

"I understand the crime scene techs discovered the heater had been on in the victim's car and the battery had run down."

Leaning forward, he asked, "And how exactly do you know that? It's not public knowledge."

"Sources." Still too smug.

"So, you're looking into the murder of Leigh Markes even though I told you not to."

I wiped the self-satisfied look off my face.

"Is that why you were at the Markes Gallery last evening?" he asked.

"I was checking to see when they'd be opening," I said. "There's a sculpture there that I'm interested in."

His eyes narrowed. "Right. What else have your *sources* told you?"

I gave in. "Not much. I do have a list of suspects, though. Want to hear them?"

A sigh escaped his lips. "Sure, Katie. Let's hear your suspects."

I ticked them off on my fingers. "Leigh's ex, Walker Stokes. He's already met with the lawyers who handle the trust James Markes left his granddaughter, Zoe. He'll have control of it until she's twenty-one, which isn't that far away, but still. It's a lot of money. And the sign on the gallery last night said it's now under new management. His management, I presume."

Quinn looked impressed despite himself.

"Does he have an alibi?" I asked. "For the actual time of death, I mean?"

He made a face. "Sort of. His wife."

I blew a raspberry. "Juliette? She'd lie for him in a heartbeat—likes the idea of him managing Zoe's money just a bit too much, in my opinion."

"How on earth do you know that?" he asked.

"It was all over her face when she told us. Iris Grant, who works here—she's Zoe's friend, and we picked her up from the airport and took her to her dad's. He was already at the lawyers."

"I see," he said slowly. "Who else is on your list?"

"Aldo Bracket. I think his given name is Alessandro."

His gaze sharpened. "Why would Alessandro Bracket want to kill Leigh Markes?" He obviously knew who Aldo was.

"He wanted to have a show at her gallery, but she refused. He does something called outsider art, but not really, I guess, because he's not really an outsider, and it's not really art." I ventured a small smile. "At least that's what I've been told."

He reached into his pocket and for the first time opened the little notebook he carried. He jotted something down, closed it, put it on the table, and looked at me with an expectant expression.

"Paisley Long was Leigh's assistant. She'd been running the gallery on her own until Leigh came back after her father's death. She could have resented losing all the power she'd had."

"I spoke with Ms. Long," Quinn said. "She was at her mother's house that evening, along with her sister and two cousins. It's been verified. Anyone else?"

"Well, Zoe Stokes probably should be on the list, but I don't think she had anything to do with her mother's death."

"You're right. We've verified that she was on campus at her university when her mother was killed."

I felt my shoulders relax a little. It was nice to know for sure the police didn't suspect Zoe. I really liked her.

"Zoe's staying with her aunt Calista instead of her dad. Calista seems like a viable suspect. She and Leigh had an argument right here in the bakery the afternoon before Leigh was killed."

"Oh?"

I nodded. "They had a book club meeting."

"Yes, I'm aware. Jo Sterling told me." There was something in his eyes.

"Ah! That's why you came by."

"That and the fact that you knew Markes was dead before anyone else did."

"I explained—"

"No, you didn't. And I can tell you're not going to."

"It was a feeling . . ."

He gave a sharp shake of his head. "Stop. Just stop. If I didn't know you better, I'd think you could have killed her."

My mouth dropped open.

Chapter 18

"Me! Kill Leigh Markes? That's ridiculous," I said.

"Oh, I know you didn't actually do it." Detective Quinn paused, his eyes boring into mine. "But maybe you saw something that night that you're not telling me about."

"I didn't."

"Where were you between eight and nine Monday night?"

I felt my eyes blaze, but then my anger faded. Quinn was just doing his job, and it *was* kind of suspicious that I'd known Leigh was dead before the police did. I couldn't tell him the truth, of course. First off, he wouldn't believe that any more than he did my premonition story.

However, sticking as close to the truth as possible was generally a good idea.

"I was on a ghost tour of Savannah with Lucy, Jaida French, Bianca Devereaux, and her daughter, Colette."

He stared at me. "You have to be kidding. A ghost tour?"

"I'd never been on one, and Jaida had free tickets. I'm not from here, you know. I don't know all the stories." I knew I sounded defensive.

"Great," he muttered and downed half of his cooling espresso. He wiped his mustache with a napkin. "Okay, back to your suspect list. Who else do you have for me?"

"I didn't finish with Calista's motive. See, her father gave her the family home but apparently no real money. However, she needs cash to start her shower cap business, and was going to mortgage the house. Leigh planned on trying to stop her by taking her to court. Now, I don't know if that would work or not, but it might slow things down and keep Calista from getting the cash when she wants it—which is now."

Quinn's eyes had widened as I spoke. When I paused, he rubbed his palm over his face. "Shower cap business."

"Yes. They're very cool shower caps," I said.

He wrote something in the notebook again. "I forgot how good you are at this stuff."

I beamed. "Thank you."

"You can stop now."

"But—"

"No, Katie. Really. Stop. You were right about Walker Stokes having a pretty serious motive, and, as it happens, no affection for his ex-wife. We're working on breaking his alibi from his current wife. Once we manage that, we'll get an arrest warrant."

I frowned. "Really? You're that sure."

He nodded.

Sitting back in my chair, I crossed my arms over my chest. "You've been wrong before."

His gaze hardened.

"I'm just saying," I said. "Not trying to be mean or anything, but you have."

He started to rise.

"Have you looked into the other book club members? What about Jo?"

Sinking back into the chair, he sighed. "Jo Sterling doesn't have a motive. Neither do the other two women who attended the book club—they were new members and barely knew the other three women."

"Do they all have alibis?" I insisted.

"Not really. Including Calista. But I don't see how anyone would kill their own sister over shower caps."

"Not shower caps per se. Starting her own business. Her family never took her seriously."

He rolled his eyes and stood. "Listen, strangling someone takes strength. Calista Markes couldn't strangle a mouse."

I heard a gasp and looked over to see that a woman at another table had overheard what he'd said. "Quinn," I warned.

He leaned down and lowered his voice. "We have our murder suspect, and now we build the case. That's how it works. You know that."

I pressed my lips together but didn't say anything.

"Go back to baking and witching or whatever you call it. I understand you knew the victim and saw her the same day she was killed, so you might have felt obligated to help. But there was nothing paranormal about this case, and no reason for you to get involved."

Unable to argue that there was a paranormal element to the case, I rose and walked him to the door. He turned before going out.

"You sure did gather a lot of information in a short amount of time, Katie. You'd make a good detective." He leaned his head forward for emphasis. "With some experience and *training*. The amateur investigator stuff has to stop, though. It's dangerous."

Smiling and nodding, I closed the door behind him.

Halfway back to the kitchen, I remembered something. Turning, I ran back and out to the street. Quinn was already in front of the Fox and Hound Bookshop. I called to him, and he stopped.

When I reached him, I said, "I forgot to tell you—there were rumors that Leigh was having a secret relationship."

One eyebrow lifted. "Oh? With whom?"

"No one seems to know. But it sounds like he's married."

"No one knows who he is, but they know that he's married?"

"That's what it sounds like. Maybe Leigh let it slip when she was talking about him?"

"Well, thanks for that nugget of non-information. I'll make a note of it."

He didn't, though. As he turned and walked away, his little notebook stayed right in his pocket.

I sure hoped he was right about Walker Stokes.

Leigh's ghost wouldn't care whether it was me or the police who found her killer, and if Quinn could prove it was Walker, it would sure let me off the hook.

Later that morning, Declan drove us to the Markes Gallery in his truck.

"What is this thing we're going to see?" He turned onto the side street I'd directed him to.

"We're going to see if Walker Stokes is at the gallery." I'd filled him in on my conversation with Peter Quinn on the way. "I'm especially interested in meeting the guy now that Quinn is so sure he killed Leigh."

"Well, I'm glad I'm with you, then."

"It's not like he's going to randomly murder someone at the gallery—" I began.

He interrupted. "You never know."

Half smiling, I said, "Anyway, the *thing* we're going to see is a rather fabulous sculpture by an artist named Hanta."

"As in hantavirus?"

I rolled my eyes. "You are such a guy."

He parked and turned off the engine.

"Yes, yes, I am. But that's not why I ask. Artists can be unusual people. There could actually be a connection."

"Oh, brother. Look." I held out my phone so he could see the pictures I'd taken of *Compassion*.

He pursed his lips appreciatively. "Hey, that's pretty cool."

"Wait 'til you see it in person."

The sign was still on the door of the gallery, but the door swung open easily. Inside, Juliette sat at the desk between the gift shop and the rest of the gallery. The chair was swiveled so her back was to us. She pointed a manicured nail and flicked her finger upward.

"Move it up about four inches," she demanded of someone in the other room. "No, a little more. Can't you see? It needs to be farther away from the other one. No, not like that!" She rose and went into the gallery, her skirt swishing behind her, completely unaware that we'd walked in.

"That's Juliette, Zoe's stepmother," I said in a low voice. I'd been keeping Declan up to speed on what had been happening—or not happening—on the case, so he knew who Zoe was even though he'd never met her.

"No, no, no! Don't be stupid. Here—give it to me."

My husband and I exchanged a wary look and then moved toward Juliette's voice. We rounded the corner to find her on a stepstool adjusting a piece of framed art on the wall. Paisley Long stood beside her, looking down at the floor, arms crossed and shoulders hunched.

A man I'd never seen before—but whose identity I could easily guess—was on her other side. Walker's eyes were brown beneath thick salt-and-pepper eyebrows. His hairline had receded, but the hair he had was thick and curling down around his ears. He wore tan slacks and a white button-down shirt with the sleeves rolled up. As he smiled at his wife, I instinctively reached toward him with my intuition. Declan gave me a questioning look when I suddenly took a step backward. I returned it with an infinitesimal shake of my head.

Beneath his mild exterior, Walker Stokes reeked of a seething anger.

Directed at whom? About what?

Aldo Bracket stood behind the stepstool and helped Juliette down when she had arranged the piece where she wanted it. I saw it was one of his collages—one I hadn't seen on my previous visit to the gallery with Bianca. This one was a mass of screws and washers and nuts arranged in clumps around a rusty screwdriver with a chip in the handle. The others I'd seen, along with a half dozen I hadn't, were already on the wall. Honestly, of all of them, the one with the screwdriver was probably the best.

Paisley's head came up, and she saw us. At the same time, I saw her eyes were wet with tears. She blinked and took a breath, then smiled at us brightly.

"Katie Lightfoot, wasn't it?"

I nodded. "And this is my husband, Declan McCarthy. I brought him by to look at *Compassion*, as you suggested. Declan, this is Paisley Long. She was Leigh Markes' assistant."

Out of the corner of my eye, I saw Walker Stokes' head swivel toward us.

"Is the piece still here?" I asked

"Oh, yes!" Paisley said. "I'll take you over to it."

Obviously, I could have located the statue again, but I got the feeling Paisley wanted to be as far away from bossy Juliette as was possible. She led us to the back of the gallery and stopped in front of the sculpture.

"This one has an effect, doesn't it?" she asked.

I murmured agreement.

"Wow," Declan said, and I could tell he meant it. "It *is* more powerful in person."

A smile bloomed on her face. "It's a wonderful piece. Inspiring. There are times that I've stood and simply looked at it for the longest time. So calming. Her other pieces are like that as well."

"How many were there?" I asked.

"Only three. She works quite slowly. Carefully. The others in this display were *Passion* and *Serenity*. They were stunning as a group."

"Did you think about buying one of them?" I asked.

She snorted a little laugh. "Oh, I thought about it. No way could I afford one, though."

"Hey! I know you!" Juliette came barreling over and pointed at me. "Walker! This is the woman who took Zoe away."

I felt Declan tense beside me, and I put my hand on his arm.

Walker came over, looking at me with a combination of suspicion and curiosity.

"You must be Zoe's dad," I said, pasting a smile on my face.

"I must be." His tone was flat. "Who the heck are you?"

"Katie Lightfoot," I said and stuck out my hand. "Nice to meet you."

He shook it without thinking, then seemed to think better of it and dropped my hand.

"It's true that I brought Zoe to your house," I said. "She's friends with Iris Grant, and she asked Iris for a ride from the airport. You know, since you apparently couldn't make it." My mouth was still smiling, but my eyes weren't.

He flushed. "I had an appointment."

"Yes. Juliette here told us all about it." I dropped the smile altogether and held his gaze. "That's why Zoe decided she'd rather stay with her aunt than in Juliette's guest room."

Walker stiffened.

I hadn't intended to confront him, but I also hadn't realized how angry I was with this guy. He'd treated his daughter horribly, and I didn't feel one whit of guilt for letting him know that I knew their house really belonged to his wife.

"Oh, it's just as well, honey," Juliette said, oblivious once again. "We don't really have room for Zoe."

"Be quiet," he said in a low, grating voice.

She blinked.

"And stop telling our business to strangers."

Her mouth opened and closed a few times; then her nostrils flared. "Well!" She stomped back to where Aldo was watching the drama unfold from across the room.

Walker looked back at me. "Interesting coincidence that you gave Zoe a ride and then showed up at my gallery, Ms. Lightfoot."

"Oh, she came in with Bianca Devereaux," Paisley said. "A couple of days ago."

"The gallery was closed two days ago," he said, turning on her.

Her eyes widened. "I opened it for them when Ms. Devereaux asked me to, you see. She's such a good customer, and such a patron of the—"

"You had no right to do that," Walker said. "I don't know who the hell this Devereaux woman is, but this is *my* gallery now. I make the decisions."

"I'm sorry, Mr. Stokes," Paisley whispered.

I found myself really hoping Peter Quinn was right. I would pay to see this guy behind bars for the rest of his life.

Declan sensed my outrage at Stokes' behavior and put his arm around my shoulders. "Well, I'm sure glad Paisley let my wife in to see this sculpture."

Walker smiled. "Well, then. Let me wrap it up for you."

I felt the blood drain from my face. "Oh, I don't think—"

"We need to discuss a purchase like this," Declan said smoothly. "I'll be in touch, Mr. Stokes."

"Sure you will," Walker said.

I gave Declan a quick squeeze, then slipped away from his arm and walked over to where Aldo was fussing with one of his compositions.

"I noticed these when Bianca and I were here the other day," I said.

"I remember," he said.

"They're very interesting. Tell me, what is your inspiration?" I asked.

"Oh, um, I, you know, gather inspiration from—" He waved his hand in the air.

"From?" I leaned forward.

"Just everything, I guess."

"Ah," I said.

"You should come to my show," he said. "It starts next week. The opening is next Tuesday evening. Everyone who's anyone will be here." He was warming up his sales pitch at lightning speed.

Walker came over and interrupted him. "I get the feeling Mr. McCarthy and Ms. Lightfoot are not so much buyers as browsers, Aldo."

"You never know," I said in a light tone. "Goodbye, Alessandro."

Mr. Outsider Artist was frowning mightily as Declan and I started for the exit. I caught Paisley's eye.

"I'll walk you out," she said.

Chapter 19

Paisley hurried to join us, then led us to the door, pushed it open, and followed us out to the sidewalk. "I'm so sorry about all that."

"Don't worry," I said.

"I'm going to go get the truck," Declan said. We'd had to park down the block, but I was pretty sure he was giving me the opportunity to talk with Paisley alone.

I nodded, and we watched him stride away. "You sure have your hands full with your new boss," I said.

She sighed. "I don't know how long he'll be my boss. That wife of his has threatened to fire me twice already today."

"Do you really want to stay?" I asked, genuinely curious.

"That's a very good question," she said. "I loved working with Leigh. She was passionate about art and expert at finding unknown talent and nurturing it. I learned so much from her." She looked back toward the gallery. "I think perhaps it's time to move on to a new mentor. One day I'd like to start my own gallery."

"Is Aldo Bracket one of her finds?" I knew he wasn't, of course, but I wanted to know what she'd say.

"God, no. He fooled me for a little while, I guess. Not Leigh. Of course, I think she knew who he really is. I heard you call him Alessandro, so I guess you know, too. I don't run in those social circles, though, so I had no idea." She leaned close. "I think he's planning to have someone buy all his work, so his show will look like a big success." An undercurrent of disgust ran beneath the words.

"And Stokes is just fine with that," a voice said behind us.

We whirled to see Aldo had silently slipped outside. Remembering how easily and quietly Bianca and I opened the door two days earlier, I could see how.

He glared at both of us. "Leigh Markes should have known better than to cross me. I always win."

I raised my eyebrows. "Is that a confession to murder?"

His lips parted in surprise. "A . . . Of course not! I'm just saying that if I'd had to, I had a little something on your sainted Ms. Markes. She was no angel, though. She was having an affair with a married man, and if she'd stood in the way of my show much longer, I was going to tell the world."

Paisley's lip curled. "Or threaten to tell the world."

"You have just confessed," I said, "to blackmail."

He smiled. "To potential blackmail. That's not the same."

"Who was she having the affair with?" I asked.

Paisley looked intrigued. She didn't like the idea of blackmail any more than I did, but she was curious.

Aldo's response was a smirk.

"Leigh's beyond caring." At least I thought so. Teddy might disagree. "And it might be pertinent to her murder investigation," I added.

He looked taken aback, then thoughtful. "Nah. I don't think so."

Not very convincing. Maybe I could talk Quinn into questioning this guy in between his attempts to nail Walker Stokes.

I changed the subject. "Why do you want a show so badly?"

Aldo's chin came up. "Because I'm an artist, and I deserve one."

Spoiled little brat.

"No, you're not," Paisley said. "If you really wanted to be an artist, why not go to art school, learn your craft, do the work?"

He fell silent for several seconds and then said, "That's exactly what I'm going to do. I just have to convince my father to allow it. And the only way I'm going to do that is if he thinks I can make money at it. Otherwise, he'll refuse to pay."

Paisley and I looked at each other, and I could see she felt a little sorry for him. Goddess help me, so did I. Which was ridiculous, wasn't it?

"By the way, no one will believe you if you spill the beans that I've rigged this show to sell out," he said, and my pity vanished. "I've got it all figured out." He turned and went back inside without another word.

Paisley took a deep breath. "Well, I guess I'd better

get back in there. I haven't been yelled at enough yet today." But she said it lightly. She'd be okay.

Declan drove up then, and I said goodbye to Leigh's assistant.

"Say, Ms. Lightfoot?" she called as I walked away.

I stopped and looked over my shoulder. "Yes?"

"Is there any chance you might buy the Hanta piece? I'd get a nice commission, and it might be my last one."

"We'll talk about it," I said. Lied, really. After paying for our wedding and before that the renovation of the carriage house, we wouldn't be buying a piece of art that expensive anytime soon.

She nodded. "My commission aside, I hope you do. It deserves a good home, and I can tell you'd give it one."

For the rest of the afternoon, my aunt and uncle and I busied ourselves getting things ready for the Halloween party at the Honeybee. Iris had worked the morning shift and had classes in the afternoon, so we were on our own. The city had closed two blocks of Broughton Street to traffic, and from four to five o'clock, a procession of the youngest trick-or-treaters had straggled past the bakery. Some were in child carriers or pushed in strollers, and all were dressed in adorable costumes and cute as heck. Many of their parents made a side trip into the bakery for a bit of sustenance or caffeine—or both—before moving on.

Halloween was always good for bakery business, despite all the goodies we gave away.

By seven o'clock, two hours after our usual closing time, Lucy and Ben were standing in the open doorway of the bakery and inviting passersby of all ages to come in and get a treat. We planned to stay open a couple more hours but would play it by ear according to how many customers were still coming in as the evening progressed. The sun had set outside, and the lights inside were down low. Foggy "smoke" swirled up from the chunk of dry ice in Lucy's cast-iron cauldron, lazily drifting to the floor and flowing around the ankles of those closest to the register.

The members of the spellbook club had stopped by earlier, all except Cookie, whom I'd talked to on the phone. Everything was set for the spell we would be casting at midnight. Cookie would be there. She'd insisted on coming, though I'd tried to get her to stay home with Isabella.

"Oscar and my mother can handle her for a couple of hours," she'd said. "This is important, and I want to be there. You'll need the whole coven."

Relieved and grateful, I'd agreed.

Thoughts of what might happen when I crossed the veil ping-ponged in my mind as I handed out marshmallow ghosties and candy corn cupcakes, jack-o'-lantern shortbread and spiderweb cookies. As the time passed, I found myself getting more and more nervous.

What if I really messed up this spell? What if I couldn't ever get Connell back for Declan? And worst of all: What if I got lost in the Otherworld, too? I'd assured Declan that I wouldn't, but there were no guarantees. Though I'd figured out some particulars about the spell, the truth was that we'd be making it up as we went along. I didn't know what would happen.

"Katie!"

I looked up from the tiny witch—pointed hat, striped tights, and all—politely asking for a cupcake to see Margie waving at me. Evelyn herded the JJs in front of her and my neighbor carried Bart on her hip. The bumblebee costume looked a bit small on him, and the wings were bent at an odd angle, but he seemed happy enough.

I delivered the cupcake to the little witch and went over to where they'd settled in the corner because Jonathan's school bus costume was impossible to maneuver between the tables. Margie had taken a large rectangular box, cut out the top and bottom, painted it bright yellow with black markings, and fashioned a short, sloping hood for the front. It had big, round headlights that I was pretty sure were made from glass salad plates, and a stop sign by Jonathan's left elbow that he extended as I approached. The whole shebang hung from two wide straps across his shoulders.

"I like it," I said to him. "Are you the driver?"

He looked at me as if I were an idiot. "No, Ms. Katie. I'm the *bus*."

"Ah. Well, you're a pretty awesome bus."

He nodded his agreement. "Mama made it."

I grinned at Margie. "Good job, Mama."

"Why, thank you, hon," she said.

I stood back to take a better look at his twin's skeleton costume. "Margie was right, Evelyn. She said you made Julia's costume cute and scary at the same time. It's great."

"Glows in the dark, too!" Julia informed me as she did a quick pirouette next to her brother.

"Nice," I said.

"It was tricky painting that leotard without anyone in it," Evelyn said. She was a sturdy woman who screamed practicality—short gray hair, no makeup, blunt fingernails, slacks and button-down shirt, low heels. "I finally stuffed it with pillows and socks. Worked like a dream."

"I love it," Julia proclaimed.

Margie patted her on the head, then put Bart down. "Oof!" She tried to adjust his catawampus wings, then gave up.

"What can I get you?" I listed the options, then went and loaded a tray with their selections. As they munched on the treats, I slid into a bistro chair and rubbed the small of my back.

"Long day for you," Evelyn said.

I nodded. "It's nice to sit down, let me tell you."

"Well, at least most of the trick-or-treaters will be done by the time you get home, and you can go straight to bed," Margie said. "I always turn off the light at nine. You only get the teenagers wanting to cause trouble that late."

"Tonight, we'll wait until ten," her mother-in-law said. "We have a few families on my street who come downtown for all this"—she waved her hand—"and then come back and hit the neighborhood later."

"We're staying the night with Evelyn," Margie explained.

I fervently—and silently—thanked the forces that be. Margie had a bad habit of sneaking out of her house at all hours to visit the stash of Twinkies she kept hidden in the backyard. Without realizing it, she'd unintentionally interrupted my late-night spell work in the gazebo more than a few times. I'd planned to use a cloaking spell around the yard, but they were notoriously unreliable and took a lot of energy. With no nosy neighbor, however much I loved her, to interfere with tonight's spell, that energy could be focused on the important work of bringing Connell home.

Declan and his fellow firefighter, Randy Post, came in then. I left the Coopersmith clan to their Halloween goodies and went over.

"Hey, darlin'," Declan said, giving me a one-armed squeeze. "I don't suppose we could talk you out of a couple of cups of coffee."

"Just made fresh. Grab something to eat while I get it."

He shook his head. "Just the caffeine. It's going to be a long night."

I whirled around with a mug in my hand. "You're still coming home tonight, aren't you?" I couldn't keep the alarm out of my voice.

Randy looked amused. "Relax. Your husband explained to the lieutenant that you don't like to be alone on Halloween, so he had to be home by midnight. We've still got a few hours to go before then is all. And *I'm* working all night."

Slightly chagrined, I raised my eyes to Declan's. "Thanks for explaining my nervousness to your boss, hon. He's very understanding."

He reddened and looked away. "Yeah. He is."

I didn't really care that Declan had made me sound like a ninny as an excuse to leave work before midnight. As long as he came home, he could tell his boss I was a raving lunatic.

They were finishing their coffees when both of their phones pinged. "Gotta go," Randy said, draining his mug and standing. "Someone's cat is stuck up a tree."

I laughed.

Declan sighed, looking at his phone. "He's not kidding."

I blinked. "Seriously? That happens?"

"The cat's not the problem," he said. "Apparently the husband climbed up after it, and he's deathly afraid of heights. Now *he's* stuck."

I laughed again, harder. "Good luck."

"Thanks." His tone was dry.

"And see you at home around eleven thirty, right?"

"Yes, dear."

"Aren't you excited to get Connell back?" I asked. Randy was already at the door.

He hesitated. "I just don't want to get my hopes up."

"Oh, honey." I didn't know what else to say. After all, I couldn't promise the spell would work.

He kissed my forehead and they left.

Margie and Evelyn headed out with the kiddos, and I did a cleanup pass. Ben was out on the sidewalk, chatting with some of the other business owners. Lucy came back in to grab more treats to give away out front. I was putting away the towel I'd used to clean tables when Iris and Zoe Stokes came in. Calista was with them. They weren't really wearing costumes, but they were dressed for the evening. Zoe wore a peasant dress, gladiator sandals, and a ton of necklaces—including the one Cookie had made for her. Glittering combs held her hair back from her face. Iris wore all black, except for a pair of dark orange Vans on her feet. The outfit plus her orange-and-black hair were spot-on for the holiday. Calista was in a tie-dyed maxi dress and had flowers in her long red hair.

"How are things going?" I asked them.

Zoe shrugged. "Okay. I'm still at Calista's, but at least Dad apologized. We're planning a memorial for Mom, but it won't be for a few weeks—he wanted to coordinate it with the big art walk, and I don't see why not. So I'll probably head back to school in a couple of days."

I gave her a hug. "That might be for the best."

"I'll miss her," Calista said. "It's been nice having the company, even if the reason my niece is here is so awful."

"Have you heard anything from the police about their investigation?" I was wondering if Quinn had tipped his hand about his main suspect.

Calista shook her head. "They questioned me, of course. Someone told the detective that I'd fought with Leigh the afternoon of her . . ." She trailed off, then suddenly gave me a sharp look. "Hmmm, I wonder if it was someone who worked here. Because our argument was right over there." She pointed to the reading area.

I quickly steered the subject away from Leigh's death. Pointing to the table set with goodies, I said, "Hard to say. Thanks for coming in. There are all sorts of treats out for you to choose from. Take whatever you'd like."

Calista's eyes lit up, and Zoe followed her to where Lucy was now womanning the register. She greeted them with a bright smile.

I turned to Iris. "You're a good friend."

She gave a sad smile. "Thanks. I want to be. I like Zoe a lot."

"Me, too. Any news from Taylor?"

Her eyes softened. "I talked to him last night for almost an hour. And you know what? I came right out and told him how I felt about him hanging out with Shawna. I mean, I know it's not supposed to be attractive when you're jealous, but I wasn't mean or anything. Just honest."

"And?" I prompted.

"He laughed at me."

I drew myself up to say something about that, but she held up her hand. "No, it's okay. He didn't really laugh *at* me. He just laughed at the idea that he'd ever like Shawna like that. Or even that she'd like him. I guess they work well together, but then they go their separate ways. She has her own set of friends, and what he called 'vapid' interests. He hangs out with some musicians he met there. Anyway, he said she's not his type at all."

"You're his type." I grinned.

So did she. "Exactly."

Chapter 20

The crowds trickled away, and we closed a little after nine. It took another forty-five minutes to clean up for the next day, including mopping the floor. Lucy had left Honeybee at home since she didn't know how her familiar would react to all the children, but Mungo had loved all the attention heaped upon him during the party.

I packed him up in my tote bag, and we locked the door behind us. Ben and Lucy had driven separately, and he headed home for the night while Lucy followed me to the carriage house. By the time the rest of the spellbook club came trickling in after eleven, we had the fire laid in the firepit and snacks and drinks ready. We'd each changed into loose, comfortable clothing that would keep us warm outside in the cool autumn night.

Jaida arrived first, and I pulled her aside. "How's Teddy doing?" I asked.

She frowned. "She has her own apartment, but she's staying with us for now. I think it makes her feel better to have people around when you-know-who won't leave her alone."

"I'm glad she can count on you guys," I said. "I take it Leigh's spirit is still bothering her."

"Yeah, though they seem to be on, shall I say, friendlier terms today." She paused. "She told me you asked her to help get Connell back."

I made a face. "That didn't go so well."

"So I gathered. I told her that's what we're doing tonight. She seemed . . . upset. I'm not sure why."

That didn't bode well. I tried to quiet the nervous flutter under my heart as the door opened and the others came in, each carrying their contribution to the evening's festivities.

"What are these?" Bianca asked, putting her purse on the kitchen chair and leaning against the counter. She was examining the plate of food Lucy had brought.

"Soul cakes," my aunt answered.

"Oh, my stars!" Mimsey exclaimed from the doorway to the living room. She bustled over to take a look. "What a perfect idea, Lucille!"

"I've never heard of them," Jaida said.

"Well!" Mimsey said, and I knew she was about to give us a lesson. "Soul cakes are traditional in England, you see. On All Souls' Day, which is actually two days after Samhain, they would hand out soul cakes to children and the poor who came to the door asking for them. It was called *souling*, and those who received cakes would pray for the dead of the family in exchange. Each cake represented a soul in purgatory, and eating the cake and praying would release that soul."

I stared at her, then turned to Lucy. "Connell *is* in a kind of purgatory."

She smiled. "I agree. Plus, they're yummy. I used lots of allspice, and maple syrup to sweeten them."

Allspice was very healing, as well as augmenting energy and determination—both of which we'd need. It was also a masculine spice, associated with fire, and we were dealing with masculine energies this evening.

"Thank you, Lucy." I gave her a hug and indicated the plate next to hers. "And I made these, based on a Samhain ritual cake, only this is more of a scone and studded with ginger and orange peel like barmbrack. I was thinking we could each have a little, and I wanted to include one in our spell as an offering to the spirit world."

"That sounds good." Mimsey gave an approving nod.

We trooped out to the firepit with the plates of ceremonial goodies and a tall pitcher of ginger sweet tea to give our spell work a little more oomph. I retrieved the candles, the jug of water, the long-handled lighter, the photograph, and the herbs and spices I'd brought out so early that morning. Jaida and Cookie took the small table from the gazebo and set it next to the copper fire bowl. I gave Mimsey the candles and put everything else on the ground next to the small table—everything except the photo in its envelope. That I kept.

Mimsey pulled an ancient-looking brass compass from the pocket of her cardigan and identified due east. Then she ceremoniously placed the candles at the compass points, starting with east and then moving to south and west and ending at north, moving deosil, or clockwise. She placed one black and one white candle at each point, the black outside the circle and the white inside. The first would serve as protection, and the second would aid in astral projection.

Because astral projection, essentially, was what I was about to try. And without the natural ability that Teddy possessed, I was going to have to wing it.

"Where is Declan?" I muttered, looking at my watch. It was already eleven thirty.

"He'll be here," Lucy assured me.

"Well, if he's not, all of this won't do much good, will it?" I knew I sounded cranky.

She smiled at me serenely. Most of the time, that calmed me. Tonight, it only made me crankier. Then I heard the sound of a truck door closing and relaxed.

That has to be him.

It was.

He came around the corner of the house still wearing his Savannah Fire Department T-shirt, but he'd changed into a pair of well-worn jeans and boots. His eyes lit up when they met mine, and my heart gave a pang.

I have to make this work. I just have to.

After everyone said hello, I directed him to a chair I'd set outside the circle. It was located where we would begin and close the circle in the east, so if we needed to open it in order to let Connell out, we could. However, I had the feeling that once Connell hit this plane again, nothing would keep him from getting to Declan. My main concern was keeping Declan safe. I called Mungo over to hang out with him—the other familiars were all absent, as sometimes they provided more distraction than help when it came to spell work.

Taking a deep breath, I sank to my knees beside him. "I need to ask you something."

"What?" He looked alarmed.

"I took something of yours this morning, and I want to use it in the spell. I believe it will help."

"Something of mine?"

Biting my lip, I reached into my pocket and pulled out the envelope. Slipping out the contents, I handed him a small square of paper. It was the black-and-white photograph of his great-great-great-aunt and the small, sprightly man she'd married in Ireland. The one who never seemed to get older in family pictures, though everyone else did.

Connell.

Declan took it. "Well, sure, Katie. You can borrow this for whatever you're planning tonight."

"Not borrow. Burn."

"You want to burn it?"

"I do. Is that all right with you? I made a copy, but the original would be better for tonight's work."

He hesitated, gazing down at the face of his guardian spirit, but then seemed to shake himself. He handed it back. "I trust you completely. Do whatever you need to do."

I stood and put the photograph back into the envelope and sealed it. "Thanks, hon." I bent and kissed him. "I love you."

Moving inside the circle, I lit the fire with reverence. I'd added a small branch from the rowan tree after thanking it for its help and had done the same with a few sprigs of witch hazel and a length of fresh rosemary. The green wood smoldered atop the drier kindling, giving the air a pungent, resinous scent as the flames grew inside the metal container.

As the fire took hold, we each had a nibble of Samhain scone and a whole soul cake. Lucy had wisely made small ones, as it wasn't good to work on a full stomach. Afterward we might be ravenous, but we'd deal with that then. After washing down the food with a bit of ginger sweet tea, we each muttered a small prayer for the release of Connell's spirit from purgatory.

Couldn't hurt.

I gave Declan a whole scone and a couple of soul cakes, along with a glass of tea. As he took them, I saw he was growing uncomfortable, and I realized he'd never seen me cast a spell. He'd seen other things, and there was that time I'd nearly killed him with the power of my Voice—that had been dicey—and he'd seen the altar I kept in the loft, hidden in an old secretary's desk Lucy had given me. However, I timed my solitary spell work in the gazebo for when he was gone. Even though he knew I practiced kitchen magic, that didn't really look like spell casting from the outside. He'd certainly never seen me work magic with the ladies of the spellbook club.

This should be interesting.

I put my reservations out of mind and turned my attention back to the task. If Declan thought what we were about to do was weird, I didn't care. Not as long as it got the job done.

We stepped inside the circle and began to put our supplies on the table next to the firepit. Lucy placed whole allspice and nutmeg in a small silver bowl. Bianca added nuggets of frankincense and myrrh she'd brought, along with a chunk of moonstone and another of lapis lazuli. She glanced upward as she did, gesturing to the nearly round moon.

"I cleared these in the light of Luna last night. It's not quite as powerful as when the moon is completely full, but they should have a little extra potency."

"Thank you," I said.

Jaida put the Eight of Wands card from the Rider-Waite tarot deck next to the bowl. "This is a powerful travel card. Seemed a good choice."

I nodded. "Perfect."

She held up another card. "This is the High Priestess. See the veil behind her?"

Squinting in the low light, I nodded. The veil was covered with images of pomegranates.

"The veil is symbolic of the seen and the unseen. It can be interpreted as the veil between planes. And the pomegranates are sacred to Persephone."

"Who traveled between this world and the underworld."

"Right-o." She added the card to the Eight of Wands.

Cookie stepped forward. "I brought the graveyard dirt."

From the corner of my eye, I saw Declan sit up straighter.

"Mimsey was going to," she continued. "But I already had some lying around."

Jaida snorted, and Cookie grinned.

Declan rubbed his palm over his face and looked at me with a combination of bewilderment and alarm.

Mimsey was next. She gently placed a single passionflower and three lotus blossoms on the table. "I've primed these to aid in astral projection. I hope they help."

"Thanks, Mims," I said. My heart felt full of appreciation, and I felt so blessed to have these amazing, generous, wise women helping me.

Lucy reached for the canister of salt to begin the circle. Mimsey grabbed the lighter. Together they'd create the magical space of safety and power.

I heard another vehicle door slam closed on the street, and my heart started thumping inside my chest. "Hang on," I said. "I think someone may be here."

Dang it! We don't need this now! Did Margie change her mind about staying with Evelyn?

I looked at my watch. My heart sank. It was a quarter to midnight. I'd planned to be well along in the spell by the time the veil between this world and the next became thinnest.

The gate creaked open, and seconds later, Teddy LaRue came around the corner of the carriage house. She stopped dead when she saw all of us, her eyes wide. We all stared at her for a long moment, and I wondered if she'd turn and run.

She didn't. She took a step toward us, then another, almost faltering, but then jogging over. "I'm here."

"So you are," Jaida said, smiling at her gently.

We stepped out of the circle of rocks and surrounded Teddy. She looked around at us, her expression wary.

"Are you . . ." I took a deep breath. "Are you here to help?"

Slowly, she nodded.

My hope soared. "Really?"

"Yes." She didn't sound very sure. Her chin lifted, and she said it again, louder. "Yes."

I threw my arms around her. "Oh, *thank you*."

When I stepped back, she was smiling. "I didn't really have a choice. Your grandmother is very insistent."

"My grandmother?" I looked around wildly. "Nonna's here?"

"Oh, yeah." Teddy sounded rueful but also a little amused. "She sure is. Showed up at Jaida's this morning and hasn't left my side since."

An image rose in my mind, of my dead grandmother's spirit riding in the car with Teddy as she drove over to the carriage house, and I suppressed a grin.

"And unlike the other spirits I told you about, she's not shy about letting her wishes be known. Nothing vague about your nonna. She said you tried to reach her this morning, very early, but that she couldn't break through to you. That you said you were going to try to act as the tether, but you can't, because you have to go get the leprechaun. That I had to help you."

I wrinkled my nose. "Sorry. I did ask for her help."

"It's okay," she said. "I think she's right. You can't do this without me."

"The idea frightened you before," I said.

Jaida put her hand on Teddy's arm.

"It still does," the young woman said. "But not as much. I understand better now what you are doing. Your grandmother gave me a lot of information. She told me what I need to do."

"Where is she?" Lucy asked. Nonna had come to me

a few times, mostly as a voice, and showed up to lecture my mother once, but she'd never come to Lucy.

Teddy nodded to the fire. "She's waiting over there. Seems a bit tetchy, really."

"Are absolutely sure you want to do this?" Jaida asked.

Teddy bit her lip. "Absolutely? No. But sure enough." She looked around at all of us, her gaze stopping on Mimsey and Cookie. "Hi," she said shyly. "I'm Teddy."

Mimsey marched up and gave her a hug, which was awkward since Mimsey was almost a foot shorter than the young woman. "Oh, honey. We know who you are. Welcome!"

Cookie came up them and offered her own hug, also enthusiastic but a little less demanding. "Yes. Welcome. And thank you for helping our friend."

"Declan," I said quietly. He'd come to his feet and hovered behind Lucy. "This is my husband, Declan McCarthy. The spirit we're going to retrieve is the one I told you about."

"Hi." She tipped her head. "He attached to you?"

My husband said, "Apparently when I was born. I wasn't the first one in the family, either. He chose one male of each generation, ever since he married one of my ancestors in Ireland."

"He's a leprechaun?" Her puzzlement was obvious.

"We think so. He looks like one, and he's not mortal," I said.

"But he married a human?"

Declan and I shook our heads.

"Love is a funny thing," he said with an affectionate

glance at me. "Though it's not like I've come out and asked him. See, Connell was more like a feeling in the back of my mind, not all the time, but when I needed to know something. Like an instinct. I didn't even know he was there until the séance brought him into my consciousness."

It had been a bit more than just his consciousness, but I didn't say anything.

Teddy glanced toward the firepit, then back at me. "I think we'd better start."

I looked at my watch. "Oh, no! It's almost twelve!"

Teddy reached for my hand. "It's okay. We have plenty of time on either side of midnight. But still. Your grandmother is getting impatient."

"Yes," Mimsey said in a take-charge tone. "Let's get started, girls."

Chapter 21

Teddy led me over to the firepit. The willowy, ethereal young woman had a surprisingly strong grip, and she strode with a sense of purpose. Unlike yours truly, she knew what to do and how to do it because of my dead grandmother.

Thank you, Nonna.

The fire flared briefly in the copper fire bowl, well-contained but burning brightly.

I grinned in that direction, knowing Nonna was nearby.

"We'll need to move the perimeter of the circle so that Katie can lie down, and I can sit beside her. She needs to be in solid contact with the earth."

"All righty." Mimsey sounded cheerful, and I could tell she was relieved to have Teddy's help as well. "Let's shift things so you two can be on the grass. Those rocks around the fire would be far too uncomfortable."

She began moving the candles so that the sacred circle would now have the firepit on one side, with an open space on the other for Teddy and me. The others moved to shift the table and its contents, declining Declan's help. He returned to watch from his seat with Mungo, an audience of two.

Teddy sat cross-legged on the ground by the outer edge of where the circle would be cast and patted the grass beside her.

I went over and said, "I'll come over after we've cast the spell."

She directed a questioning look toward the fire, then nodded. "Your grandmother says the others will cast the spell," she said. "You need to be here, relaxed and ready when it's finished."

Frowning, I said, "But I need to help—"

"Nonsense," Mimsey said from behind me in a tone that brooked no argument. "Your nonna's spirit is right. Your job is to journey to the other plane and bring back Connell. Teddy's job is to keep you tethered to this plane. And our job is to cast the spell that sends you on the journey. Lie down, Katie."

"Okay," I said, but held up a finger in the universal just-a-minute sign. "I need to talk to Lucy first."

I went over to where my aunt was rearranging the items on the table. She kept glancing toward the fire, and I knew she wished she could see her mother standing there. When I approached, she looked up and smiled.

"Feel better about things?" she asked.

I let out a whoosh of breath. "You have no idea. Listen, I need you to add this to the burning spell." I handed her the envelope. "Because apparently I'm going to be *relaxing* while the rest of you work." Not being part of the spell work felt strange.

Lucy gave a little laugh and took the envelope. "What is this?"

"It's a direct link to Connell. That's the intention I put on it, anyway."

She didn't ask for particulars, just simply put the envelope on the table with everything else.

"Thanks," I said.

"Of course." She gave me a tight hug. "It's going to be fine."

"I know."

Sort of.

Back where Teddy was waiting, I lay down on my back, arms straight beside me. "Like this?"

She snorted a laugh. "Is that how you relax? Katie, you need to get into a meditative state. Close your eyes. Take some deep breaths. Ready yourself for travel."

"The idea of astral projection is anything but relaxing," I grated out.

Bianca came and stood over me. "Try breathing through only your left nostril."

Jaida joined her. "Try inhaling to the count of four, then hold to the count of seven, and exhale to the count of eight."

Cookie elbowed her way between them. "Look at her. Yikes. Anyone have a valium?"

"Leave her alone, girls." Mimsey's tone was mild.

"Thank you," I called to her, sparing a mild glare for my coven mates.

Cookie grinned.

"I'm told you can go ahead and close the circle," Teddy said, ignoring all of us.

"Come along," Mimsey said.

I turned my head and saw she was already standing at the easternmost set of candles. The others drifted away. Determined to calm down, I closed my eyes again.

I heard the lighter click. Seconds later, Mimsey said, "We call upon the archangel Raphael and the element of air to protect and aid us." There were footsteps on rocks and then she said, "We call upon the archangel Michael and the element of fire to protect and aid us." As she lit the next candle she called upon the archangel Gabriel and the element of water, and finally the archangel Uriel and the element of earth. I knew she'd finish the circle by walking to the now-lit black and white candles in the east.

"Above, below, and within," the others intoned together.

The ritual was familiar and predictable. Comforting. I found my muscles loosening as I listened. Next, they would gather by the fire and contribute the different elements of the spell. Turning my head slightly, I slitted my eyes open enough to see what they were doing. First Mimsey added her flowers, then Lucy tossed in the herbs. Bianca contributed the resinous frankincense and myrrh. The air filled with their intense, heady scent, and I inhaled deeply, again and again. Jaida added the tarot cards then, and Cookie sprinkled a bit of graveyard dirt on the new flames. As each new item was added, the fire became smokier and smokier.

Then Lucy added the picture of Connell in the envelope, and the smoke coalesced into a narrow column that rose from the center of the fire. The five witches stepped back, forming a ring around the fire. They clasped hands, and I felt their powers flare as they combined with each other and with the innate power of the elements.

"Katie," Teddy said beside me.

I closed my eyes again, seeing that hazy column of smoke in my mind's eye.

"Follow it, Katie," Teddy said. Her fingers closed firmly around my wrist, solid and real. "Follow the smoke. Ride with it. Rise with it."

How the heck am I supposed to do that? I can't. I just can't.

Panic began to build in my throat.

Then I heard a word, soft, so soft, almost inaudible. No, actually inaudible. It came from within the circle and yet beyond the circle.

Trust.

It was Nonna. She said it again, a mere breath of meaning in my mind. *Trust.*

"She's right," Teddy said. "You have to trust us all. It's all right. I won't let go. I promise."

Low and steady, the word rose now, coming from the lips of the spellbook club members as if they were in a trance.

Trust, trust, trust.

The sibilance of the word drew out, turning into a hiss that reminded me of the curls of smoke rising from the fire.

Ride the smoke. Trust Teddy. Trust that I can do this.

I breathed in the scents of fire and spice, of frankincense and myrrh, of rowan and rosemary, of passionflower and lotus. I took them in, filled my consciousness with their miasma mixed with . . .

. . . smoke.

The ground became nothing, falling away from my awareness though I knew I still lay on it. I could see, though I knew my physical eyes were closed, and I could still feel Teddy's fingers wrapped around my wrist. Rather than seeing the other women or Declan and Mungo or my own backyard, I saw a swirling nothingness, a kind of colorless fog filled with light and dark. Some of the dark billowed into a human shape, but then was gone. Another section of gray mist loomed, then disintegrated.

I was standing upright, I realized as I looked down and saw my own feet below me, resting on . . . nothing. However, I took a step, and felt something solid beneath my soles. I was walking. Lifting my arm, I saw the only shred of color anywhere in the grayscale smokescape: a bright scarlet cord tightly wrapped around my wrist.

A tether.

Teddy.

"I'm on the other side of the veil," I said out loud to myself.

I could hear the sound of my voice. Was I really speaking? Could the others hear me? I didn't think so, but I couldn't be sure. It didn't matter, because I had to call.

"Connell!"

I waited. There was no response.

"Connell!" Louder this time.

Still no answer. The silence was so thick it filled my mind. A panicky claustrophobia tried to claw up from my subconscious. I pushed it back down.

Not now!

I took a few steps and called again. Nothing. I began to slowly walk, but not in a particular direction because there didn't seem to be a particular direction. Instead, I chose to move away from where the cord trailed from my wrist, figuring that I would be moving farther into the veil. The tether snaked along with me, keeping track but not holding me back.

There was no ground, yet I walked. I heard the sound of no sound. None of the pungent fragrances from the spell fire reached me. There was only the odd caress of something like air against my cheek.

I called again.

No answer.

I walked faster, calling Connell's name. The scarlet cord trailed out behind me, tight around my wrist, keeping me safe. I began to run, still calling.

Suddenly the tether grew taut. It wasn't trailing anymore; I was pulling on it.

I stopped, frightened by the tension of the cord. Desperate, I screamed, "Connell!"

Was that a far-off voice?

I screamed his name again, putting everything I had into it.

This time the response was a little closer.

I called one more time.

There was movement in the gray. Then more. Connell emerged, grinning wide.

"Lassie, am I ever so glad ter see ya!"

"Oh, Connell." I took a step and reached for him.

As I did, I felt the cord loosen. Looking down, I saw it begin to unwrap from my wrist. I screamed and reached for it with my other hand.

Missed.

No longer tethered to me, the scarlet line slithered away. I started after it.

In a flash, Connell leaped ahead, grabbed it with one hand, and then grabbed me.

Sobbing in relief, I grasped the tether with both hands. Together, we followed it back the way I'd come. Gradually, after a time, the cord wrapped itself around my wrist again, but I kept the fingers of my hand curled around it for good measure. Connell kept step with me, one hand clasping my shoulder, while the other held my free hand.

The sound of alarmed voices and a dog barking filtered through the nothingness. We kept going toward them. Suddenly Connell stopped.

"What's wrong?" I asked.

He pointed.

I turned to look. "Nonna!" She appeared in full color and looked like my memory of her when she'd been alive. Her long auburn hair was streaked with bright white, and her green eyes gleamed with affection. Her laugh lines deepened as she smiled at us.

She wasn't alone, either.

"Welcome back, Katie," she said. "And you must be Connell."

"Indeed I am! Charmed ter know ya!"

I smiled. How could I have forgotten that Connell shouted more than he spoke, and every word was laced with his heavy brogue?

He waggled his considerable eyebrows at Nonna, and she laughed.

"Stop flirting," I told him as I turned my attention to

the woman beside her. Spirit. Whatever. I recognized her as Leigh Markes—which made sense, really, because she was sticking with Teddy, and Teddy was here. There. Wherever.

Leigh looked more relieved than pleased that I'd made it back.

"Please don't worry," I said. "I'm working to find your killer."

She reached out a pale hand toward me in apparent supplication. It held the dragonfly scarf, and even though I didn't technically have a body on this side of the veil, I shivered.

"Can't you simply tell me who it is?" I begged.

I mean, it was the logical question. I'd tried to get a spirit to tell me who had killed him before, and it hadn't worked. That had been the séance that brought Connell out of the woodwork. But now I had the actual ghost of a murder victim right in front of me, as it were.

She shifted and wavered, and I suddenly just *knew*, out of nowhere, that she couldn't tell me. Maybe couldn't remember. That was why she needed me.

"Why can't she talk to me like you can?" I asked Nonna.

"You and I have a magical hereditary connection, Katie. She's new and was never trained. Most spirits aren't like me."

No doubt.

"Goodbye, my darling," she said. "Know that I'm always around when you need me."

"Wait, Nonna! Can't you—"

She shook her head.

"It's time. The others are frantic with worry. They

almost lost you, you know." She and Leigh both stepped back, and the veil took them. The last thing I saw was the end of the blue and green dragonfly scarf.

Connell squeezed my shoulder, and we started moving toward where the tether led. Moments later, I saw the backyard and the sacred circle with the spellbook club members still standing in a ring around the fire, though now they were talking back and forth and did, indeed, sound frantic. Next to Declan, Mungo was whining. Teddy sat on the ground, hunched over me. Suddenly, she looked up, and I could tell she saw me.

"Oh, thank goodness," she said.

Mungo fell silent. He was looking at me, too.

Pop!

The ground felt cold against my back, and the night air had grown quite chilly. Shivering, I struggled to sit up. Teddy called to the others, and they rushed over to help me. Declan was standing next to the chair, looking worried. Mungo bounded to the outside of the circle.

Yip!

"Oh, Katie." Lucy's voice trembled as she bent over me.

I patted her hand. "Don't worry. I'm okay. Connell?" I called. "Connell, are you here?"

"Quickly, girls," Mimsey said. "We must open the circle."

She trotted to the eastern candles and blew them out, muttering thanks to Raphael and air, then widdershins around the circle to the north, the west, the south, and back to east, blowing out candles and giving thanks as she went.

Bianca and Jaida helped me up, and I ran out to where Declan was standing, Mungo on my heels.

My handsome husband held out his arms to me. I fell into his embrace, soaking up its comfort for a long moment, then stood back and searched his face. His throat was working, and his eyes were wet.

Stunned, I put my hand on his cheek. I'd been so sure it had worked. "Oh, Declan," I stammered. "I thought . . . I thought . . . He was right here with me."

Something shifted in his gaze, in the planes of his face, in the way he held his body. I recognized the shift, and joy pierced through me.

"Ah, things are not always as they seem, lass!"

Oh, that brogue.

Connell/Declan laughed and gave me a huge hug that lifted me off my feet. "Thanks ter ya, lass! So happy ter be back here, where ah belong, with yer man!" He let me go and turned to Teddy.

She was staring at him with a combination of wonder and dismay on her face. When he ran over and swooped her off her feet, she gave a little cry of surprise.

"Also, my gratitude ter this one!" Connell shouted. "Fer holdin' on ter tha red cord for our Katie here!"

"Connell," I admonished him, "you're scaring her."

"Hey!" a voice came drifting from the house on the other side of Margie's. "Be quiet, or I'll call the police. It's the middle of the night!"

And like that, Connell was gone and my own sweet Declan was looking out from behind those beautiful blue eyes. He was grinning like a fool as he stepped back from Teddy.

"Er, sorry. That wasn't really like me."

Lucy put her hand over her mouth, but her eyes were dancing. She snorted out a giggle, then another one. Cookie was next, then me, until we were all laughing hysterically, releasing the tension still riding the air, relief passing through the group like a virus.

"Shh," I finally managed. "I don't know how we could explain this if that guy actually calls the police."

When we'd managed to get ourselves under control, Teddy said to Declan, "No, it wasn't like you. It *wasn't* you." She took a deep breath. "That's amazing."

He nodded happily. "It really is."

Then he came over to me, and took me in his arms, and I felt his love and gratitude filling my heart.

"You can feel that he's there?" I asked.

Declan nodded. "He's back."

Chapter 22

In books and movies, there is always a price to pay for magic. At the least, it's supposed to enervate the practitioner. But once I began spell casting, I discovered it energized me. However, I hadn't actually practiced any magic during the spell to find Connell, and it seemed that astral travel could take the wind out of this witch's sails. I slept for a solid seven hours, and only woke when Mungo *yipped* me awake, impatient for his morning visit to the yard.

Lucy had insisted I take the day off from work, so I let my familiar out to the backyard, then crawled back into bed. Snuggled up next to Declan, I basked in his warmth beneath the covers, content and happy.

For a while at least.

Finally, I flopped onto my back and stared at the ceiling. No way was I going back to sleep. Leigh's spirit had still been following Teddy the night before. That meant there was still a murderer to be brought to justice.

Maybe that was just a matter of time, though. Quinn had seemed so sure that Walker Stokes had killed his ex-wife out of greed. It made sense. Building a murder case to take to the district attorney wasn't a fast process, at least I assumed. Perhaps I simply needed to be patient.

And yet . . .

Ah, things are not always as they seem, lass!

I realized that Connell's words, spoken in Declan's voice, had haunted my dreams and half dreams all night. Even awake, I couldn't get them out of my mind.

What isn't as it seems?

The time of death hadn't been as it seemed at first. What else, though? The murder method seemed pretty sure. Strangulation with a silk dragonfly scarf.

Wait.

Quinn said that strangling someone takes strength. That was probably another reason he thought Walker had done it. As a man, he would have been able to over-power Leigh. However, did he? Aldo was also strong enough—physically, at least. I didn't know if he had the mental fortitude for such a thing.

Who else?

The image of Jo Sterling came to mind. Tall, muscular, a former professional athlete who no doubt kept in shape at her own gym.

She could have done it. The thing is, she seemed like the only one besides Zoe who was really sorry Leigh was dead.

And what about Calista? She could be stronger than she looked. She wasn't much bigger than her sister, but adrenaline and rage were known to provide extra strength. Still, unless she was mentally unstable to a spectacular degree, she was a long shot. She loved her shower caps, but Quinn was probably right. It wasn't a good enough motive.

Then there was the affair Leigh had supposedly been having. Who had it been with? Did Aldo really know? Could he have made such a thing up? No, that didn't make sense. He couldn't blackmail a gallery owner with fictional dirt. Plus, her daughter had also been under the same impression.

Something was not as it seemed. That was for sure.

My stomach growled. Loudly.

I got up and padded out to the kitchen. It felt strange to be home on a weekday morning, and I should have reveled in not having to be in the kitchen at o'dark thirty. Instead, I brought Mungo back in from the yard, and he watched from a kitchen chair as I started breakfast.

By the time Declan came wandering in, his hair a disheveled mess, T-shirt awry, chin rough and scruffy—gorgeous, in my opinion—the counters were laden with French toast made with heavy cream and Grand Marnier, a small pitcher of warm maple syrup, a platter groaning under crispy slabs of thick, applewood-smoked bacon, and freshly squeezed grapefruit juice.

"Hungry?" I asked with a grin.

"I am now." He looked at the spread. "And you obviously are."

"Famished, as a matter of fact. Let's eat out back."

We carried our plates, piled high, out to the table on the patio. Mungo got one bite of bacon, which he did not think was nearly enough, and a scrambled egg. He wolfed it down in ten seconds and sat back next to his placemat, looking up at me as if trying to convince me that I hadn't fed him at all.

"Nice try," I said around a mouthful of French toast. "You're this far from going on a diet, sir."

Yip!

He turned and ran away to the far side of the yard.

I finished breakfast and sat back in my chair. "Oof. That was good."

"If you do say so yourself," Declan said. "I agree, though. Fed and rested. Can't ask for more than that."

"It's a start." I looked at my watch. It was certainly late enough to call Quinn.

After carrying our plates into the kitchen, I brought my phone back out to the patio. The detective answered on the second ring.

I got right to the point. "How's that case against Walker Stokes going?"

He sighed. "Katie . . ."

"What? You asked me to leave it up to you, and I'm curious about how that's going."

Silence fell on the line for several seconds, and then he said, "There's a fly in the ointment."

I sat up straighter.

"His neighbor confirmed his alibi."

"Uh-oh."

"I still think the guy did it," he almost growled. "Maybe he hired someone. We're looking into his financials to see if they support that theory."

"I don't like the guy," I said. "Not one little bit, but I don't think he did it. I don't think he's got enough money to take a contract out on his ex-wife, either."

"You have a better suspect?"

My mind returned to my thoughts earlier that morning. "Maybe. Let me check on a couple of things, and I'll get back to you."

"Katie, don't do anything stupid."

"Don't worry. I'll call you when I know something. I've been in enough dicey situations to know I don't want to be in any more."

"What's up?" Declan asked after I'd ended the call. "Did you have a eureka moment?"

"Maybe," I said slowly. "I just keep wondering about this affair everyone said Leigh was having, but no one knows who it was with. Or they're not telling, at least." I picked up my phone again. "One person claims to know." I started to tap on the screen.

"Who are you texting?"

"Steve Dawes."

"Oh."

I glanced up at Declan from under my eyebrows. "I need a phone number. He's a resource."

He shrugged.

Do you have Aldo Bracket's phone number?

Steve responded in less than a minute.

Nope. Why?

Can you get it?

Maybe. Why?

"Of course, he's being difficult."

Declan's response was a noncommittal "Mm."

I considered what to say. Decided on:

Because I want to ask him something about Leigh Markes. I need your help.

That did the trick.

I'll hit you back.

I put my phone away. Now I had some waiting to do.

On a day we both had off, we should have done something fun—gone for a hike at Skidaway Island State Park, hung out at the beach on Tybee Island, at least had a picnic in Forsyth Park. But no. We cleaned the carriage house and worked in the yard.

Mind you, we still thought of that as fun. We loved our little place, and we loved taking care of it, and we loved hanging out together. Declan mowed, and I weeded the garden beds. Inside, he vacuumed, and I polished.

"You know, that rose on the side of the house has gotten too heavy for the trellis it's on now," he said. "That can be my next project in the woodshop."

"Sounds fancy."

"Not so much. But I'm still learning. You wait—I'll be making you elaborate gewgaws in no time. For now, though, I'm going to go clean up the workshop."

I laughed and went to put the laundry in the dryer.

It was afternoon, and Steve still hadn't texted. The whole time we'd been spiffing things up around the homestead, I'd been pondering how to approach Aldo Bracket so he'd give me some answers. However, in the meantime, I could check in with Calista. After all, she had to have heard the rumor about Leigh's affair from someone.

How to get her number? I could text Iris, and Iris could text Zoe, who was sure to have her aunt's number, or . . .

. . . I could see if she was listed in the telephone book. We weren't so old-school as to keep a printed copy around, but the white pages online would have Calista's number if she had a landline.

A few minutes on my laptop revealed that she did. I called her immediately.

There was no answer.

Of course there wasn't. *Grr.*

I texted Iris. After two minutes, she hadn't texted back. She was at work, and often left her phone in the office. Most of the time I admired that, but not so much today. I picked up the phone to call the Honeybee landline, but on impulse tapped the number I'd just called.

This time Calista answered.

"Hi, it's Katie Lightfoot."

"Hi, Katie! What's up?"

"I have kind of a weird question for you."

She laughed. "Okay."

"The other day, you mentioned your sister had been seeing someone."

Her response sounded reluctant. "I probably shouldn't have said anything about that."

"No, it's okay. I don't judge. You don't know who it was?"

"No . . ."

"Was Leigh the one who told you about him?"

Her laugh sounded harsh. "God, no. Leigh would never confide such a thing to me. She barely tolerated me."

Ignoring the reference to their dysfunctional relationship, I asked, "Who did tell you, then?"

"Jo did. Leigh told her things like that. Jo was her best friend."

"Did she tell Jo who it was?"

"I honestly don't know. Jo knows how to keep things under her hat, if you know what I mean. But you know . . ." She trailed off.

"Yes?" I prompted.

"Jo might have been Leigh's best friend, but she didn't seem very happy about her new love interest. So maybe she did know who it was."

I went out and sat on the steps of the gazebo for a few minutes, staring into space. Zoe hadn't seemed to know who her mom was seeing, either, had only heard her at the gallery having an intimate conversation with a man.

Or thought she'd heard that.

Things are not always as they seem.

"Hey, neighbor!" Margie called over the fence.

I got up and went over to chat. "How was your evening at Evelyn's?"

"Fun. The kids love it over there." Her eyes twinkled. "I'm sure it wasn't as much fun as you guys had here. Why didn't you tell me you were having an after-hours party?"

"Oh, well, when I found out you weren't going to be here—"

"And I'm glad I wasn't." She grinned. "Sort of, at least. Mr. Vicks in the house on the other side of ours had a lot to say about it. Sounds like a pretty wild wingding."

I snorted and decided to stick as close to the truth as possible. "Hardly. Some of the ladies from book club came over with Aunt Lucy, and we sat around the fire. Not very wild at all. We weren't even drinking alcohol."

Her head reared back. "What? That's no way to party."

"Right? There was some loud laughter is all. It was

late, and I guess we woke up Mr. Vicks. He wasn't shy about giving us his opinion about it, though."

"He never is," Margie said with a shake of her head.

My phone buzzed, and I looked down to see Steve had texted a number. "Oops. I've got to go, Margie. We'll have that glass of wine soon, okay?"

Chapter 23

I checked on Declan. He was happily puttering away in his workshop, organizing screws and nails by size in itty-bitty bins. I kissed his still-rough cheek and went back inside to call Aldo.

Settling on the couch, with a sweating glass of iced tea on the coffee table, I took a deep breath and made the call. After several rings, he didn't answer. I hung up when his voice-mail message came on.

This is getting old.

Of course, he didn't know my number. I often let calls go to voice mail when I didn't know the number, and most of the time they were telemarketing calls. I'd try again, and if he still didn't answer, I planned to text him and say I knew someone who might be interested in his art. He might even believe me.

However, he answered the second time around. "Yeah?"

As the day had gone on, I'd decided how to question Aldo Bracket. It was one of the reasons I'd wanted to make sure Declan was out of earshot.

I was going to use my Voice.

"Aldo, this is Katie Lightfoot. Do you remember me?"

"Maybe."

"We met at the Markes Gallery. Twice."

"How did you get this number?" He didn't sound very happy to hear from me.

I gathered and focused power behind my Voice but tried to keep it subtle. I'd never be as good as Mimsey, but I hoped to one day not be such a bull in a china shop with that element of my witchy talent.

"Who did you tell that Leigh Markes was having an affair?"

"Leigh Markes . . ." He was struggling against answering the question.

I asked it again, adding a little more ginger to the words.

"Jo," he said, as if he couldn't help it. Which, let's face it, he couldn't.

"Who did you tell Jo Leigh was involved with?"

There was a long silence. I was about to ask the question again when he said dreamily, "Her husband."

Leigh was seeing Walker? What? No, wait. Leigh was seeing *Jo's* husband.

The handsome Rhett.

Oh, Lordy.

I had to confirm. "Jo Sterling's husband, Rhett, was having an affair with Leigh Markes."

"Yeah . . ." He groaned as if with great effort, and the line went dead.

Well, that was one way to stop my Voice from working. But I had what I needed.

"I hate it when you do that," Declan said from the doorway that led out to the backyard. We'd left it open all day. "It makes me feel like ants are crawling in my brain."

"Stop sneaking up on me," I snapped.

He gave me a look.

"Sorry." I was. He'd scared me, though. I took a deep breath to calm my heart rate and told him what I'd found out.

"But I thought this Aldo character said he hadn't told anyone," Declan said. "That he wanted to use the information as blackmail."

"That's what he told me when we were at the gallery." I considered. "But he must have been lying."

Things are not always as they seem.

"I wonder . . ." I squinted in thought. "I wonder why he would tell Jo at all? I mean, Aldo isn't the kind of guy who does something like that out of altruism. What if he'd already tried to blackmail Leigh, and it hadn't worked? I can certainly see her telling him to go fly a kite if he threatened her. She wasn't a woman to take any guff." I sighed. "But if it's true, I can see why she'd want to keep it secret from her best friend." I rubbed hands over my face. "What a mess."

I dropped my hands in my lap. "What if by telling Jo, he was trying to cause upheaval in Leigh's life?"

Declan dropped into his old rocking chair. "Why?"

"Maybe he thought that the more distracted she was, the more likely he'd get his show."

Or the more dead she was.

As I changed out the laundry again, I thought about whether to call Quinn with what I'd found out or make one more call. I decided on the latter.

"Sterling Fitness. How may I help you?"

"Hi," I said. "Is Jo Sterling available?"

"Just a minute. I'll get her." Suddenly, I was on hold listening to Olivia Newton John singing "Physical."

It seemed like a lot longer than a minute before the voice came back on the line. "I'm sorry. Jo can't come to the phone. She got a phone call and says she has to leave in a few minutes. I might be able to snag her on her way out if you want to leave a message."

I cursed to myself. "No, thank you. Can you tell me when she'll be back?"

"I'm not sure. She was scheduled to work until nine tonight."

"Okay. I'll call again later."

Only I wouldn't. Something had frightened Jo, and I had a feeling it was one Alessandro Bracket telling her I'd called him asking questions.

Great. Quinn is going to kill me.

I braced myself and called the detective anyway. At least I'd figured out a better suspect than Walker Stokes.

Quinn didn't answer his phone. Figuring I'd lucked out, I left a lengthy voice mail.

"How do caprese BLTs sound for supper?" Declan asked after I hung up.

A glance at my watch informed me it was already five thirty. I grinned at my husband. "Really good. I can't believe we're even talking about eating again after that breakfast, though."

"Not just eating again, but eating bacon again."

We had sourdough from the Honeybee, leftover bacon from breakfast, and tomato and basil fresh from the garden. However, one of us had to run to the store for fresh mozzarella.

"I need to wash up," Declan said. "Then I'll go."

"No worries. I'll go right now, while you're showering," I said quickly. Maybe a little too quickly because Declan gave me a puzzled look.

I ignored it. "Want to go for a ride, Mungo?"

Yip!

I grabbed my wallet and hurried out to the Bug. Mungo jumped into the passenger seat. I buckled him in before backing out of the driveway.

"We're going to take a little detour," I said.

My familiar cocked his head and looked at me quizzically.

"Jo Sterling was at her gym a few minutes ago. Maybe I can still catch her."

He made a noise in the back of his throat.

"At the gym," I clarified. "I'm not going to confront her on the street, for heaven's sake."

He huffed and looked out the window.

I drove to Sterling Fitness, admittedly a bit too fast. When I ran through a very stale yellow light at West 37th Street, Mungo gave me a stern look.

"Sorry," I said. There was a sense of urgency running under my skin, a feeling of crisis boiling up on the horizon like a thundercloud despite the reality of easy autumn light beginning to slant across the city toward sunset. It had begun when I remembered Connell telling us things weren't always as they appeared and had grown exponentially as the day wore on and I thought about the case.

I careened into the Sterling Fitness parking lot and

buzzed around the outside loop of the lot toward the front of the building. As I did, Jo came out of the front door and strode to a white Jeep Wrangler.

Squinting, I tried to make out the license plate number. I made out the letters and numbers and read them off to Mungo, which helped me to remember them. Not only that, I saw it was a custom tag, an uncommon one that I'd nevertheless seen around town on a few cars. It said PLAY GOLF GEORGIA on the bottom and had a picture of a golf ball and a gold flag with the number 18 on it.

Quickly, I grabbed my phone and texted Quinn.

He responded right away.

In a meeting. Got your voice mail. Will follow up later.

Frustrated, I put my phone down. He wasn't taking me seriously. Should I just go home?

No. See which direction she's going, at least. Maybe she's on her way home, and I'm overreacting.

On the other hand, if Aldo had called her, she could be running—on the lam, as it were.

However, it quickly became apparent Jo Sterling was not trying to skip town. Keeping as far back as I could, I followed her down Lathrop Avenue to Louisville Road. She turned left toward downtown, and we stayed on Louisville until it turned into Liberty Street. By then, I had a notion where she might be going, and sure enough, she turned right onto Whitaker. I fell back even farther as we arrowed straight through the Historic District, drove along the edge of Forsyth Park, and headed toward Midtown. I was pretty sure Jo had never seen my car but figured a celery green Volkswagen Bug might stand out in someone's rearview mirror after a few miles. When she reached the side street that led to the Markes Gallery, I slowed to a crawl, waiting until I was sure she was well down the block before making the turn myself.

Jo parked half a block away from the gallery, got out of her car, and sauntered along the sidewalk as if out for a casual stroll. I made a U-turn and parked a full block away and on the other side of the street, then twisted to watch her through my back window. As Jo walked, she kept looking up, turning her head, searching the light poles and buildings. A couple of times, she looked over her shoulder, toward her car.

What's she doing?

When she got to the gallery, I rolled down all the windows and asked Mungo to stay in the car. His eyebrows drew together·in a doggy scowl.

"I'll be right back," I said, getting out of the car.

Slowly, I walked toward the gallery along the opposite sidewalk. She turned up the walk to the door and pulled on the handle, but it didn't open. I looked at my watch. It was after six o'clock. The gallery was likely closed for the day. I prepared to duck down if she turned around, but instead she went around the corner and along the side of the building.

I scooted across the street and peered around the corner as she went around the back. I ran lightly along the side of the building and stopped to listen. I heard the sound of a key turning in a lock and peeked around the corner just in time to see the door closing behind Jo.

She was inside the Markes Gallery.

My first thought was to find an unobtrusive place to wait and then see where she went next. But what was she doing in there? My curiosity felt like an itch under my skin. Could she be stealing something? Could she be planting some kind of evidence that would implicate someone else? Or maybe she was just . . . no. I couldn't think of a good reason for Jo Sterling to be in the Markes Gallery after it closed.

She does have a key, though.

I didn't know what to think. Leigh had been her best friend, she'd said. Had that really been true? Could she have really killed her if she thought Leigh was betraying her? Most women would take revenge on their cheating spouse. I could be completely wrong about Jo. Maybe she was innocent, and Quinn was right about Walker.

Then I realized what she'd been doing as she walked down the street. She'd been looking for cameras—traffic cameras, surveillance cameras, and security cameras on buildings.

Security cameras. Like the ones inside the gallery. I'd noticed them the first time I'd been there, with Bianca.

I wasn't wrong. Jo was acting hinky because she was guilty of something.

Quickly, I texted Quinn again, telling him where I was and that Jo had gone into the gallery. After a few seconds of hesitation, I texted Declan, too. I didn't want to worry him, but I was alone, and Jo was a killer. I'd certainly proved that I could defend myself before, and from some pretty scary people—having the power of a lightwitch had its advantages in tight situations—but there was no need to be stupid.

Still, I had to know what she was doing in there. Taking a deep breath, I turned my phone ringer off and the camera on. I needed some kind of evidence. My hope was to snap a few pics of whatever Jo was doing and high-tail it out of there. Gathering all my intuition and asking for aid from the four elements, I slowly opened the back door and slipped inside, closing it quietly behind me.

The sound of raised voices made me freeze. The door opened onto a small hallway with an office on one side and a bathroom on the other. The alarm keypad by the door showed the security alarm was off. I tiptoed to the office and peeked inside. Another door led to the gallery proper. It was open, and I could see Paisley Long standing with her hands on her hips.

"I'm clearing out my stuff," she said. "I'm quitting tomorrow. Right now, though, I'm still an employee of this gallery, and I have a right to be here. You don't, and you shouldn't have that key."

"Oh, relax. Leigh gave me the key." Jo's tone was dismissive.

"Why would she do that?" Paisley demanded.

"She wanted me to pick something up for her a while ago."

"So why are you here now?"

"There's something in the office I need. I'll get it and be on my way."

I saw Paisley's eyes narrow in suspicion. "What is it?"

"None of your business!" Jo's voice sounded closer, and I moved to duck back into the hallway.

"I think you should just be on your way. Come back when the gallery is open tomorrow and Walker is here," Paisley said.

Jo swore at her.

"That's it. I'm calling the police."

"Put that down!" There was real anger in Jo's voice. Paisley cried out.

I ran through the office and out to the gallery. Jo was standing over Paisley, who was sitting on the floor with her arm up in a defensive position. Their heads turned as I barreled in. When they saw me, they both gaped.

"I've already called the police," I said and held up my phone as if that were proof, then took a picture of them.

Fury infused Jo's face. In a flash, she strode over and knocked my phone out of my hand.

"Hey!" I said.

She ignored me, leaning down to pick it up. I groaned to myself as I saw the camera was still on, so Jo didn't need my passcode. Barely sparing me a glance, she tapped the screen.

"You haven't called anyone since earlier this afternoon. Somebody named Peter. Nice try."

"Detective Quinn's first name is Peter," I said. "You remember him questioning you about Leigh Markes' murder, don't you?"

"Sure," she said. "And you're on a first-name basis with him? I don't think so."

"Katie's solved murders before." Paisley scrambled to her feet. "She was in the paper."

I silently cursed her.

"I thought I recognized you when Ms. Devereaux brought you in, and looked online," she explained.

Great.

Jo was watching me warily. She looked down at the phone, tapped again.

"You didn't call, but you did text this Peter just a few minutes ago. And someone named Deck."

"He's my husband. They both know I'm here—and that you're here."

Her wariness increased.

"You might as well give up," I said.

Jo put my phone in her pocket and looked around the gallery, eyes intense with desperation. Her gaze fixed on the display of Aldo Bracket's outsider art. Two strides with those long legs took her to the one I'd seen the day before with the arrangements of screws and nuts—and the rusty screwdriver in the center. She grabbed the whole thing off the wall, then ripped the screwdriver away from the background it was mounted on and held it out in front of her.

"What are you doing?" Paisley sounded bewildered. "Why are you acting like this?"

"Because she killed Leigh Markes," I said, looking up at the camera on the wall, hoping it was recording all this. At the same time, I felt myself pulling energy from around me, concentrating it in case I needed to defend myself against Jo.

Paisley shook her head. "But why on earth would she kill Leigh? They were friends."

"Because she had an affair with my husband," Jo grated out. "She met him right here." She looked around in disgust. "My *best friend*. Oh, I know people think my husband's a player, and he's a terrible flirt, but he's never strayed. Not once. Not until Leigh. I've lost my career, my income from endorsements, and all I have now is my husband and our business together. I even put off having kids for my career, and now he thinks it's too late to start a family. Rhett is—"

Paisley gasped and put her hands over her face. She

stared over her fingertips at Jo, who had stopped speaking. Leigh's assistant dropped her hands and suddenly bent over, breathing in huge gasps, hyperventilating.

"What's wrong with you?" Jo demanded sharply.

A terrible thought came to me.

Things are not always as they seem.

I went over to Paisley, pointedly ignoring the weapon Jo held in her hand.

"Are you okay?" I asked.

Paisley straightened and nodded. "I'm okay. It's just—" She met Jo's puzzled gaze. "Rhett's *married*?"

Jo frowned at Paisley, then suddenly her face cleared. "*You* were the one who was here with him those nights." She sounded stunned.

"Your husband didn't have an affair with Leigh," I said. "She didn't betray you."

"But Rhett did!" Paisley's horror had morphed into righteous anger. "He told me he was in the middle of a divorce. That his wife was a shrew, and they'd been separated for years."

Jo lifted the screwdriver, and for an instant, I thought she was going to come after us. However, she looked at it for a long moment, then let it drop to the floor. She sat down, her back against the wall beneath Aldo's art.

"I killed her for no reason." Her eyes filled with tears. "I killed the wrong person."

Paisley looked alarmed.

"She's innocent, too," I said. "Rhett lied to you, and he lied to her."

Jo put her head in her hands.

I went over and moved the screwdriver farther away from her with my foot.

"May I have my phone back?"

Sighing, she leaned her head back against the wall and reached in her pocket. I took the phone and called Quinn.

"Katie, you have to stop—"

"Jo Sterling has confessed to murdering Leigh Markes. We're at the Markes Gallery now. I'm pretty sure the security cameras caught everything, and she seems ready to turn herself in."

"Oh, good Lord," he said. "We'll be there right away."

"Good. The back door's open."

I called Declan next. He'd just seen my text and was heading out the door to come to the gallery. "Don't worry," I said. "Everything is copacetic, and Quinn is on the way."

He insisted on coming over anyway.

I hung up and sat down beside Jo to wait. After a few moments, Paisley joined us.

"That's why you were here, isn't it?" I asked Jo. "To erase the security footage from Monday night?"

"Yes," she said quietly. "Leigh and I came by the gallery after the book club meeting. I'd been trying to decide what to do about her and Rhett. How to approach her. I was going to beg her to stop."

This was not the story I'd expected.

"But when I asked her about it, she acted like she didn't know what I was talking about."

Because she didn't.

Beside me, Paisley started breathing fast again.

"We argued here, but then I dropped it. I couldn't figure out why she'd lie right to my face like that. It wasn't until after we'd had dinner that I brought it up again. In her car. She not only denied it again, but she *laughed* at me. It was so humiliating. I kind of—" She rubbed her face with both hands. "I kind of lost my mind. The scarf was already around her neck and . . ." She trailed off.

"And you knew you'd been seen together at dinner, so you left the heater on in Leigh's car to fudge the time of death."

Jo looked at me in surprise. "How do you know about that?"

"The forensics techs figured it out pretty quickly," I said, and then added, "Alessandro Bracket told you about the affair."

Jo nodded. "He told me he lives near here and drives by the gallery a lot. He belongs to our gym, so he knew Rhett, and he knew his car. He told me I could see for myself how my husband's car was here after hours. I came by twice, and sure enough, Rhett's car was parked across the street."

"I wonder if Aldo knew it wasn't Leigh in here," I mused out loud.

"What?"

"The guy practically stalked Leigh," I said. "Bugging her, trying to get his show so his father would take him seriously. Don't you think he knew whether it was really her in the gallery or not?"

"You mean you think he . . . wanted Jo to go after Leigh?" Paisley asked.

Jo looked sick.

"I don't know," I said. "I'm not sure I'd put it past him, though." Then a thought occurred to me. "Paisley?"

"Yeah?"

"Where were you the Friday night before Labor Day?"

She thought and then must have remembered because she swallowed hard. "I was here for a while."

"Alone?"

Slowly, she shook her head. "Not alone."

"It's been going on that long?" Jo whispered.

"I'm so sorry," Paisley said.

We all fell silent then, deep in our own thoughts. Mine consisted of what Zoe had told me about hearing her mother in an intimate conversation with a man that night. She'd been right about the conversation she'd overheard through the back door of the gallery, just not about who had been having it.

The sound of voices came from the office, and Quinn strode in followed by two uniformed officers, and then Declan. The three of us got to our feet, Jo moving slower than Paisley and me.

She walked toward the man who was there to arrest her and held out her wrists to be cuffed.

Chapter 24

Iris and Lucy had taken down the Halloween decorations when I was off the day before. Now I stood at a counter in the kitchen packing cobwebs and felt mice into a large plastic container to store until next year. Over at the sink, Lucy scrubbed the bottom of her Dutch oven with kosher salt.

"There's a nip in the air today," she said. "I think I'll cook a pot roast in this tomorrow. Carrots, potatoes, mushrooms, onions. Lots of red wine, thyme, and bay leaves."

I groaned. "Stop it."

"You and Declan can come for dinner. He doesn't start his forty-eight until the next morning, does he?"

"Nope," I said, happy for the invitation. Lucy's pot roast was . . . magical. "We'll be there. What can we bring?"

"More red wine," she said promptly. "I'll grab something from here for dessert."

"Deal."

"Keep those silk autumn leaves out," she said. "We can use them for the Thanksgiving decorations."

I sighed and put them aside. Honestly, I wasn't ready for another holiday quite yet.

Ben came back to the kitchen and grabbed a still-warm molasses cookie off a baking sheet, crammed half of it in his mouth, chewed, and swallowed. "Things are slow out there right now. You said you'd talked to Peter Quinn earlier. What did he have to say?"

"Hang on," I said. "Just let me put the lid on this." When I was done, I leaned my hip against the counter. "Detective Quinn told me that he arranged for Jo to meet Aldo in a restaurant. He recorded their conversation." I paused and took one of the molasses cookies myself. "Jo confronted Aldo, and eventually he admitted that he told her about her husband cheating because he hoped she'd go after Leigh. He denied that he knew it was really Paisley that Rhett was meeting, and he claimed he didn't intend for Jo to kill Leigh. Still, Quinn plans to charge Aldo with incitement to commit a crime."

Ben looked skeptical. "Will that stick?"

I shrugged. "It's a good question. Daddy has awfully deep pockets."

"The Aldo Bracket outsider art show at the Markes Gallery was canceled," he said. "It was in the paper this morning."

"Good." Lucy set her cast-iron pot on a burner and turned it on low. "I'm glad Walker Stokes stepped up and did what was right."

"If that's what he actually did," I said.

Ben nodded. "From what you've told us, he might simply have realized that now that Aldo is in trouble with the law, he might not be able to afford to buy all his own work."

"And no one else is going to." I reached for the decorations. "Ben, can you put this out in your truck? Lucy said you'd take all this home and put it in storage."

"Sure." He stuffed the rest of his cookie in his mouth and took the container from me. I opened the door to the alley. Iris came in as Ben went out.

"Nice hair," he commented.

"Wow," I said, looking her up and down. "You look fabulous."

"Thank you." She pirouetted so that her black taffeta skirt flared. She wore a sleeveless red silk shell with it, and the color made the fairy tattoo on her arm pop. And sure enough, the orange streaks that had been in her hair for Halloween were now bright red. "Taylor's coming home for the weekend, and we have a date later."

Lucy smiled. "I'm glad it turns out he's not a jerk."

She laughed. "I did call him that, didn't I? Well, I'm glad, too." She reached for an apron large enough to cover her skirt. "Now, what shall I do first?"

I was ringing up a customer at the register when my cell phone buzzed in my pocket. Quickly, I checked to see who it was.

Teddy.

"Thank you, and have a great day," I said as I gave the customer her change. Then I gestured Ben over to help the next customer and took the call.

"Hi, Teddy. How're you doing?" I closed the office door behind me. "You know, in the aftermath of keeping me from disappearing into the ether. Jaida said you slept all day yesterday."

"I did! Oh, and I feel so great now. Thank you, thank you, thank you."

"Er, shouldn't I be thanking you?"

"No, I mean for finding who killed that poor woman. Katie, she's gone." Relief threaded her words. "Her spirit passed on to wherever she needed to go next."

"Oh, that's wonderful!" I felt tension ease out of my shoulders. "I'm happy for her, and I'm happy for you. I don't suppose my grandmother is still hanging around, is she?"

Teddy laughed. "Sorry. She left right after you and Connell came back."

"That's what I figured."

"Katie? I want you to know how much it means that you believed I could help you. No one ever thought my ability to see the spirit world was a good thing. Mostly, no one even believed it was real. You and the other ladies accepted me at face value. I'm starting to realize I might have a gift rather than a curse. That means a lot."

"Of course we accepted you. Honey, I'm so glad we met," I said. "I know I've thanked you, but it doesn't seem like enough. I hope you know how very grateful Declan and I are for your help in retrieving Connell."

"Oh, gosh. You're welcome, Katie." Teddy was silent for a few beats and then asked, "Do you think we could stay in touch?" She asked the question almost tentatively, as if I might say no.

"Absolutely!" I assured her. "You can call me any time. Any of us, really. And I think I know a certain little girl named Colette who wants to be your new best friend."

She laughed. "I'm hanging out with her on Saturday while Bianca goes out with her boyfriend."

"That's great, but isn't Saturday a big ghost tour night?"

"Usually. But I've decided to explore a new kind of work. Just because I can see dead people doesn't mean I have to make a career out of it. Jaida and Gregory say they need a paralegal, and they want me to start working for them while I'm going to school to learn the ropes."

"That's terrific! You take care of yourself, and stay in touch, okay?"

"I will."

Iris had left for her date with Taylor and we were about to close, when Zoe and Calista came in.

"Hey, you two," I said. "What can I get for you?"

"Hi, Katie," Zoe said, fingering the necklace Cookie had made for her. I realized she'd been wearing the comfort amulet every time I'd seen her and was happy to see it appeared to be helping her.

Calista smiled. "Nothing for us today, I think." She glanced at her niece, who nodded. "We're here to bring you a little present. A thank-you, I guess." She held out a paper bag.

Lucy came over as I took it, unfolded the top, and looked inside.

"Oh!" I said, taking out three shower caps. "These are great!"

With my short hair, I wouldn't use them, but Lucy looked very interested. She held up one that was a bright orange paisley with a giant bow on the front.

"This is really cute," she said.

"Thank you," Calista said. She looked truly happy. "I'm going ahead with my Shower Chapeaus business."

I tried to look encouraging, wondering if Zoe was still upset about Calista's plan to mortgage the family home.

"Zoe's going to be my partner," Calista said, pride in her voice. "She's studying business and will help with that side of things. That way I can concentrate on the artistic aspect."

Surprised, I looked at Zoe, who looked as happy as her aunt. She nodded. "I talked with one of my professors, and she agreed that I could do a business plan for Shower Chapeaus as my special project this semester. Then she'll give me feedback, so we'll know we're doing it right. Calista agreed to wait until that's done before we make any financial commitments. And between the two of us, we should have enough money to get us started without mortgaging the house."

Lucy made a noise of alarm. "You're using your own money?"

Zoe nodded. "My dad is in charge of my trust for the next year and a half, but it turns out my grandfather made sure that could only be used for expenses related to my education. Juliette isn't too happy about that, but my dad seems okay with it." She half smiled. "We've been talking."

"I'm glad," I said. And I was. I still didn't like Walker, but it seemed good for Zoe to have a relationship with her father. The jury was still out on her stepmother.

"In the meantime, Mom left me her house and, well, a good bit of money outside of the trust." She looked a little sheepish, and I wondered how much money she was talking about. "I don't know what I'll do with the house—probably sell it—but for now I'm staying with Calista when I come home from school. That way we can make our business plans." She looked at Calista. "And maybe fix up that old house a bit."

Her aunt put her arm around Zoe's shoulders. "She's going to keep me on the straight and narrow, aren't you, honey?" She was beaming, and I could sense the affection between them. Jo had said Leigh's family was all about how things looked, but I thought she was wrong.

After all, Jo Sterling had been wrong about a few other things, too.

The door opened, and Mrs. Standish came in. I was surprised to see her, as she'd already been in earlier, and I couldn't imagine what else they'd need before the next day.

She bustled over to the counter, then gave a little cry when she saw the orange paisley shower cap Lucy had laid by the register. "Oh! That is absolutely *adorable*!" She grabbed it and twirled it in her hands. "Oh, where can I get one? Oh! And this one!" She had spied a turban-style cap in classic black with a white ribbon wound around the base. "Where did you girls find these?"

I nodded to Calista, who was beaming. "Calista

Markes, this is Mrs. Edna Standish. Mrs. Standish, meet Calista Markes, owner of Shower Chapeaus."

Mrs. Standish put her hands on her hips. "Calista Markes? I knew your father. Well, no wonder these are so fabulous. Yours is a creative family indeed."

"Thank you," Calista breathed.

"Do you have a website?" Mrs. Standish demanded. "I need at least a half dozen of these to begin with."

Zoe stepped forward. "For now, you can order them from our Etsy shop."

"I'll do that."

Zoe gave her the information, and then said she and Calista had a dinner reservation. They left and I turned to Mrs. Standish, about to ask if I could get her something from the pastry case before we closed.

"Oh! There he is!" she exclaimed, and rushed to the front door. She held it open for Skipper Dean, who was carrying a large box. With a nod to us, he continued back to the reading area. It looked heavy, which was confirmed when he sat it down on the coffee table with an *oomph*.

"Skipper parked in the loading zone out front, dears, so we only have a moment," Mrs. Standish announced. "Come along and see what we've brought."

Lucy, Ben, and I exchanged curious looks, then followed obediently behind. We gathered around the mysterious box. Mrs. Standish stepped forward and grasped the handles on top and tugged. The lid slid up smoothly to reveal the contents sitting on a heavy marble base.

It was the Hanta piece from the Markes Gallery. *Compassion*.

As soon as I saw it, I felt its calming effect. The very air around us seemed to be softer and more caring.

"Oh, my," Lucy breathed. "That's stunning." Gingerly, she reached out as if to touch one of the metal tendrils that twisted up from the center. Then, as if suddenly remembering herself, she snatched her hand back.

"Wow," Ben said, short but sweet. He regarded the sculpture with frank admiration.

"Yes, it's a *marvelous* piece," Mrs. Standish all but brayed.

I was so delighted she'd bought it that I wanted to hug her, but she'd never struck me as the hugging sort. So I just said, "It will look so lovely in your home."

It would, too. Mrs. Standish and Skipper Dean's large antebellum house boasted surprisingly modern décor. At least it had surprised me when I'd been there.

"Oh, no, Katie, my dear. Not our home."

"Are you donating it to one of your charity causes?" Lucy asked.

"Well! I certainly wouldn't call it that. No, Lucille, we're giving it to you."

My aunt blinked in surprised. "*Me*?"

"Oh, not you, per se." Mrs. Standish waved her arm in an encompassing gesture. "To the Honeybee Bakery."

Ben and I exchanged glances. "Mrs. Standish, I happen to be familiar with this piece," I said. "You can't possibly give it to us."

She waggled her finger at me. "Oh, I certainly can. And I am. You see, Dean was over at the Markes Gallery earlier. He read about that so-called outsider artist canceling his show, and he wanted to take the opportunity to step in with some advice for Walker Stokes. Dean has discovered a rather wonderful young woman who really is an outsider, and a genius to boot, he says."

I looked at Skipper Dean. He smiled back at me, silent. When his paramour was around, Dean was usually the Teller to her Penn.

"Walker listened to Dean, of course," Mrs. Standish said. "And Dean will help coordinate the young woman's show." Her rings flashed as she waved her hand. "But never mind all that. While Dean was there, he was talking with that lovely Paisley Long."

"Paisley's still there?" I asked. "I thought she quit."

Dean shook his head and spoke for the first time. "Walker realized he couldn't run the place without her. He hired her back—with a big raise."

Good for you, Paisley.

"Anyway," Mrs. Standish went on. "Your name came up, Katie. Paisley told Dean quite the story about what happened. Goodness! You do find trouble, don't you, honey? She told Dean about the sculpture you took such a fancy to, and he asked to see it, and Bob's your uncle."

Uncle Ben looked amused.

"I'm sorry," Lucy said. "I'm afraid I still don't understand."

"Lucille, we love this place," Mrs. Standish said. "Ever since it opened it's been our home away from home. You make the most delectable treats, you listen to this old woman go on and on—"

I started to protest, but she held up her hand.

"Now don't fuss. This is our present to the bakery. I know you wanted it for your own home, Katie, but Paisley had the feeling you couldn't, um, manage it." She reddened.

"You mean Declan and I couldn't afford it? She's right about that. Which is why it's just too much."

"Darlin', believe me—I can afford it. And I did. And now you can enjoy it every day, here in the Honeybee, and all your customers can, too." She peered at me. "Is that okay? To have it here rather than your charming carriage house?"

I felt tears threaten. "It's more than okay. It's much, much better for more people to enjoy it." I went and threw my arms around her, not caring if she was a hugger or not.

"Oh! Well, that's nice."

"Thank you," I said.

Lucy and Ben chimed in with their own thanks, and then Ben said, "I'll get a pedestal for it tomorrow. It can sit over here where everyone can see it."

"That sounds—Dean!" Mrs. Standish interrupted herself as something outside caught her attention. "They're trying to give us a ticket." She barreled to the door, Dean following behind. "Listen, you can't give that car a ticket," she called to the parking enforcement officer. "It's in a loading zone, and we were unloading something. Ben! Come tell this person we were unloading."

Ben grinned at Lucy and me. "Excuse me. I'm needed outside."

We laughed and turned our attention back to the sculpture.

"That was very generous of her," Lucy said. "She's a kook, but she's kind to her core."

I nodded and gave her a one-armed hug. "Compassionate, you might say."

Mungo and I drove home and parked in the driveway. When we got out, the whine of Declan's table saw drifted from the open garage. I walked up, dropped my tote, and covered my ears with my palms to block some of the noise before looking inside. Mungo took one look and headed to the other side of the yard. Too much of a racket for him.

My industrious husband was ripping a two-by-four in half, carefully feeding the length of it down the whirring blade. A stack of similar pieces of wood sat on a nearby bench. I guessed he planned to use them for the hefty new trellis he was making for the Cherokee rose bush that grew beside the carriage house. He wore ear protection and eye protection and hadn't seen me. I was about to creep away, figuring the last thing I wanted to do was startle a man using a table saw, when I saw him suddenly straighten. A nanosecond later, one of the halves of the two-by-four suddenly bucked up in the air, narrowly missing his face.

My gasp was inaudible in the din. If Declan hadn't straightened when he had, we would be on the way to the emergency room at that moment. But he *had* straightened.

Something had told him to.

Connell was back.

I was trembling when Declan looked up and saw me. He looked chagrined for a moment, then suddenly smiled. I smiled back, weakly at first, then full force. He turned off the saw, and silence descended as he walked over and wrapped his arms around me. I leaned into his chest, sliding my hands around his shoulders, inhaling his scent, basking in his warmth.

Life was good.

Acknowledgments

As always, I'm grateful to my fabulous editor, Jessica Wade, and to the rest of the team at Berkley Prime Crime, who took my story and made it into a real live book. I am in awe of their talent and hard work. A big thank-you also goes to my agent, Kim Lionetti. The members of the Old Town Writers Group—Laura Pritchett, Laura Resau, and Todd Mitchell—once again provided insightful, wise, and oh-so-helpful feedback on the manuscript. And then there's Kevin, with his constant support and love combined with the occasional kick in the pants and a ton of laughter. Thank you.

Recipes

Spiced Molasses Cookies

24 cookies

2¼ cups all-purpose flour
2 teaspoons baking soda
½ teaspoon salt
1½ teaspoons ground cinnamon
½ teaspoon ground allspice
¾ teaspoon ground cloves
¾ cup (1½ sticks) unsalted butter, softened
½ cup dark brown sugar, packed
½ cup granulated sugar, plus ⅓ cup for rolling cookies
1 large egg
1 teaspoon vanilla extract
⅓ cup molasses

Preheat oven to 375 degrees F. Whisk together the flour, baking soda, salt, cinnamon, allspice, and cloves in a bowl until thoroughly combined and set aside.

Using an electric mixer, cream the butter for 2 minutes. Add the brown sugar and ½ cup granulated sugar and beat until light and fluffy, about 3 minutes with mixer set at medium speed. Add egg, vanilla extract, and molasses. Beat until combined, about 30 seconds. Scrape down the sides of the bowl with a rubber spatula.

Add dry ingredients and beat at low speed until just combined, about 30 seconds.

Place remaining ⅓ cup of granulated sugar in a shallow bowl. Working with 2 tablespoons of dough at a time, roll dough into 1¾-inch balls. Roll balls in sugar and place on ungreased cookie sheets, spacing them 1½–2 inches apart.

Bake until the outer edges of the cookies begin to set and centers are soft and puffy, about 11–13 minutes. Cool cookies on sheets for 2–3 minutes before transferring them to cooling racks.

Be careful not to overbake. The centers of the cookies should be somewhat soft and spongy when you take them out of the oven.

Blood Orange Thyme Cake

2½ cups unbleached white flour
2½ teaspoons baking powder
4 large eggs
1½ cups granulated sugar
1 cup light olive oil
1¼ cups freshly squeezed blood orange juice
Zest from the oranges used for the juice (usually
    3 or 4)
2 teaspoons fresh thyme (or 1 teaspoon dried)
1 teaspoon pure vanilla extract

Preheat oven to 350 degrees F. Grease two standard loaf pans. In a medium mixing bowl, whisk together the flour and baking powder. In a large mixing bowl, cream together the eggs and sugar until light and fluffy—about five minutes. Switching mixer to low speed, slowly drizzle in the olive oil until thoroughly combined. Keeping the mixer on low speed, slowly add the blood orange juice, blood orange zest, thyme, and vanilla extract. Add the flour mixture, mixing just until combined. Do not overmix.

Pour the batter into the greased loaf pans. Bake for 50–60 minutes, or until a cake tester inserted in the middle comes out clean.

Allow cakes to cool completely on a rack, then store in an airtight container for up to five days. A lighter, not terribly sweet olive oil cake, the loaves can be sliced and served as is, or dusted lightly with confectioners' sugar. This cake freezes quite well.

If you love Bailey Cates' *New York Times* bestselling Magical Bakery Mysteries, read on for an excerpt from the first book in Bailey Cattrell's Enchanted Garden Mystery series,

Daisies for Innocence

Available now wherever books are sold.

The sweet, slightly astringent aroma of *Lavandula stoechas* teased my nose. I couldn't help closing my eyes for a moment to appreciate its layered fragrance drifting on the light morning breeze. Spanish lavender, or "topped" lavender—according to my gamma, it had been one of my mother's favorites. It was a flower that had instilled calm and soothed the skin for time eternal, a humble herb still used to ease headache and heartache alike. I remembered Gamma murmuring to me in her garden when I was five years old:

Breathe deeply, Elliana. Notice how you can actually taste the scent when you inhale it? Pliny the Elder brewed this into his spiced wine, and Romans used it to flavor their ancient sauces. In the language of flowers, it signifies the acknowledgment of love.

Not that I'd be using it in that capacity anytime soon.

But Gamma had been gone for over twenty years, and my mother had died when I was only four. Shaking my head, I returned my attention to the tiny mosaic pathway next to where I knelt. Carefully, I added a piece of foggy sea glass to the design. The path was three feet long and four inches wide, and led from beneath a tumble of forget-me-nots to a violet-colored fairy door set into the base of the east fence. Some people referred to them as "gnome doors," but whatever you called them, the decorative miniature garden phenomena were gaining popularity with adults and children alike. The soft green and blue of the water-polished, glass-nugget path seemed to morph directly from the clusters of azure flowers, curving around a lichen-covered rock to the ten-inch round door. I wondered how long it would take one of my customers to notice this new addition to the verdant garden behind my perfume and aromatherapy shop, Scents & Nonsense.

The rattle of the latch on the gate to my left interrupted my thoughts. Surprised, I looked up and saw Dash trotting toward me on his short corgi legs. His lips pulled back in a grin as he reached my side, and I smoothed the thick ruff of fur around his foxy face. Astrid Moneypenny—my best friend in Poppyville, or anywhere else, for that matter—strode behind him at a more sedate pace. Her latest foster dog, Tally, a Newfoundland mix with a graying muzzle, lumbered beside her.

"Hey, Ellie! There was a customer waiting on the boardwalk out front," Astrid said. "I let her in to look around. Tally, sit."

I bolted to my feet, the fairy path forgotten. "Oh, no. I totally lost track of time. Is it already ten o'clock?"

The skin around Astrid's willow-green eyes crinkled in a smile. They were a startling contrast to her auburn hair and freckled nose. "Relax. I'll watch the shop while you get cleaned up." She jammed her hand into the pocket of her hemp dress and pulled out a cookie wrapped in a napkin. "Snickerdoodles today."

I took it and inhaled the buttery cinnamon goodness. "You're the best."

Astrid grinned. "I have a couple of hours before my next gig. Tally can hang out here with Dash." She was a part-time technician at the veterinary clinic and a self-proclaimed petrepreneur—dog walker and pet sitter specializing in animals with medical needs. "But isn't Josie supposed to be working today?"

"She should be here soon," I said. "She called last night and left a message that she might be late. Something about a morning hike to take pictures of the wildflowers." I began gathering pruners and trowel, kneeling pad and weed digger into a handled basket. "They say things are blooming like crazy in the foothills right now."

Astrid turned to go, then stopped. Her eyes caught mine. "Ellie . . ."

"What?"

She shook her head. "It's just that you look so happy working out here."

I took in the leafy greenery, the scarlet roses climbing the north fence, tiered beds that overflowed with herbs and scented blooms, and the miniature gardens and doors tucked into surprising nooks and alcoves. A downy woodpecker rapped against the trunk of the oak at the rear of the lot, and two hummingbirds whizzed by on their way to drink from the handblown glass feeder near the back patio of Scents & Nonsense. An asymmetrical boulder hunkered in the middle of the yard, the words ENCHANTED GARDEN etched into it by a local stone carver. He'd also carved words into river rocks I'd placed in snug crannies throughout the half-acre space. The one next to where Dash had flopped down read BELIEVE. Mismatched rocking chairs on the patio, along with the porch swing hanging from the pergola, offered opportunities for customers to sit back, relax, sip a cup of tea or coffee, and nibble on the cookies Astrid baked up each morning.

"I am happy," I said quietly. More than that. *Grateful.* A sense of contentment settled deep into my bones, and my smile broadened.

"I'm glad things have worked out so well for you." Her smile held affection that warmed me in spite of the cool morning.

"It hasn't been easy, but it's true that time smooths a lot of rough edges." I rolled my eyes. "Of course, it's taken me nearly a year."

A year of letting my heart heal from the bruises of infidelity, of divorce, of everyone in town knowing my—and my ex's—business. In fact, perfect cliché that it was, everyone except me seemed to know Harris had been having an affair with Wanda Simmons, the owner of one of Poppyville's ubiquitous souvenir shops. Once I was out of the picture, though, he'd turned the full spectrum of his demanding personality on her. She'd bolted within weeks, going so far as to move back to her hometown in Texas. I still couldn't decide whether that was funny or sad.

I'd held my ground, however. Poppyville, California, nestled near the foothills of the Sierra Nevada Mountains, was *my* hometown, and I wasn't about to leave. The town's history reached back to the gold rush, and tourists flocked to its Old West style; its easy access to outdoor activities like hiking, biking, and fly fishing; and to the small hot spring a few miles to the south.

After the divorce, I'd purchased a storefront with the money Harris paid to buy me out of our restaurant, the Roux Grill. The property was perfect for what I wanted: a retail store to cater to townspeople and tourists alike and a business that would allow me to pursue my passion for all things scentual. Add in the unexpected—and largely free—living space included in the deal, and I couldn't turn it down.

Sense & Nonsense was in a much sought-after location at the end of Corona Street's parade of bric-a-brac dens. The kite shop was next door to the north, but to the south, Raven Creek Park marked the edge of town with a rambling green space punctuated with playground equipment, picnic tables, and a fitness trail. The facade of my store had an inviting, cottagelike feel, with painted shutters above bright window boxes and a rooster weathervane twirling on the peaked roof. The acre lot extended in a rectangle behind the business to the front door of my small-scale home, which snugged up against the back property line.

With a lot of work and plenty of advice from local nurserywoman Thea Nelson, I'd transformed what had started as a barren, empty lot between the two structures into an elaborate garden open to my customers, friends, and the occasional catered event. As I'd added more and more whimsical details, word of the Enchanted Garden had spread. I loved sharing it with others, and it was good for business, too.

"Well, it's nice to have you back, sweetie. Now we just have to find a man for you." Astrid reached down to stroke Tally's neck. The big dog gazed up at her with adoration, while I struggled to keep a look of horror off my face.

"Man?" I heard myself squeak. That was the last thing on my mind. Well, almost. I cleared my throat. "What about your love life?" I managed in a more normal tone.

She snorted. "I have plenty of men, Ellie. Don't you worry about me."

It was true. Astrid attracted men like milkweed attracted monarch butterflies. At thirty-seven, she'd never been married, and seemed determined to keep it that way.

"Astrid," I began, but she'd already turned on her heel so fast that her copper-colored locks whirled like tassels on a lampshade. Her hips swung ever so slightly beneath the skirt of her dress, the hem of which skimmed her bicycle-strong calves as she returned to the back door of Scents & Nonsense to look after things. Tally followed her and settled down on the patio flagstones as my friend went inside. I saw Nabokov, the Russian blue shorthair who made it his business to guard the store day and night, watching the big dog through the window with undisguised feline disdain.

Basket in hand, I hurried down the winding stone pathway to my living quarters. "God, I hope she doesn't get it into her head to set me up with someone," I muttered around a bite of still-warm snickerdoodle.

Dash, trotting by my left heel, glanced up at me with skeptical brown eyes. He'd been one of Astrid's foster dogs about six months earlier. She'd told me he was probably purebred, but there was no way of knowing, as he'd been found at a highway rest stop and brought, a bit dehydrated but otherwise fine, to the vet's office where she worked. Of course, Astrid agreed to take care of him until a home could be found—which was about ten seconds after she brought him into Scents & Nonsense. I'd fallen hard for him, and he'd been my near constant companion ever since.

"Okay. It's possible, just possible, that it would be nice to finally go on an actual date," I said to him now. Leery of my bad judgment in the past, I'd sworn off the opposite sex since my marriage ended. But now that Scents & Nonsense wasn't demanding all my energy and time, I had to admit that a sense of loneliness had begun to seep into my evenings.

"But you know what they say about the men in Poppyville, Dash. The odds here are good, but the goods are pretty odd."

A hawk screeched from the heights of a pine in the open meadow behind my house. Ignoring it, Dash darted away to nose the diminutive gazebo and ferns beneath the ancient gnarled trunk of the apple tree. He made a small noise in the back of his throat and sat back on his haunches beside the little door I'd made from a weathered cedar shake and set into a notch in the bark. Absently, I called him back, distracted by how sun-warmed mint combined so nicely with the musk of incense cedar, a bright but earthy fragrance that followed us to my front door.

Granted, my home had started as a glorified shed, but it worked for a Pembroke Welsh corgi and a woman who sometimes had to shop in the boys' section to find jeans that fit. The "tiny house" movement was about living simply in small spaces. I hadn't known anything about it until my half brother, Colby, mentioned it in one of his phone calls from wherever he'd stopped his West-falia van for the week. The idea had immediately ap-pealed to my inner child, who had always wanted a playhouse of her very own, while my environmental side appreciated the smaller, greener footprint. I'd hired a contractor from a nearby town who specialized in tiny-house renovations. He'd made a ramshackle three-hundred-twenty-square-foot shed into a super-efficient living space.

There were loads of built-in niches, an alcove in the main living area for a television and stereo, extra foldout seating, a drop-down dining table, and even a desk that tucked away into the wall until needed. A circular stair-case led to the sleeping loft above, which boasted a queen bed surrounded by cupboards for linens and clothing and a skylight set into the angled roof. The staircase par-tially separated the living area from the galley kitchen, and the practical placement of shelves under the spiral-ing steps made it not only visually stunning, but a terrific place to house my considerable library of horticulture and aromatherapy books.

Most of the year, the back porch, which ran the seventeen-foot width of the house, was my favorite place to hang out when not in the garden or Scents & Non-sense. It looked out on an expanse of meadow running up to the craggy foothills of Kestrel Peak. Our resident mule deer herd often congregated there near sunset.

After a quick sluice in the shower, I slipped into a blue cotton sundress that matched my eyes, ran fingers through my dark shoulder-length curls in a feeble attempt to tame them, skipped the makeup, and slid my feet into soft leather sandals. Dash at my heel, I hurried down the path to the shop. I inhaled bee balm, a hint of basil, lemon verbena, and . . . what was *that*?

My steps paused, and I felt my forehead wrinkle. I knew every flower, every leaf in this garden, and every scent they gave off. I again thought of my gamma, who had taught me about plants and aromatherapy—though she never would have used that word. She would have known immediately what created this intoxicating fragrance.

Check her garden journal. Though without more information it would be difficult to search the tattered, dog-eared volume in which she'd recorded her botanical observations, sketches, flower recipes, and lore.

A flutter in my peripheral vision made me turn my head, but where I'd expected to see a bird winging into one of the many feeders, there was nothing. At the same time, a sudden breeze grabbed away the mysterious fragrance and tickled the wind chimes.

Glancing down, I noticed the engraved river rock by the fairy path I'd been forming earlier appeared to have shifted.

For a second, I thought it read BEWARE.

My head whipped up as I wildly searched the garden. When I looked down again, the word BELIEVE cheerfully beckoned again.

Just a trick of the light, Ellie.

Still, I stared at the smooth stone for what felt like a long time. Then I shook my head and continued to the patio. After giving Tally a quick pat on the head, I wended my way between two rocking chairs and opened the sliding door to Scents & Nonsense.

Nabby slipped outside, rubbing his gray velvety self against my bare leg before he touched noses with Dash, threw Tally a warning look, and padded out to bask in the sunshine. A brilliant blue butterfly settled near the cat and opened its iridescent wings to the warming day. As I turned away, two more floated in to join the first. As the cat moved toward his preferred perch on the retaining wall, the butterflies wafted behind him like balloons on a string. It was funny—they seemed to seek him out, and once I'd seen two or three find him in the garden, I knew more blue wings would soon follow.

ABOUT THE AUTHOR

Bailey Cates believes magic is all around us if we only look for it. She is the *New York Times* bestselling author of the Magical Bakery Mysteries, including *Witches and Wedding Cake*, *Cookies and Clairvoyance*, and *Potions and Pastries*. Writing as Bailey Cattrell, she is also the author of the Enchanted Garden Mysteries, which began with *Daisies for Innocence*.

CONNECT ONLINE

BaileyCates.com

Ready to find
your next great read?

Let us help.

Visit prh.com/nextread